THE FIGHTING SEASON

BRAM CONNOLLY
THE FIGHTING SEASON

ALLEN&UNWIN

SYDNEY · MELBOURNE · AUCKLAND · LONDON

First published in 2016

Allen & Unwin
83 Alexander Street
Crows Nest NSW 2065
Australia
Phone: (61 2) 8425 0100
Email: info@allenandunwin.com
Web: www.allenandunwin.com

Cataloguing-in-Publication details are available
from the National Library of Australia
www.trove.nla.gov.au

ISBN 978 1 76029 038 2

Set in 12/18pt Minion by Midland Typesetters, Australia
Printed and bound in Australia by Griffin Press

To my sons, Matthew and Andrew.

AUTHOR'S NOTE

I always knew I would join the army. As a young boy I spent hours reading *Combat and Survival* magazine and watching *Tour of Duty*. On weekends my best friend Sam Townsend and I would ride our bikes into the bush not far from where we lived and practice the skills needed to survive on the battlefield: patrolling, ambushing, observation and reporting. It was always just part of what made me tick.

On my seventeenth birthday I went to the recruiting office in Adelaide and sat the interviews and tests required to join the army. My first day was 5 February 1991, and what followed was twenty years of hard work. It wasn't the glamorous, glossy life depicted in the pages of *Combat and Survival*, but in many ways I had a very fortunate career, and sometimes I was just in the right place at the right time. I attended the first Commando Selection Course in 1996 for the newly raised 4th Battalion Commando, of which I was a founding member. I was also a founding member of the Tactical

Assault Group-East (TAG-E). My operational deployments included Somalia as a forward scout (1993), Timor as a reconnaissance patrol commander (2001), and Timor again as the 3rd Brigade special operations liaison officer (2006). I deployed twice to Afghanistan, the first time as a company operations officer (2008) and the next time as a commando platoon commander (2010).

I owe much to the army and the men and women I served with, way too much to detail as an author's note. Suffice to say, I am the person I am now because of these amazing life experiences, the formal training I received throughout my career and the strong bonds and relationships I formed with fellow warriors. But enough about me…

Matt Rix is my way of taking you, the reader, into battle.

Let me tell you now that close combat is exciting: your senses are on overdrive, your awareness is amplified, and you can do the seemingly impossible. The relief that rushes over you when those first rounds start cracking overhead is something you have to experience to believe. You feel elated, and once you've tasted it you want more, so much more.

Let me also tell you now that combat is terrifying: the fog of war can overwhelm your senses and make you ineffective as rifle shots and machine gun fire, screams and explosions all flood the mind. The adrenalin alone can cripple the fittest man and make you gasp for breath. The easiest tasks become totally unachievable and once you've experienced it you never want to again.

Matt Rix has experienced both these dimensions of combat. He is a flawed person. At times he is a great leader and at other times he is ineffectual. He isn't real, nor are his platoon or any of the other characters in the book, save for the obvious historical figures.

What is real, however, are the descriptions of combat and the landscape in which he operates. I have tried to capture the frictions of war that I personally experienced and describe the stress it puts on leaders and their soldiers.

Finally, much is said and implied in the book of the relationship between The 2nd Commando Regiment and The Special Air Service Regiment. This relationship can occasionally be strained. When two units live by their mottos, 'Without Warning' for 2nd Commando and 'Who Dares Wins' for the SASR, this is going to happen. It is important to note, however, that both units are full of exemplary Australians who have devoted their whole lives to the defence of Australia and put themselves deliberately in harm's way again and again to ensure mission success, at home and abroad. Some of these men have given everything. On behalf of all Australians, and to both these units, thank you.

To you, the reader, I hope that you enjoy Matt Rix's deployment as much as I did.

Bram Connolly, DSM
facebook.com/BramConnollyAuthor

I would like to thank Mark Abernethy for his mentorship and guidance and Jane Elsolh for her patience and diligence in correcting the first draft.

'Combat turns quickly to chaos. The orderly plan conceived in the relative calm and safety of the headquarters becomes a shambles, influenced by violence, confusion and fear. The commander's role is to hold the plan together, for as long as possible in an effort to exert his unit's will over the enemy, and ultimately win the confrontation.' — Bram Connolly DSM, 2016

1

CAMP RUSSELL, TARIN KOWT

As he looked out into the darkness, the young infantry soldier from outback Queensland could smell something out there, something peculiar. Perhaps being scared magnified the senses. Whatever it was, the smell carried to him on the breeze, and it made him all the more anxious.

A couple of minutes earlier, Joel's Afghan counterpart had left him without a word, and now he sat in the wooden guard box overlooking the rear gate of the Australian military base alone. Perhaps Mohammed had gone to relieve himself? Maybe it was time for him to pray again?

Joel looked at the glowing hands of his watch. It was now approaching three in the morning. It was just his luck that he had pulled sentry duty the day before his birthday. The next day, 28 June 2010, he would be twenty-one. Right now he just wanted to get through to see the light of this day. The hair on the back of his neck stood up as the faintest sound came from the shadows. Eyes straining to penetrate the dark, Joel focused on the large concrete blocks designed to slow approaching cars, trying to discern what could have made that noise. A feral cat? There were plenty running around the base.

A crisp breeze cut though the sweltering night, drying the sweat on his face. The heat was almost unbearable at this time of year – summer, referred to by the Taliban as the fighting season. While the cool draught of air brought some respite from the searing heat, it also carried the smell to him again, a pungent odour. Joel shivered. Staring into the night, he could barely see the outline of the mountains behind the lush Mirabad Valley. Though only eight kilometres from the coalition base, Mirabad may as well have been a hundred: it was a different world out there. Hidden evils lay in wait for the unsuspecting at every turn. Rushed patrols, or those that had not been planned properly, never ended well. Joel had been part of a patrol that had been ambushed the week before. Two of his friends had been killed and at one point the section was almost overrun. When they finally returned to the base the section commander was relieved from his position, deemed not up to the task. It had been a shambles and the events had terrified Joel.

He looked over his shoulder for his fellow guard. Working with the Afghan partner force could be challenging at times, but for the most part it was rewarding. Mohammed was a decade older than Joel, a family man, and had been working with the Australian infantry platoon for the last two months. He was a fast learner and something of a practical joker. The Australians had warmed to him. He kept some of the other Afghans in check and had already been earmarked as a future commander.

'Mohammed? Psst, Mohammed!' Joel hissed through his teeth.

Another noise came from the direction of the concrete barricades in front of Joel's position: the distinctive tap of metal on metal – definitely not a feral cat. Joel swallowed hard, wishing he had his night-vision goggles. But they were attached to the helmet he'd left perched out of reach on a pile of sandbags several metres away from where he sat behind the machine gun. The Kevlar helmet weighed a ton; after only a minute of wearing it he had a stabbing pain in the top of his head. Some long-forgotten colonel, sitting in an office in Canberra, had thought the helmet looked good in a glossy brochure and signed off on the deal; the Australian infantry had been wearing it now for a decade. Correction: should have been wearing it. He just hoped his complacency wouldn't cost him too dear.

Squinting into the darkness, Joel thought he could make out shapes moving in and around the barbed-wire barricades, the second line of defence. Perhaps his mind was playing tricks on him now? If only he had on his NVGs. The lights of the camp behind him cast a shadow right in front of the guard box, creating an extra layer of darkness extending beyond the perimeter. Further on, past the road, it was pitch-black. Joel felt exposed with the light behind him and had the sudden realisation that he was silhouetted for anyone out there to see. In the daylight this area of the airfield looked flat and open for a thousand metres. However, on closer inspection, it was full of crevices and ditches, small creek beds and earthworks. These all combined to create a landscape where you could move around in the dark undetected. And something out there was definitely moving . . .

The stairs behind Joel creaked. Half jumping out of the wooden chair, he swung around.

'Fuck, Mohammed, you scared the shit out of me. Where the hell have you been?!'

Mohammed arrived at the top of the stairs, holding his AK-47. Joel noticed he had the security gate keys in his front hand – the same hand which was holding the hand guard of his weapon.

'What are you doing with those?'

Mohammed opened his mouth to speak but no words followed.

Joel looked at his face. 'What's wrong, mate?'

Before the Afghan could respond, Joel caught a flash of movement in his peripheral vision. He turned quickly and couldn't believe his eyes. A group of Taliban, maybe thirty or more, came sprinting out of the darkness, their white and black robes flowing behind them as they ran towards the guard box.

'Oh, shit! Shit – Mohammed!'

Smashing the alarm on the side of the desk with the palm of his left hand, Joel grabbed at the trigger of the machine gun with his right. The bolt flew forward and slammed into the breech with a loud clunk and then – nothing.

It had been unloaded earlier in the day to be cleaned and now the belt of rounds lay useless on the sandbag next to the gun.

'NO!' Joel spun around to face Mohammed. 'Quick, lock the top of the stairs, lock them now!' he ordered.

The alarm started to wail and Joel could hear shouts from the depths of the base behind him as soldiers automatically moved into their well-rehearsed drills. A voice came over Joel's radio, the headset hanging to one side of his body armour. He looked at Mohammed who seemed to be frozen solid with fear. This was all happening so fast.

'For Christ's sake, lock the stairs, come on – lock them!' Joel urged, gesturing frantically.

Mohammed was a statue, his eyes wide. Then he let out an involuntary sob. 'I'm sorry,' Joel heard him say in English as he squeezed the trigger.

The first round slammed into Joel's body armour and the force sent him crashing back off the chair and onto the floor. In an instant the second and third rounds followed, smashing into the wood beside Joel. The last round made a loud cracking noise as it ricocheted off a nail and zipped around the guard box.

• • •

Mohammed gazed at the Australian infantrymen lying barely conscious on the floor, bleeding profusely from a large cut on his head sustained as he fell off the chair. Satisfied that his role was complete, the Afghan felt as though an enormous weight had been lifted from his shoulders. Turning, he half slid and half ran to the bottom of the steep stairs. Dropping his rifle on the ground, he sprinted through the gate he had opened only minutes before.

Standing at the wide-open perimeter gate was Ahmed Defari, the local Taliban commander. As Mohammed disappeared into the night, Defari lifted his radio to his lips and gave a quick set of instructions. Thirty kilometres down the valley, the two Pakistani thugs from the border regions who were stationed in Mohammed's home released Mohammed's terrified wife, two-year-old daughter and six-year-old son. The couple's eldest child was Rashid, a cheeky nine-year-old and the village favourite. He now lay dead on the dusty floor; his throat had been cut with the rusty blade of an old kitchen knife. The cost to Mohammed would have been much greater if he had not complied with Defari's demands.

2

CAMP RUSSELL, TARIN KOWT

'Yankee Alpha! Yankee Alpha!' he heard her scream.

Skiing off piste, Matt Rix miscalculated a sharp turn and smashed into a tree.

'Yankee Alpha!' she screamed again.

Why is she using my call sign? he wondered. As the commander of Yankee Platoon from the 2nd Commando Regiment, Matt was referred to as Yankee Alpha – but not by her; it was as confusing as hell.

The soft cold snow, her sweet British voice filled with terror, the violent impact of his high-speed crash: it was all repeated over and over. Then he felt her soft hands on him, shaking him gently as she yelled.

'Yankee Alpha!' Her voice grew deeper, harsher; her hands became strong and hard and the shaking became violent.

'Yankee Alpha! Boss! For fuck's sake – Matt!'

Matt opened his eyes in bewilderment to meet the steely gaze of his platoon sergeant, Yankee Bravo, otherwise known as Jack Jones, or JJ. A giant of a man and an accomplished martial artist, JJ was a no-nonsense straight-talking commando sergeant, just what a platoon commander needed in Afghanistan.

With his eyes open now, Matt surveyed the small room. It was flooded with red light and through a gaping hole in the ceiling he could see the clear night sky above Camp Russell. The bright stars seemed to be flickering in time to the bursts of machine-gun fire on the perimeter. In the background, various alarm bells were ringing and people were yelling out fire control orders, panic in their voices.

'Gun Group, fifty metres, at the base of the tree, five enemy lying in the creek bed, rapid FIRE!' A section from the infantry company next door had their area of responsibility well under control. The section commander's voice boomed out over the camp.

Matt looked at his feet; the skis were gone, and his heart sank with the realisation that Rachel, too, was gone.

An explosion reverberated through the camp and then another impact blew out the hallway wall, causing Matt to lift from the bed.

He looked at the sergeant. 'Shit! What the hell was that?'

'Christ, boss – c'mon, wake up!'

Boom! Boom! Boom! Matt recognised the sound of mortars in the adjoining camp firing an illumination mission, trying to bring clarity to the confusion. A couple of seconds later the night above him became an eerie yellow day.

'MATT! The men fucking need you – right now!' JJ screamed as Matt became fully conscious to the events unfolding around him. They were under direct attack!

JJ grabbed the brown t-shirt and combat pants from the chair next to Matt's bed and pushed them into his chest.

'Hurry! Put these on.'

'What the hell's going on? What time is it?' asked Matt, almost stumbling in his haste as he pulled on his pants.

'It's three thirty in the morning and it's a fucking mess out there, boss! What the hell do you think is going on? Listen!'

'Right, right – got it.' Matt grabbed his body armour and threw it over his head, doing the Velcro up with one hand while snatching his M4 rifle off the wall rack with the other. Two huge explosions interrupted the distinctive sound of AK-47 fire.

Handing Matt his helmet, JJ bundled him out the room and into the hallway.

'Suicide bombers, boss – I think there are about fifty or more Taliban out there and they seem well organised.'

The two of them ran out of the smouldering building and into a night thick with the smell of cordite and burning paint.

'They're inside the wire. The platoon is moving to their defensive position now. The HQ building is locked down and the enemy is being held back in the vehicle yard.'

Machine-gun fire was followed by what sounded like grenades.

'Where are the SAS guys?' Matt demanded.

'They're still an hour away, out on some time-sensitive targeting mission in the mountains up above the Chora Valley.'

Another rocket-propelled grenade whistled overhead, exploding harmlessly past the dining facility. Matt calculated that it had come from the open-sided shed being used as a vehicle yard located on the outer perimeter. While the yard didn't guarantee the Taliban immediate access to the inner perimeter, and therefore free run of the base, it was only a matter of time and Matt knew it. He looked around as they passed the last accommodation block. He could see that most of the damage was contained to the accommodation blocks themselves.

'How come these pricks always have so much ammunition?' JJ yelled.

They were running past Yankee Platoon's vehicles now. The soldiers had been packing the Bushmasters earlier that afternoon, and the protected mobility vehicles lined the road in front of the accommodation.

'I don't know, mate, but it's lucky all the gun cars are still sitting here on the ring road and not where they should be in the vehicle yard.'

Matt and JJ arrived at the forward area of the internal perimeter. Beyond this was the vehicle yard. It had thirty-foot Hesco walls, a type of rapidly deployable defensive structure filled with dirt. At either end of the yard was an access gate. The Taliban had passed the external guard tower with its big steel gates and, instead of heading straight into the main camp, they had turned right and were now trapped inside the yard. As Matt settled in behind a sandbag wall his radio came alive.

'Yankee Alpha, this is Yankee One – over.' It was the Team One commander. Matt's platoon had four teams, each comprising six commandos that made up his platoon.

'Send it,' replied Matt.

'This is Yankee One. All four teams are firm in location, the enemy are contained in the outer perimeter and we are awaiting further instructions – over.'

Matt thought for a second then replied, 'Roger. All call signs, this is Yankee Alpha; hold position and wait for further orders – out.'

Matt pulled down the NVGs on his Ops-Core helmet and surveyed the area. Tracer rounds flashed backwards and forwards and the sounds of 40mm grenades echoed on the perimeter. Matt fixed his eyes on the guard box. Spotting some movement, he nudged his sergeant. 'JJ, is someone up in the guard tower?'

The sergeant quickly turned his attention from covering the top of the Hesco wall and adjusted his NVGs. 'Ah, yep – looks like Australian camouflage pants, boss. I can only make out his legs from here.'

'Bloody hell, that changes the situation a bit, mate. We've got to get him out of there.'

'He's already dead I reckon, boss. Can we clear it after we sort these guys out?'

'No, I'm pretty sure I saw him move. Either way, he's one of ours and worth a punt, right?'

Matt looked back towards the accommodation block and the vehicles parked along the road and then across to his men, who were lining their defensive positions and sending controlled fire back at the Taliban. The booming sound of AK-47s was interspersed by the tap-tap of the smaller calibre, suppressed M4 rifles, the favoured weapon of elite Special Forces units the world over.

'Allahu Akbar! Allahu Akbar!' The scream came from the yard and then a Taliban sprinted out of the gate towards the inner perimeter fence.

Whack! He fell stone dead, shot by the commandos a few metres from the exit of the vehicle yard. He detonated seconds later; the ground shook as the explosion rocked the area, sending bits of bone fragment, mixed with rocks and earth, into the air.

'Another suicide bomber,' JJ said calmly.

'No shit.' Matt grabbed his radio fist mic. 'All call signs, this is Yankee Alpha – radio orders, prepare to copy – over.'

The teams replied and waited for their instructions. Matt surveyed the frontage and the adjoining base. The regular infantry guys were doing a great job in holding their own perimeter. So far they had maintained discipline and fire control. The small Special Forces base known as Camp Russell was an extra extension of the main Dutch-controlled Tarin Kowt base. While primarily the Australian Special Forces secured the smaller base, it shared a guard tower that had dual access from either perimeter. The smaller base was able to be supported and in turn also support the larger adjoining base occupied by the Dutch and the regular Australian infantry battalion. For the moment it seemed as if the Taliban attack had stalled – though if there were more suicide bombers to come, and if they could penetrate the inner perimeter, the situation could change significantly.

Matt chose Yankee One and Yankee Two as the assault teams. Their purpose would be to clear the vehicle yard of all enemy forces. The locked southern gate was the safest entry point for Matt's plan, as the yard was a dogleg and therefore the gate wasn't directly across from the northern gate. This would offer his men a covered entry point on break-in. Yankee Three would support the plan by taking two gun cars and breaking into the yard through the northern gate, blocking the enemy's withdrawal and providing direct fire support to the assaulting teams. JJ would wait near the main power box and on Matt's command cut all the lights to the base. That way the commandos and their NVGs would hold the advantage.

Matt relayed his orders.

Yankee Three immediately mounted the Bushmasters. The engines were started and the .50-cal machine guns on the remote weapon stations whirred into life. These vehicles were never designed to be an infantry fighting vehicle, but all the commandos considered them capable and trained with them often with this scenario in mind.

The final part to Matt's plan was to have Yankee Four move behind the gun cars and break off at the last safe moment to secure the guard tower. From the guard tower they could then be used as the assault force from the opposite gate should the main assault be defeated.

Team Four pulled back to meet up with the Bushmasters and JJ also left his position to access the main electrical fuse box near the mess hall. This was the most dangerous moment, as all the teams were moving into their positions and the perimeter was manned only by a handful of cooks and engineers. Two more suicide bombers were dropped short of their objective in the few minutes it took the commandos to reach their start positions.

Matt keyed the mic. 'All call signs this is Yankee Alpha – GO! GO! GO!'

The lights went out around the camp. The Bushmaster vehicles screamed to life, accelerating fast they smashed through their own defensive gate and towards the vehicle yard. At the northern gate they screeched to a halt. The .50-cal machine guns thumped into action, spraying bullets across the yard. The rattle of the heavy weapons made the air shake. Dust rose up from inside the vehicle yard and a brown cloud fell over the whole frantic scene. The tracers from the large calibre guns mixed with the dust to create a murderous laser show. An explosion inside the yard told of the presence of more suicide bombers.

Yankee One and Two, with Matt following close behind, raced on foot around to the other end of the yard and the locked gates. The lead man stopped and put down covering fire into the yard, as another team member placed an explosive snib charge on the iron chain that secured the gates. The chain disintegrated in a flash and moments later the two teams poured inside, racing down either side of the yard. At the other end of the yard Team Four ran to the guard tower and the commandos scaled the stairs two at a time. Within seconds they had secured the tower.

Matt's radio crackled into life.

'Boss, this is Yankee Four, we've got a man down up here. Four/Four is stabilising him and then I'm sending two guys to drag him back into the perimeter.'

'Roger that.' Matt fired his suppressed rifle at a Taliban who ran across his front, directly between him and one of the guys from Team One. The two rounds slammed into the enemy's chest and dropped him in a crumpled heap. Matt adjusted his NVGs and tightened the chinstrap of his helmet. His sweat had made the goggles slide around on his face.

The vehicle yard could hold nearly sixty vehicles and was a couple of hundred metres wide. There weren't too many places to hide in there, especially as it was largely empty of vehicles. Matt and the commando teams were now in and among the remaining enemy fighters, some of whom had found a ladder and had propped it against a wall to try to escape back out to the airfield. The Taliban who were yet to scale the wall ran around in the dark, firing desperately in all directions. But with the commandos' NVGs and invisible lasers it was hardly even a fight. The commandos moved in and around the shadows, firing at the enemies' illuminated faces. The subdued recoil of the commandos' suppressed M4s was in stark contrast to the deafening explosions of the AK-47s, but every time there was a little tap-tap another Taliban would fall dead into the dust. The fight was brutal, one-sided and over in less than two minutes.

Matt and JJ surveyed the carnage contained within the vehicle yard. Metal hitting flesh and bone does strange things to the human body – the scene was nothing like how it would have appeared in a movie. The enemy lay in twisted heaps surrounded by dark red pools where their life had flowed from their bodies. Most had single holes in the centre of their faces and the back of their heads had all but disappeared. The unluckier ones had multiple holes in their chests. Their legs or arms had been blown off from the force of bullets turning after striking internal bone. It was a grotesque scene.

JJ moved from body to body collecting their biometrics and taking photos for the evidence boards. The men collected equipment. It was gathered and tagged to ensure that the right equipment matched the biometric samples of the dead enemy fighters. They mostly worked in thoughtful silence.

'That was intense,' JJ said.

'Yeah, it was. Turned out all right in the end though.' Matt looked up at JJ while unloading one of the enemy weapons. 'Mate, why were the Bushmasters still in front of the barracks? I'm sure the RSM told you yesterday that he wanted them secured in the yard and out of the way.'

'Come on, boss, that was a bullshit order and you know it.' JJ had little time for the regimental sergeant-major. The most senior non-commissioned officer, he was responsible for standards and discipline on the base. JJ thought his efforts would have been better focused on the men's morale.

'It doesn't matter if it was bullshit or not; an order is an order. You should have just done what the RSM frigging asked.'

'Boss, all he gives a crap about is having the place tidy, everything packed away where it should be. We have to live and fight off those vehicles and so they need to be packed and the guys have to have access to work on them. Having them kept six hundred metres away in the vehicle yard makes it near on impossible.'

'You can't pick and choose the orders to follow, Jack!'

The exchange between the two was catching the platoon's attention.

'Boss, if the cars were in the yard this might have been a different gun fight.' JJ pulled the white surgical gloves from his hands and wiped the blood off his face with the bottom of his shirt.

'JJ, you're clutching at straws, mate. For the last time – follow orders and do what you're told. For your sake and the platoon's. I don't need the RSM all over us like white on rice every chance he gets, pal.'

'Jesus, you're such a fucking boy scout!' JJ yelled as he threw an AK down into the dirt. 'I suppose you never break the bloody rules?'

'I'm going to let that comment go through to the keeper – just this once.' Matt glared at JJ, who looked away.

JJ was a good man, Matt knew, but prone to emotional outbursts – and because of his sheer size these outbursts could be terrifying to those who didn't know him well. He was usually able to control his temper, but it had been a rough evening. The vehicles had been a contentious issue for a few days. JJ had decided to forget to tell the guys to move them. He thought the regimental sergeant major was a dick. Actually, Matt thought ruefully, everyone on both sides of the Special Operations Task Group, the SAS and the commandos, shared that opinion.

The RSM had never deployed in a combat role and knew little of the realities of combat. He aspired to be the Command RSM one day and needed an unblemished record to achieve it. The commandos represented a real issue for him. They were hard to control and pig-headed. Unlike the SAS guys, he complained, they were not quiet achievers. Everything they did was either for dramatic or strategic effect. They were a product not only of their training, but also their own self-belief, which was fuelled by their higher command's open bias against them.

In the two weeks since the commando platoons had rotated into the camp, the RSM – who was from SAS – had tried to break them. He had been hot on having the place look like a military base and despised disorder, however functional it might have been. The gun cars left lined up in front of the accommodation blocks had been the last straw. He had launched into a tirade about the commandos' lack of discipline and standards and then somehow linked it all to haircuts and beards before settling on slamming the door to the operations room and storming off. The RSM didn't have to wait long for the problem to be halved though. Whether by design, good fortune or a mixture of both, the Commando Company had been broken up for this rotation. X-Ray Platoon, commanded by Chris Smith, was now providing a Quick Reaction Force to the NATO Special Operations Force based out of Camp Baker at the Kandahar airfield. They were bouncing all around Regional Command South, either securing helicopter landing zones, dropping in on gunfights to break any deadlocks or pulling out other Special Forces units that had bitten off more than they could chew. Meanwhile, back in Tarin Kowt, the Yankee Platoon was left to check and double check that their weapons were zeroed on the Tarin Kowt range and work on their room entry drills. It was growing old with Matt's men at a rapid rate.

'Okay lads, let's get back to the barracks and get cleaned up. The MPs are here now, they can deal with this. JJ, hand over your notes, mate,' Matt said.

'Sure thing and not soon enough. I've had a gutful of this for one night.'

Matt looked down at his own hands and noticed that they were shaking. He took a deep breath and focused on calming his central nervous system. A year's previous training with the platoon on counter-terrorism duties had taught him a thing or two. He looked around at his men and some of them were going through the same drill. They all looked exhausted.

3

KANDAHAR

Captain Sam Long, the military intelligence officer from the Australian Special Operations Task Group, placed his pen down next to his writing pad. Sipping on a cool glass of water he looked around the room. The other twenty or so intelligence officers from the various task forces were all listening intently to Leon Panetta, the director of the CIA, as he outlined the agency's strategy for the next five years in Afghanistan. The intelligence officers had worked through the night sharing information and cross-referencing their facts. Even when news had come through of the attack on Tarin Kowt they had kept to their agenda.

Finally we might all be on the same page, thought Sam. He was impressed by Panetta's opening address. When the director made an offhand remark about the Taliban and the insidious relationship between the governments of Afghanistan and Pakistan, Sam chuckled and caught the eye of Steph Baumer.

He smiled across at her. Steph gazed back at him, her face giving nothing away.

Sam watched as the American CIA agent ducked her head to flick through some papers in a manila folder. Even dressed as she was in tan cargo pants and a black T-shirt, her strawberry-blonde hair pulled back in a tight ponytail, he found her attractive.

'As you are all now aware, we are continuing to hear that the Taliban are planning a decisive blow at the end of Ramadan this year. In fact, we have heard their senior leadership discuss it openly. They are up to something big; all the indications are that it is going to be some type of bombing campaign. Some of the information suggests that the Taliban have obtained a new type of suicide vest. We don't know exactly what that means and we don't have any indication as to the intended target.' Panetta paused and looked around the room. 'Let's have a five-minute break, guys, and then we'll go round the room for your monthly action items.' With that the brains trust made their way to the coffee urns, toilets and smoking areas to decompress.

• • •

Steph stayed in her seat and continued looking through the files on her desk as her colleagues returned to their seats and the meeting resumed. She tapped one particular folder with her finger, deep in thought. The file, which bore the title ODIOUS, was a dossier of indications that Iran was getting actively involved in the region. Through her network, she had gathered enough information over the last few months to draw the conclusion that the Iranians were supplying weapons to the Taliban. She had painstakingly pieced it all together and searched for any evidence that supported her theory.

Her father had been an accomplished CIA operative and also best friends with William Buckley, the Beirut CIA Station Chief who had died at the hands of Hezbollah in 1985. Buckley's death had had a profound effect on Steph's family. Her mother and father separated a year later, after her father turned to the bottle looking for solace, and then, in the early 1990s, her father committed suicide. After that Steph became obsessed with joining the CIA and even more obsessed with the Middle East, in particular.

Steph looked up from her papers to listen briefly as Sam Long gave his monthly report to Panetta. She shook her head and went back to her own folder. She had never really liked Sam. He had always seemed awkward and uncomfortable in her presence. But there was more to it than that: Sam was a genius and she didn't trust him. He always held back his analysis until the last minute and then would play a lay down misère, seemingly not wanting any accolades but not allowing others to take the glory either.

'Ms Baumer, what have you to report?' asked Panetta as he came to Steph for her update. It was already well past midnight and he was pushing to get a conclusion to the meeting. She had been so lost in her own thoughts that she had completely missed the others as they updated the director.

'Well, sir, I have secured another three informants across Regional Command South. They are new and still being groomed.'

'Good, go on.'

'There's a rumour on the streets that Khazi's brother is intending to flee the country to the United Arab Emirates, although that seems to be a common theme we hear before every fighting season.'

'Okay, yes, that confirms what Jackson said in his brief.' Panetta nodded at Jackson.

'I wish the whole family would just up and leave – perhaps then we could get some traction with the government,' chimed in one of the other intelligence officers, others nodding their agreement.

Steph dismissed him with a wave of her hand. She looked up at Panetta. 'There is one more thing, sir.'

'Yes?'

'Well, it's just a theory at this stage – it's about the Iranians.'

There was a chorus of groans from the group.

A Marine Corps intelligence officer interjected, 'Seriously, here we go again. Do you have anything concrete this time, Steph? The last time we went down this path we had half of the 24th Marine Expeditionary Unit wasting six weeks looking for supply lines that never even existed.'

Steph ignored him and looked directly at Panetta. 'Sir, there is strong evidence that the Iranians are seeking to keep us tied here while they exert further influence regionally. They're supplying weapons to Syria and advisers to Yemen, not to mention the ongoing Hezbollah support.' Steph held up her thick folder. 'My theory is that they are the ones supplying the IEDs and weapons to the Taliban through their southern border and up through Pakistan. Once in Pakistan they're moving things with impunity to Quetta and then into Afghanistan.'

'That theory has more holes in it than a sieve, Steph,' Sam argued. 'I just don't see how that's viable. We've found their IED factories here in Afghanistan. We know that most of the weapons here were leftovers from the Soviet occupation. Sure, there's no doubt that the Iranians are involved in smuggling, and that low- or no-metal content IEDs are coming across the border, but these are mostly criminal elements. There's no evidence to suggest that it's state-sponsored.'

'I totally disagree.' Steph smacked her folder on the table and glared across at Sam.

Sam glared back. 'Your information is always based solely on your own network's sources, Steph, rather than corroboration from all our combined networks.'

'I have an idea, Steph,' said Allie van Tanken, a Dutch intelligence officer. 'Why don't we pretend that we are giving your sources some information in return for the information they have? It might save us some time and lead us directly to Iran – misinformation manipulation, espionage 101.'

Panetta stepped in. 'Steph, let me reiterate what I have said to you before: this is an interesting theory –' his gaze swept around the room to encompass the gathered intelligence officers '– and let me remind you all that Steph is here because she provides the strategic viewpoint.' He paused and then rose from his seat. 'Listen, Steph, Captain Long is right: involve the others more. Share your information and cross-check it against what the other networks are saying. When you have a solid lead on Iran, something concrete to support your theory, then bring it back to me. In the meantime, you guys have to play nice together.'

The director smiled at the group. 'Okay, everyone, that's the end of the update. It's been a long day and a much longer evening. I'll be back in four weeks and we can do this again. I expect that in that time you will all prepare your briefs for my review prior to the Senate's committee hearing next month.' Panetta began to pack his piles of papers into his leather holdall, still talking. 'Ladies and gentlemen, reach out to your sources – go over the intelligence; I have a bad feeling that we are about to be sucker-punched.'

As the director left the room, Steph shot Sam a furious look.

As if oblivious to her annoyance, he walked over. 'Sorry,' he apologised. 'I didn't mean to sound so dismissive.'

Steph ignored him and started to gather her papers.

'Perhaps we can sit down together some time,' he suggested, 'share some information – see if we can find any trends that might support what you're chasing. Over a coffee, maybe?' Sam smiled.

Steph rose from her seat and pushed the chair under the table. She picked up her folders and files and placed them in her small camouflage backpack.

'Whatever, Sam.'

• • •

Sam watched, bemused, as Steph walked off. Obviously Panetta's exhortation to play nice had gone over her head. He shrugged and looked down at his watch. He had better get moving if he was going to get his gear packed; the next flight back to Tarin Kowt left early that afternoon.

4

'He can't hear you, Omar, the explosion hurt his ears.'

Ahmed Defari pitied his older brother; he had never truly seen the death that was part of a jihad.

They had travelled all through the day in an old pick-up truck to bring Ghasul home. Now the young fighter lay bleeding under a blanket, close to death. The villagers had stood outside his room and mourned for him until his mother arrived by his bedside and kissed his cheeks – then they celebrated.

'How did this even happen, Ahmed?' Omar demanded. 'You were only meant to attack the front gate. You were going to draw them away from the base and into your trap, you said.' Omar's face reflected the pain that he felt over the imminent death of his young nephew.

'The situation changed, brother. We found a way inside their base, into the very lair where they sit and plot our destruction.'

Ahmed took a step back from his son and turned to face the others. 'We couldn't pass up the opportunity to show them they are not safe, no matter where they hide.'

Omar stroked the forehead of the young Taliban, not yet in his twenties. 'And now this, Ahmed – your eldest son? Bleeding from the nose and ears like a yard cat that has been beaten around the head with a stick?' As if to reinforce his point, the old man smashed his walking stick into the hard ground.

'Yes, it's very sad that he was not martyred like the others, but it was not his time.' Ahmed smiled across at his sibling. 'Listen, brother, we tried it your way, but the infidel didn't listen; now we must do it this way, the way of the fighter. I have the approval of Quetta. Think of it, Omar: God willing, if this succeeds, I will be the governor before the new planting season and we will rule all these valleys again.'

Omar scoffed under his breath. 'Abdul Rahman, you stand there very quiet – do you agree it is worth the bloodshed? The loss of twenty brothers, most of them family?'

Abdul Rahman looked at Ahmed and then around at the others gathered by Ghasul's bed. 'Omar, old friend, you know my feelings on this. The council has chosen your brother, Ahmed Defari, and now we need to follow him. I will fight to my last breath if it is God's will.'

The real truth of the matter was that Abdul Rahman would much rather be tinkering with motorbikes, and the young chai boys, in his Tarin Kowt workshop. He also knew that he wouldn't be asked by Ahmed to be a foot soldier any time soon. He was best utilised as a conduit of information and distributor of Ahmed's weapons.

Omar sighed and looked around at the group. 'I fear you may yet fight to your last breath if you follow Ahmed. I fear it will be his will for us all.'

'It is true that the attack did not go to plan, brother,' Ahmed conceded. 'The bearded devils arrived. They are special: the infidel use them when they feel most threatened. They are different from the others; they can see in the dark and they are deathly silent. If they catch you, it is said that you disappear forever.' Ahmed became animated talking about the Australians. He had come to respect them, almost to idolise them, rather than fear them like the others.

'I hear that they use explosions to open walls, Ahmed, that they come into the homes in the dead of night and rip you from your bed and that they have wolves with them with teeth the size of fence posts,' an awed Abdul Rahman added.

'Yes, yes, that's right, Abdul. But I have noticed a weakness. I have watched them for many years now. Every fighting season they are different men from the years before.'

'What have you learnt, Ahmed?' asked Faisal Khan. He had appeared bored, standing in the corner watching the grieving family, but now his eyes were alive.

'They make the same mistakes, Faisal. They always take the same paths – even when there are no roads, they seem to drive the same way as the years before. They park their tanks in the same places and they look in the very same houses.'

'I have seen that the traitors with them are Hazara Shi'a!' Faisal Kahn added. He walked across to the group and put his hand on Abdul's shoulder.

'Yes, Faisal, this is true. They bring the Hazara from the north.' Ahmed was not surprised that Faisal had observed this; he was highly regarded as an intelligence officer within the Haqqani network. The senior leadership in Quetta had decided to promote Ahmed but only provided he took the counsel and guidance of Faisal. It was said that Faisal had been hand-picked by Mullah Omar himself for the task.

Before Ahmed had met Faisal Khan, he had been a low level fighter with modest aspirations. His small village had been peaceful and had always grown pomegranates in the land between the mountains and the walls that circled the village. It was a hard but honest way to make a living and the village was wealthy compared to most.

When Faisal arrived, so too did the processed opium from Helmand Province for shipment to Pakistan and beyond. At first, this made Ahmed uncomfortable; they were Muslims, yet this poison they were helping al-Queda and the Taliban supply to non-believers had found its way to their own people as they, too, became addicted. Abdul Rahman's brother was managing the profits from Kabul, and he seemed always to have money whenever Ahmed needed it. Over time Ahmed grew to trust Faisal and the closer he worked with him the more powerful and successful he became and the less of a concern the drugs were to him. He knew where the money ended up.

Ahmed turned to look once more at the still form of Ghasul. 'Things are going to change soon, my friends,' he said soberly. 'Let's move outside – I want to speak to you about something important'. He motioned towards his wife. 'Mouza, tend to our son now.'

Mouza rose like a spirit from the corner of the dusty room just as a moan came from Ghasul. She had been sitting crouched in her burqa, hidden from the men's view in one of the dark corners.

She was listening intently and watching Ahmed's every gesture and movement. His control of the group and the power that he now wielded within the tribal area filled her with excitement. Soon, she was certain, her family would be rulers of the lands between Tarin Kowt and Kandahar, just as her father had once been.

'What's so important that you can't discuss it in front of a dying boy, Ahmed?' Omar asked.

'Your nephew is not the concern, brother – I want to be under the stars so that Allah himself might look down upon our discussion.'

Ahmed walked through the doorway and out into the open courtyard. The compound itself was modest in size, but it looked over the entire valley below and its thick stone walls and single entrance had ensured that it remained unconquered for hundreds of years, as had the family within.

'In the coming months, we are going to receive a new weapon,' Ahmed revealed when the men had assembled again outside. 'I am told by Quetta that it will change the fight.'

'What, Ahmed – what is this weapon?' Omar asked, wide-eyed.

'They are uniforms made of a special material. Explosive is woven into the fabric. With these we can get inside the government and police buildings and destroy their leadership. A single vest will kill a group of ten men standing together. They were tested in Pakistan, against a government spy and his family, and the best part is that the foreigners can't see them with their wands.'

'You mean that clothes are the new weapon, Ahmed? How is this possible?' a toothless Abdul said, smiling to disguise his anxiety. He sensed that he was going to be receiving the new shipment of weapons very soon, which always made him nervous.

29

Omar, too, was puzzled. 'How will this help, Ahmed? They listen to us, they see and hear everything. How are we meant to fight them when they have all these machines, these planes, and all we have is clothes?'

'I told you, brother, they will not detect these, not like the vests you send the young Pakistanis out in – and we will make a plan: they will all go off together, in every police station and army HQ in the district. There will be no one left in power. The American puppets will be finished and then we will step in to run the province.'

It was true, Omar thought, the Pakistanis were less than effective, especially being such weak, sick creatures. He'd had little success with them in recent months.

'The same way the Mujahedeen fought the Soviet Army.' Faisal smiled.

A high-pitched squeal came from inside the house and then the door burst open. Mouza came running out, one hand holding her abaya above her ankles to allow her to move more freely.

'Ahmed, Ahmed – Alhamdulillah, Ahmed, praise be to God! Ghasul has left, he is a martyr now. Oh, Ahmed, it was meant to be.' Mouza could barely contain her joy now that her eldest son had died and gone to the afterlife. 'We must make preparations. Come now, we must send him off properly. Come, come, Ahmed.'

Ahmed looked up into the brilliant night sky. 'Alhamdulillah. You see, Omar? God was listening to our prayers. Abdul Rahman, make preparations to receive the weapons in the secret place. And Faisal? Use your contacts. Keep them looking the other way. I need some time to plan this well.'

5

Following the assault on the vehicle yard, the Australian Defence Force Investigation Service asked to interview every guy in Matt's platoon. Matt knew that they would be thorough and ask probing questions. Prior to the interviews, Matt talked to the platoon and reminded them to be honest and not to embellish their actions. It had taken three days to collect everyone's statements. Matt and JJ were the last to go through.

Having finished his own interview, Matt waited outside the demountable for JJ to come out. From inside he could hear JJ laughing with the ADFIS warrant officer.

'Alright, mate?' asked Matt as his sergeant exited the building.

'Yeah, no dramas, boss – he was pretty good. He did say that I might get some grief over cutting the power. Apparently the hospital needs it to do surgery. Who would have thought?'

'I should think they'd have backup power – he's talking out his arse.'

As far as Matt was concerned, the investigation was just a formality. His own interview had been straightforward. He had described to the investigator his thinking and actions in detail; the ADFIS man had kept fairly quiet, only remarking, 'I see. So you decided to take matters into your own hands when no information came to you from the headquarters.'

Matt and JJ headed in the direction of the Yankee Platoon office to develop a training package for the next few days. The commandos were scheduled to train with the partner force out at the mock-up Afghan village.

'Sir!' Matt's signaller, Daniel Barnsley, jogged over to the pair. 'I've been looking everywhere for you, boss – you too, JJ. The CO wants to see you both in his office urgently.'

Matt and JJ looked each other, then shrugged and changed course to the headquarters.

'How's this going to go down, boss?' said JJ as they made their way up the steps of the HQ building.

'No issues, mate. I've been trying to get hold of the CO for a couple of days to explain what happened, but he has been busy with wrapping up that SAS operation – I assume he just wants to know what the ADFIS guys were asking.' Matt rapped on the door of the CO's office then led the way in.

Expecting something of a hero's welcome – they had successfully repelled a Taliban attack, after all – he was taken aback by the reception accorded him and the sergeant.

'What in God's name did you cowboys think you were doing the other day, Rix?' the CO shouted before they were even fully through the door. At six foot three inches, standing in front of his desk and dressed in MultiCam fatigues, he cut an imposing figure.

The CO had been a top performer since joining the military and had experienced a meteoric rise from his beginnings as a troop commander in the Special Air Service Regiment. He was young enough to still be in touch with the men; however, his ascendance had been to the detriment of his actual combat experience. Unlike the CO, the majors and captains below him had nearly all led their units in combat and he had something of a chip on his shoulder about it.

'The base security plan clearly outlines that you are to hold your position and wait for the Quick Reaction Force to respond to any incursion. And what the hell do you think you were doing by smashing your vehicles through our own goddamn gates, Rix?' The CO glared at Matt and then at JJ. 'Do you have any idea of the repair bill we're facing?' The CO held up a notepad of scribbled numbers, probably a quick estimates report carried out by one of the other officers on the camp, thought Matt.

'Jack, I expected more from you, champ.' The RSM was standing in the corner with a self-righteous smirk. Still addressing JJ, the RSM gestured to Matt. 'Can't you control this dickhead?'

Before JJ could respond, Matt said, 'Well, I guess that all depends on your interpretation of control. If you are suggesting that JJ should be telling me how to command my platoon, then I guess the answer is no, he can't control me. And come to think of it, I didn't actually see you out there.'

'That's because I was in here with the CO, doing my bloody job, sir.'

'And my platoon was out there doing our bloody job,' Matt retorted. 'Killing the enemy.'

The CO, perhaps furious at being left out of the exchange, threw his notebook against the office wall. It fell onto the table and knocked an open water bottle over a pile of papers. The RSM rushed to mop up the spill, tripping over a power cord on his way and pulling the computer monitor off the side of the CO's desk. It hung suspended by the power cord just off the floor.

'Jesus, RSM.' The CO picked up the monitor and placed it back on the desk and the two of them went to work lifting papers to move them out of the way of the ever-expanding puddle of water.

Matt watched on in disgust. He remembered those dignified officers and tough old warrant officers from the Jungle Training Centre in northern Queensland. They were Vietnam veterans and would muck in with the lads for the duration of the training. They had been men leading men, not bumbling twits like this. Where had that type of warrior gone?

'So how do I explain this to the task force commander? That my commando platoon used in excess of two hundred rounds of fifty-cal inside our own base walls, then used the Bushmasters as infantry fighting vehicles against suicide bombers, smashed out of our perimeter gates and left their fucking positions, rather than follow the base reaction plan?' The CO had gone red in the face and was clearly about to unleash another round when he was interrupted by the phone.

'Sir . . . yep . . . uh-huh . . . Yes, of course, sir.' The CO shifted awkwardly. 'Yes, that's correct, it occurred on the twenty-seventh of June, sir. That's right, three days ago. He's with me now. You want me to write it up for you? Right, I understand, of course, sir.'

The CO was looking down but Matt could see that his brow was furrowed, though whether in concentration or consternation Matt couldn't tell.

'Okay, I will pass that on, sir. Yes, definitely, sir, I will be sure to pass that on.' He paused and turned away from the others with the phone pressed hard against his ear. 'Yes, exactly, I agree. Right, will do. See you then. Thank you, sir.'

The CO hung up the phone and turned to look at Matt. 'That was General Towers, the Commander of Australian Forces in the Middle East Area of Operations.' The CO paused as if struggling for the words. 'He's furious. He's coming to the base next week. Rix, mark my words: if you *ever* deviate from our base plan again, or if you or any of your men so much as step a foot out of line, I will have you court-martialled.'

But Matt was determined to have his say. 'Sir, the enemy tried to penetrate into the heart of our base. We took the initiative. A commando platoon is not going to just take a defensive posture and hope that the enemy attack fails; the moment was right to strike back at them.'

The CO started to shake his head, but Matt ploughed on. 'Now the infantry guys know that we have their backs and the Taliban will think twice before trying that again.'

'I have heard just about enough, Rix. You are treading a fine line, mate.' The CO looked across at the RSM, who twitched the corner of his mouth in a wry smile.

The CO nodded his concurrence on what was obviously a preconceived plan. 'Go and see the intelligence guys, Rix – I want you to head out tomorrow on a disrupt operation; I don't want to see you or your platoon for two weeks.' The CO looked from Matt to JJ then back again. 'Sam Long is waiting to provide you with an update.'

The CO breathed in and out, and then resumed his usual, more measured tone. 'Right, you two can go now – just get out of my sight.'

Matt looked down at his feet to disguise the fact that he was secretly quite pleased with his new orders. Vehicle disrupt operations sucked, but at least he and his men would be out among the population – and, hopefully, the enemy.

'Right, understood, sir.' Matt looked at JJ. 'Let's go, Sergeant.'

JJ's face was bright red with rage. Matt knew that he had longed for Matt to unload on the RSM and at the very least argue some more with the CO.

As he and JJ left the CO's office, Matt decided he would catch up with Sam Long later, after his temper had cooled. Not that he had a problem with Sam; the intel captain had been a classmate of Matt's back in the Royal Military College and was a walking brain to boot. He was now attached to the SAS but hadn't let that get in the way of their friendship.

'So that went well,' said JJ as they started down the hall.

Matt's response was interrupted by the appearance of Terence Saygen.

'Hello there, lads.'

Terence commanded the SAS troop that made up the second combat element of the Special Operations Task Group. Matt had a theory that to be an SAS officer you needed a cool name, had to be at least a level two certified Crossfit coach, an expert in the subject of yourself and have amazing hair. Terence had all these attributes. His ability was dwarfed by his own self-opinion and his men emulated his strutting persona. Matt hated him with a passion, and Matt's men hated his troop. It had gone past friendly rivalry some years ago.

'Saygen,' Matt said under his breath as he edged past the other man with JJ close on his heels.

They walked on a few metres then JJ turned to face Matt. 'That guy is such a dickhead. I'd like to punch his perfect teeth the other side of his chiselled jaw.'

From the office they just left, they heard the CO warmly welcoming Saygen and heaping praise on his troop's latest performance. 'Great outcome last night, Terence – not who we were after, but at least some of the network won't give us any more trouble.'

'In and out, sir, easy days – no contest really.' With that the door to the CO's office closed.

Matt and JJ continued down the hallway and out into the courtyard. They walked in silence for a few minutes towards the barracks, then Matt spoke.

'Do you want to know a secret?' he asked.

'Sure, why not.'

'I slept with Saygen's girlfriend. You know, before they were together.'

They walked a few metres more in silence.

Then JJ started to chuckle. 'Ha! That's hilarious.' JJ laughed until he had tears in his eyes. When he'd managed to compose himself, he said, 'So I have to ask – did you get freaky with her? You know, tie her up or handcuffs, establish a safe word and delve into some choking?'

Matt looked sideways at him. 'Jesus, JJ. Why does it always end up with someone getting choked with you, mate?'

'I don't know, because I am a Judo black belt, I guess – you know?'

'No, I don't know. And no, I didn't choke her out. Jesus. I actually really liked her; she's cute, sporty and great in bed.

A good catch actually. Anyway, I didn't play it very smart. That being said, though, if I could do it all again . . .' Matt paused, looked up at the sky, and sighed. 'I would definitely choke her out.'

They both laughed.

'Does he know?' JJ asked.

'No, I'm saving that bombshell for once they get married – I figured that would be more fun.'

'What? Christ, and you're worried about me? You're a nasty piece of work, boss. Surely you're over her by now, anyway. What about that chick you met in Italy? What was her name, the one you keep talking about?' JJ opened the door into the accommodation block, surprising some of the local contractors who were already hard at work repairing the damage from the past evening's events.

'Rachel? I haven't heard from her. I think it was a holiday fling. She works for some leftie magazine and doesn't seem the type to want a relationship.' Gentle and calm, she was like every other girl he had ever been with and every other girl that it hadn't worked out with.

JJ strong-armed the door to the common room and it slammed open against a box overflowing with various magazines. Copies of *Top Gear*, *Australian Penthouse* and *FHM* slid in all directions across the tiled floor. Matt strode in behind him and Yankee Platoon fell quiet, looking up at their commanders. Most of them sat around one of the three tables in the common room. The men had been down at the range all afternoon conducting scenario training and had just finished cleaning their weapons, ready for any eventuality. They sat around now in dusty combat fatigues. The room smelled of sweat and Nescafé.

'Right – well, that's the last time we protect *this* base,' JJ said.

The men shifted uncomfortably, correctly interpreting JJ's sarcasm to mean that the meeting with the CO hadn't gone so well.

Matt dropped heavily onto the couch in the corner of the room and let out an involuntary sigh. The men resumed their conversations.

Matt slowly shook his head and then reached for a car magazine that lay on the couch. He flicked through it, still too steamed up to concentrate, then tossed it aside and stood up.

• • •

Matt shared a special bond with his men. Most of the guys had endured the same commando selection course he had some years back. Half way through the course, the candidates had to complete a 25 metre underwater swim. When they'd finished, the warrant officer had the men form up in two lines by the side of the pool, screaming that one of them had cheated by coming up for a breath before the end. He demanded that the cheat own up. No one did. A solid ball of muscle, the warrant officer had the men do push-ups until the cheat owned up or he was dobbed in. To a steady stream of abuse, the guys did push-ups for half an hour straight, until most of them collapsed to the ground in a shaking mess. No one owned up, though.

'Now listen very carefully to me, men,' the warrant office then said in a quiet and measured tone. 'We're going to start doing push-ups again but this time to my count. Any man that fails to stay in time with me will be stood up and put on the bus home, right here and now. Do you understand me?'

Matt knew that the bus would fill up fast; most of the men didn't have another push-up in them. 'It was me, Sergeant Major. I took the breath.'

'Really, I see, sir. Well, this is a bit of a problem isn't it? Not only are you a cheat but you also have made these men endure punishment that they didn't deserve. Off you go then, sir. Go pack your gear and get on the bus.'

Matt was floored. This hadn't gone to plan at all. There was no arguing at this point. He had miscalculated and would now have to return to his unit. 'What the hell have I done?' he thought as he walked away.

Just then a captain stepped forward.

'As I recall, it may have also been me that took a breath, Sergeant Major,' said the young officer.

'Yeah, I think it was me, too, sir,' said a corporal, stepping forward and standing next to the captain.

'And me, sir,' said another young soldier.

'Me too.'

'You know what, I just remembered that I didn't even actually swim underwater, sir,' said one smart arse.

'Was there a swim test?' asked the guy from the Air Force who was part of the Joint Terminal Air Controller Program.

'Captain Rix, get back over here now! It seems the lot of you are a bunch of liars and cheats. Seems that we have much convict blood in our veins. The only way to lose that trait is to run it out of you. Grab your shit and fall in, the lot of you! We're running the fifteen kilometres back to the camp. With me, let's go.' And with that the men fell in and followed the steady pace of the warrant officer. Matt caught up to the back of the group, grateful to be there.

The afternoon's events had gone perfectly, like clockwork, just as every selection before. Only the actors had changed. The men all smiled at each other as they ran in silence. They thought they had won a small victory. The training staff also shared a quick glance between themselves. They knew that a lesson in loyalty had been driven home today.

Six years on and many of those same men were now in Matt's platoon. To say they were friends would not be doing the relationship justice. They knew Matt was loyal, but the gap between a private and a captain in Special Forces could change depending on the context and the circumstance. On the battlefield, or in the office, it became noticeable. The men could see that Matt was expected to perform as a leader. When they rested after an arduous activity, he had to plan for yet another operation or do some other task. In the common room, however, Matt was afforded the luxury of a safe place among friends.

• • •

'Right, lads, I'm off to see the intel guys. We're heading out tomorrow afternoon on a vehicle patrol,' he told them. 'Get the Bushmasters ready. Eddie, tell the guys who aren't here that preliminary orders will be later this evening.'

'No worries, boss. How long are we going for?'

'A couple of weeks, mate, we should be back on the sixteenth or seventeenth of July,' Matt replied, moving towards the door.

'What's the task and how far are we going, boss?' Derrick, one of the older commandos, asked innocently from behind a book.

'Come on, mate,' Matt snapped. 'I haven't even seen the bloody intel guys yet – give me a break.'

Johnno threw an empty water bottle at Derrick; Derrick shrugged it off and went back to his book.

As he left the building Matt cursed himself for snapping; there was no need to take out his frustration on the blokes.

Glancing into the kitchen hall as he passed, he saw Terence Saygen and the RSM sitting at one of the long tables, deep in conversation. He wouldn't mind taking out his bad temper on those two though, he thought, wondering what they were talking about. Whatever it was, it probably didn't bode well for Matt and his men.

6

KANDAHAR

Steph Baumer adjusted her glasses on the bridge of her nose and, still staring at the computer screen, picked up a half-chewed pencil and placed it between her lips. The information she was looking at concerned her. Picking up a mobile phone she opened a new SMS and typed in the letter O and then sent the message to a number saved under favourites. Sucking on the end of the pencil, she raised her eyes to meet the gaze of Corporal Dawson, who sat at the desk opposite hers. The American intelligence analyst's eyes darted away and then back to Steph.

'Fucking problem, Dawey?' she said.

Corporal Dawson looked back at his computer screen and shifted awkwardly in his chair. Even Steph, with her elfin features and lack of personality, was attractive eight months into a fourteen-month tour, especially in those glasses.

'No, ma'am, I was just thinking about something.' Dawson knew as he said it how lame it sounded; he could feel his face turning red with embarrassment.

'Well, kindly don't look at me when you're doing it.'

The oval-shaped room was empty. During busy periods there could be up to twenty analysts, a mixture of military and CIA, all poring over computer screens, analysing reams of data and compiling urgent reports. It was quiet now, though, with just Steph and Corporal Dawson, and a low murmur of voices coming from a set of military radios on one of the desks.

'Sorry, ma'am. Hey, why are you even in so early? It's like you never sleep. I mean, I have to be here, it's my shift – but it's a weekend, you could be sleeping in.'

'Dawey, I have six more months in this shithole then I'm back stateside to take up some mandatory desk job analysing the conversations between Mexican drug cartels and LA gangsters.' Steph took off her glasses and placed them on the desk. 'All these other shmucks are just trying to survive over here; I have a higher purpose.'

'You mean you need to make a name for yourself?'

'Dawey, you're not even in the ballpark. The more success a CIA operator has over here, the less likely they are to be sent to some intelligence backwater. I'm not going to compete for a station chief position by learning Spanish and interviewing Mexicans discovered in the trunks of cars. My place is here in the Middle East.'

Steph's desk was a clutter of handwritten notes and screwed up Post-its. A small black Nokia vibrated among a pile of different phones on the shelf next to her computer. She switched her focus from the corporal to the phone. Its screen was lit up with a single word: ODIOUS.

About time, she thought. She grabbed the tattered Moleskine notebook sitting in her top drawer and another analog mobile phone that was underneath it. She checked it was charged and stuffed it into the pocket of her cargo pants.

'I'm going for a coffee on the boardwalk, Dawey. I'll be back at ten if anyone needs me, otherwise they can ring my cell number.' Steph attached the paddle holster to the belt of her pants and adjusted the Sig Sauer 9mm on her hip.

'Yes, ma'am,' Dawson replied to the closing door. 'Bitch,' he added, as he turned his attention back to the episode of *South Park* that was playing on his computer screen.

• • •

The small Starbucks was empty; not unusual for this time of the morning. Steph surveyed the surrounds and noticed that she was mostly alone, save for a few guys playing volleyball on the sandy pitch inside the confines of the boardwalk, the covered walkway that skirted the multiple playing fields. A private construction company had made a fortune building it. The boardwalk had become the focal point of the Kandahar base. It housed military equipment shops, cafes and all the major American fast-food outlets; all providing the troops with a sense of civilisation in an existence that veered between mundane and violent. The workers were mostly imported Filipinos and some locally hired staff, the mixture of cheap labour and low operating costs making the boardwalk stores highly profitable.

'Yes, ma'am?' said a bored-looking Asian woman.

'Give me a grande skinny cappuccino, to go,' said Steph.

'To have here, ma'am?'

'What? No!' Steph said. 'That's why I just said *to go*.'

'Okay, ma'am, one grande skinny cappuccino to go. That's five dollars, thank you.'

Steph handed her a five-dollar bill from the back of her notebook. The phone in her pocket vibrated again. She checked the caller ID. It was Faisal Khan.

She turned away from the cashier. 'Faisal, hi, how are you? Are the family all well?' Her voice, which had been gruff and sarcastic moments before, was now high and girlish.

'Yes, I am good, thanks be to God. Some of the younger brothers are not so well but our big brother got away safely, thanks to you and the information that you gave me yesterday.' Faisal coughed and Steph could hear him spit onto the ground.

Steph had painstakingly pieced together the life of Faisal Khan. From their conversations she knew that he was from a well-off Afghan family who had supported him as he studied English at Lahore University back in the eighties. He had then stayed in Pakistan through much of the nineties, living in the network of madrasas around Islamabad before disappearing for another decade as a guest of Pakistan's Inter-Services Intelligence, or ISI as it was known in spy circles.

Steph was still unsure of exactly where his loyalties lay. Some of their conversations gave her the feeling that he had grown to despise the West. She thought it strange that he had resurfaced in Afghanistan not long after US forces had ousted the Taliban. Perhaps he had some local government aspirations or maybe he was working for the Taliban. It was even probable that he was on the bankroll of ISI. No matter the case, Faisal was one of Steph's best sources and she needed to handle him as such. She had reconciled that they were using each other, which is often the case between a handler and an informant.

'That's okay, Faisal. I'm glad he's safe.' Steph grabbed the coffee that was placed on the counter for her and walked outside to a table in the morning sun.

'These bearded devils are a problem for us, sister. Maybe we need to go away until they leave Uruzghan.'

Uneasy at the prospect of losing such a valuable resource, Steph hastened to reassure him. 'Faisal, they're not an issue – I will let you know when they're close. As long as you keep giving me what I need, I will be able to protect you. You have to trust me, Faisal. So, tell me, do you have anything for me today?'

'I do have something for you.' He lowered his voice and she pictured him looking around to see who was watching him. Speaking in English on a mobile phone was a sure way to get shot in the back of the head by an overzealous patriot or, worse still, reported to Quetta as a spy – because then you would surely wish you were dead. 'You need to look at the pomegranates going into Iran,' he whispered. 'The Iranians control it all and instead of money coming back it's weapons, tonnes of them.'

'That doesn't make sense, Faisal. What would the Iranians want with pomegranate?'

'Pomegranate is worth 10 million dollars a year to them, but it's not just pomegranates, Sister. It's wheat, corn and any other crop they get their thieving hands on. The sanctions placed against Iran have cut them deep, but they have found ways around it.'

'Of course, and the one thing they have an abundance of is old Russian weapons.' Steph was joining the dots together now. 'So they come over and buy off the farms and labour in exchange for weapons and in that way they are able to increase their trade in areas where they are not held against a sanction. Pomegranate juice made in Iran and shipped to the US, except that the pomegranates are from Afghanistan, farmed by Afghans with the proceeds going to Mahmoud Ahmadinejad.'

'Yes, I think now you get the picture.'

'Right, well, that is interesting, Faisal.' Steph could feel the excitement tingle in her spine – finally someone was confirming her theory that Iran was actively involved in this mess; this was the smoking gun she had been looking for.

'Yes, the locals all know about it; most of the pomegranate orchards are owned by Uruzghan farmers, simple people, while the Taliban maintain the poppy fields so that the Americans think that it is the main export and don't go looking elsewhere.'

Steph sensed that she could make a huge deal of this; she hardly dared to think of how quickly this would advance her career. But she needed to play it smart. The CIA director was chairing another meeting in a few months' time, and if she could get enough information together, she could present this in front of the other regional intelligence directors while he was there. There was no telling how much traction she would get with the director. Certainly her profile would be lifted and they would talk about her in Washington.

'Faisal, I suspect your friends in the police can't touch them?'

'No, of course not, and it has become difficult for the local farmers and the families, they are living on scraps while the bulk of the crops disappear over the border.'

Steph thought again for a moment, trying to work out Faisal's angle and why he would part with such important information. 'Right, and so if we liberate these farms from the Iranians, it will help to make the Uruzghan clan that you work for more powerful and give them a greater hold over the area.'

'Yes, of course, and the farmers will receive money again for their crops, with the money staying here in Afghanistan and the flow of weapons will stop.'

'Okay, this is good information, Faisal. Do you have names, contacts, somewhere I can start looking?'

'Give me some time sister; a loaf can't be baked before the ingredients are mixed. I will see what I can get.' There was a pause and Steph could hear the sounds of young children playing in the background near Faisal.

'Now, do you have something for me?' Faisal demanded. 'When are the bearded devils moving again?'

'Well, Faisal, I saw today that they are going in their cars to the Chora Valley, so they shouldn't be a bother to you at all. There is a mixture of Australian Special Forces and Afghan army. They are delivering medical supplies so they won't be looking for a fight.'

'Not in the helicopters this time, that's good. We will watch out for them. How long are they going to be here?' Steph noted that he sounded more at ease now.

'Fourteen days,' she replied. She gave him all the details that she had seen in the Yankee Platoon's concept of operations brief, including their withdrawal route, which saw Yankee Platoon crossing briefly into the Mirabad Valley before moving through the dasht back to Tarin Kowt.

'Hmm, I see. You know, the other girl that I talk to doesn't tell me very much – and she doesn't pay me very much either.' Faisal laughed under his breath.

'We've talked about this before, Faisal. Don't ever mention me and don't try to play us off against each other. I would prefer it if you didn't talk to her at all. You know that.' Steph was annoyed now; he had given her this gem and then wrecked it with his usual crap.

'I'm joking, sister. I have a different phone for her and I only use my middle name.'

'Right, and how many Faisals are there in Tarin Kowt? Yours is a fairly uncommon Muslim middle name.' Steph had the shits now. *God these guys are useless*, she thought. Steph had been trained to handle post-Cold War operators in Eastern Europe. There was nothing in her training that had prepared her for the complete idiocy of the locals here.

'It's okay, all my brothers and uncles have the same middle name.' He laughed. 'I must go now, sister, it's time for prayers.'

'Faisal, remember, only use the phone I gave you to call me and don't ever call anyone else on it and don't talk about me to anyone, do you understand?'

'Yes, of course, nothing has changed; I will wait for the message, then text the first number and then ring the second. I understand, sister, rest easy. God willing, our friendship will be of benefit to us both.'

'Good, let me know when you have some more information and I will tell you when the devils are moving again.'

Steph hung up her phone and made some notes in her Moleskine. She sipped at her coffee and thought deeply about what

Faisal had just revealed as she watched the guys on the pitch start to organise another volleyball match. *The Iranians are controlling the crops and exchanging them for weapons to maintain the Taliban.* 'Well, that is interesting, the rest of the intelligence community thinks it's heroin,' Steph said out loud. She was enjoying this new game. She allowed herself a brief moment to imagine where she might be this time next year and wondered if there was a Starbucks in the White House.

7

CAMP RUSSELL, TARIN KOWT

'Sir, we have an issue.' Sam stopped the commanding officer as he was making his way from the gym back to his private accommodation.

'What is it, Sam? Make it quick, I have a teleconference with Regional Command South in twenty minutes.' The CO chugged down the last of the water in his plastic bottle and threw it effortlessly into the large rubbish bin by the side of the dirt track.

Sam quickened his stride in an effort to keep up with the CO.

'We intercepted some low-level fighters talking among themselves about some military vehicles that are heading up to the Chora Valley. They know when Yankee Platoon is going to leave the base and exactly how long they'll be in the valley. They also know that it is a mixture of our guys and Afghans delivering supplies.' Sam stumbled over a small pile of rocks and dropped the map he had been holding.

'What?' The CO stopped walking and turned to face him. 'How can they possibly know that? It must be someone from here, right?'

The noise of a C-130 landing on the airstrip just outside the wire drowned out all the other sounds and Sam waited for the engines to die down.

'Maybe, sir, I'm not sure yet. I only gave Yankee Alpha his update brief this morning. I don't think that he's even given his men their orders yet. So the only people here that know about the plan are the headquarters staff and Matt.'

'Well, that narrows it down somewhat.'

'Not really, sir. We have to ask the command in Kandahar for their approval of the concept of operations. They inform Regional Command South as well as brief the commander of Special Operations Command in Kabul. Then there are the Dutch; we cross-level all operations daily in the intelligence update brief – though I haven't given them the update brief yet; that's set for later this morning.' Sam's face was red from the heat. He was uncomfortable standing in the morning sun in his full combat fatigues. A bead of sweat ran down his cheek and he wiped it away with his sleeve.

'I'm aware of the process, Sam,' the CO said impatiently. He looked past Sam and off into the mountains in the distance.

'Well, I'm just saying, sir, that it's a convoluted process and there are many points at which it could be intercepted.'

'Hmm, yes, I agree.' The CO continued to gaze at the mountains.

'Sir, what was highly unusual about this intercept was that one of the handsets belonged to a human intelligence source working for the Dutch Intelligence Officer Allie van Tanken.'

'So are you saying *she's* responsible? We should move straight away if that's the case.' The CO was annoyed now.

Sam shrugged. 'Like I said, sir, the Dutch haven't even been briefed on the plan yet; it just means that their guy is getting his information from someone in the know. But it could also mean that the Dutch are aware that there is a leak, or they're conducting an operation that we don't know about. Maybe they're selling our information for some sort of gain.' Sam remembered the comment by Allie to Panetta in the intelligence update briefs the day before, when she'd suggested that Steph Baumer feed misinformation to her networks. He looked up at the CO to gauge his response and could see that this possibility had annoyed his boss even further.

'Right, well, that is an issue. Go and see the Dutch, find out what they know about this. Clearly the human intelligence networks need a shake-up.'

'I have an idea, sir.' Sam's mind was racing as he considered how to present it; if he didn't get the CO's buy-in, he might well shoulder the blame for this himself in the not-too-distant future.

'What are you thinking, Sam?' The CO started to walk again, but more slowly now.

'Well, if the leak is occurring after we submit our concept of operations plans up the chain of command, then we could use that to our advantage. We could send false concept of operations plans to the command in Kandahar . . .' Sam fell silent as they walked past four lads from Yankee Platoon who were returning from cleaning the heavy weapons in the vehicle yard.

'Go on,' the CO said when they were in no danger of being overheard.

'If we send generic plans that detail one thing, we could then do the opposite and perhaps uncover the leak within the human intelligence network.'

The CO thought for a moment, then nodded to show he liked where this was going. 'Or even better still,' he suggested, 'we could brief exactly what the commandos are going to do and then use it as a trap for the SAS to action against.'

'No, that's not exactly what I meant, sir.'

'Think about it, Sam.' The CO was sounding excited now. 'We would be showing only part of the plan – the part that concerned the commandos – while keeping the SAS involvement secret. We don't need to file concept of operations briefs with Kandahar if Terence's lads are responding or reacting to intelligence that is time-sensitive. In most cases, we should be able to judge when the enemy are going to launch an attack on the commandos and then be poised, ready to counterattack.'

He was practically rubbing his hands in glee and Sam had a pretty shrewd idea what he was thinking: the key performance indicator for the SOTG tours had always been Taliban leadership killed in action, and drawing them out like this would surely make them even easier to target.

'Yes, sir, that makes sense, I guess,' said Sam feeling the situation getting away from him.

'I like it, Sam. Let's set our own traps for the Taliban leadership. Good thinking.' The CO slapped Sam on the back.

'Thanks, boss,' Sam said, a little uneasily, not being sure how this had suddenly become his grand idea.

'Do you have a name for this operation, Sam?'

'No. Oh, hang on. What about Operation Ferret, you know, because we are using Yankee Platoon to ferret out the enemy?'

The CO gave Sam a bemused look. 'Really, that's the best you could come up with?'

'I've got it. Odin's Raven, sir. The commandos see themselves as modern day Vikings and Yankee Platoon are out forward of everyone for the time being, very much like Odin used his raven's in Viking folklore.'

The CO stopped abruptly and turned back to face Sam. 'That's good, Sam. Brief the Dutch, in as much as we need their help to try and find the leak. They don't need to know the rest.'

The CO started to walk away and Sam had to almost trot to keep up.

'The Dutch might smell something fishy if we present it as a counter-intelligence operation and then have Yankee Platoon's plans detailed within it, plans that they are actually going to go and execute.'

'Rubbish. They won't look that closely at the concepts, Sam. And if they do, we will cross that bridge as we come to it. Now get cracking mate, let's get this underway.'

'If you give me a couple of hours I can set up a brief and outline the situation so far – what we know and don't know, so to speak. We could then get Matt and Terence in and bring them up to speed.'

The CO stopped walking and fixed his gaze on Sam. 'No. No need to tell Captain Rix. Get something together and we'll update Terence.'

'But, sir,' Sam protested, 'Matt needs to know. I mean, otherwise they're going to be walking into a trap every time they leave the base, with no knowledge of what's going on.'

'Ah, they'll be fine. What they don't know won't hurt them, mate. I'm sure Captain Rix's planning is good enough to counter whatever the Taliban throws at him – and if we're going to fool the enemy, it's best if the commandos' responses are authentic.

No, this is just for you, Terence the RSM and myself. Besides, the less people who know about this, the less likely it is to be leaked and the better the results will be.'

'I see,' said Sam, though he wasn't sure he saw at all. He really didn't like the direction this conversation was taking. 'I think I get it, sir.'

'Good, that's settled then. I'll go round up Terence and the RSM, and we'll swing by the den at eleven am. Is that enough time?'

'Yes, sir, that's fine. But I've been updating the intelligence package for Matt's patrol and I asked him to come back at eleven.'

'Well, put him off,' the CO said brusquely. 'Tell him to drop by after dinner this evening. He can pick up the intelligence package from your guys then.'

'From my guys, sir?'

'This new information changes things, Sam. We can use this leak to our advantage. Pack an overnight bag, mate. I want you to come back with me to Kandahar today so that you can sift through the latest target deck and get a good feel for the leadership we're going to target with this. Let's chat about it some more at eleven.'

The CO took a few steps in the direction of his accommodation, then paused and came back. 'Oh, and Sam? Good work. You're a fine officer and I have a gut feeling that you're going to have great success with this.' He slapped Sam on the back and strode off.

Sam turned to go back to the intelligence building. He wasn't so sure about the CO's 'gut feeling'. His own gut was telling him the complete opposite, that he was going to be the fall guy if this went south.

8

THE INTELLIGENCE DEN

The CO stopped talking, closed his diary and put down his pen. The silence was broken by an incoming message on Sam's secret computer system in the corner of the room. Two more messages came in quick succession. Looking around at the three other men, he tapped his finger against the table waiting for a response. Sitting around the oval table, the men all thought about what the CO had just said. The room had been witness to many of the most important decisions the SOTG had made over the last few years. Various COs, some great and some not so great, and their staff had discussed operations and targeting serials on that shiny table that sat on an old tattered Afghan carpet. No bigger than an average dining room, the place was packed with computers, printers, secret fax machines, phones and monitors.

'So, do you understand the situation and what I need you to do, Terence?'

Saygen nodded. 'Yes, sir, I think I understand.'

'RSM, Captain Long, how about you two? No issues?' The CO narrowed his eyes. It was clear that he didn't want there to be any issues; particularly not in relation to using Yankee Platoon as bait.

'No, sir – all good.' The RSM said matter of factly.

'Good, it's understood then. We'll act under the assumption that the enemy has access to the concept briefs sent to the NATO HQ for approval. We'll use Yankee Platoon to draw the enemy out, and Terence will target off the back of the Taliban taking the fight to Matt's guys.'

'Yes, sir.' Saygen made a few more notes in his small notebook.

'So, Sam, why don't you update us on the most recent developments,' the CO suggested.

Sam brought up a chart on the big screen showing the local Taliban network within the province. These were primarily black-and-white cartoons depicting the traditional Arab, nondescript and wearing the headdress typical of the region's Bedouin. Below each image was the real name that the intelligence community assumed belonged to the objective, and above was a code name. There were over eighty of them in total. They were arranged from foot soldiers and low-level fighters to medium-value individuals and high-value targets.

'Okay, sir. We have this guy in recent developments. We don't have a definite name for him yet, but it is believed he might be Mullah Ghal. We think he is now in charge of much of the Taliban in the area and is thought to be operating from Quetta.' Sam clicked on one of the cartoon images and a fact sheet came up.

'He's an HVT, a high-value target. It's assumed that he's in his early fifties, has black hair and is of medium build. There's a scar running the length of his left cheek and a hole where the left eye once was – he doesn't wear an eye patch, either, as he believes the grotesque look earns him the fear and respect of his foot soldiers. He has a distinctive limp; local legend has it that he lost his foot and his eye when he stepped on a Soviet mine, but some say that in fact he has a club foot.'

'So we're not going to find the ugly fucker at the local Tarin Kowt square dance meet then,' said the RSM.

'No, RSM, it's believed he was once a close friend of Mullah Omar, who is still believed to be alive and well and leading the Taliban from a safe haven somewhere in Pakistan. This guy is a senior tribal judge who administers the border regions of Zabul bordering the Panjwai and Khakrez provinces. We are more likely to run into him managing a huge tribal meeting, what the Afghans refer to as shura. Not much else is known of him. We had a report in late January that he was spotted in Uruzghan by one of the human intelligence network, riding a Helmand 175 motorbike. This sighting wasn't corroborated nor was it from a very reliable source and it's now five months old so not of much use anyway.' Sam paused to give the other men time to study the fact sheet before bringing up the next screen.

'As you know, the main network is operating in and around Uruzghan Province. The latest operation the SAS conducted greatly attrited a large proportion of the lower-level fighters, as shown here.' Sam clicked his mouse and a series of more than twenty red crosses went through the bottom two tiers of foot soldiers.

Saygen looked across at the CO, who smiled at him.

'Well done, Terence – sterling effort from you and the lads, mate.'

They both turned their attention back to Sam, the CO observing. 'So, we are making some inroads; good work all around, eh, Sam?'

'Yes, sir, it's going well.' Sam clicked the mouse and another fact sheet came up on the big screen. 'This is Dahwood Wardak. Our sources indicate that he was here last week on the night of the attack on Camp Russell. This in itself is interesting, because in recent years he has taken a back seat from the fighting to focus primarily on making homemade explosives for IEDs. No known photo. What we do know about him is that he is tall and in his early forties. After the attack on the camp, one of our agents identified a possible location for his compound. It's the other side of Sorhk Lez, just past the Mirabad Valley, seventeen kilometres as the crow flies.'

'Only a few minutes' flight from here,' Saygen remarked.

'That's right,' Sam agreed. 'Just a stone's throw away, really – across the open dasht and out the other side of Tarin Kowt, then over the Mirabad Valley; with some deception thrown in, it's about fifteen minutes' flying at the most.'

'Dasht?' the RSM queried.

'Afghan word for the desert plains, RSM.'

The RSM nodded. 'Got it.'

Sam took a folder from his desk. 'Terence, here's the target pack, maps and all the reports on the area, just in case you need it in the coming days.'

'Right, thanks, Sam.' Saygen took the proffered file. 'Is there a trigger to launch on this punter – what's his name . . . Dahwood?'

The CO stood up and walked over to a large map hanging on the wall. He turned side on to the group. 'That's where Rix comes in. His platoon is going to patrol through this corridor here and move past these key areas over the next couple of weeks.' The CO turned back to the map and traced a wide arc through Tarin Kowt up to the Chora Valley and back around. Terence watched him, silently wondering what that would mean for Matt and his platoon.

Sam nodded in agreement. 'We can't be exactly sure when he will be there. He rarely stays on a phone or radio for very long, unless he's reporting information and most of the neighbours want nothing to do with any of our field agents. It's going to have to be a drop-in on his compound, triggered by Yankee Platoon's movement in that area. Then you either kill or capture him and turn the place over looking for evidence of IEDs. You'll know pretty quickly if you have him as we suspect that his fingerprints are all over the IEDs that were found on the last rotation.'

'Understood. Thanks, Sam.' Saygen tapped the folder.

'Go over the package, Terence,' said the CO, 'and brief me tomorrow afternoon when I return from Kandahar.'

'Roger that.' Saygen got up to leave.

'Oh, and Terence?' The CO looked at Saygen and then his gaze swept over to encompass Sam and the RSM. His expression was serious. 'The situation with the commandos is compartmented. No one is to discuss it outside of this group. I hope I make myself clear.'

9

TASK GROUP GYM

Terence Saygen racked the hundred and twenty kilos back onto the bench press and jumped up onto the heave beam. With his hands shoulder-width apart he quickly lifted his body until his chin was above the beam, then he slowly controlled it down again. He raised himself up easily ten more times, admiring himself in the mirror as he did so. On the last chin-up he saw Matt Rix walking past the gymnasium door in the direction of the intelligence hut.

'Poor bastard,' Saygen said under his breath as he dropped off the beam.

'What's up with that joker, skipper?' said Sledge, one of Saygen's older troopers, as he walked past to place some weights back on the shelf.

'Nothing, mate – I suspect in the next few days he's going to get his arse handed to him by the Taliban, though.' Saygen half laughed as he ran his sweaty hands through his jet-black hair.

'No big deal, we can pull 'em out of the shit as always.' The trooper dropped the two forty-five-kilogram dumbbells on the rubber matting. The dull thud reverberated throughout the gym.

Saygen kept his eye on Rix as the Yankee Platoon leader walked past the gym windows and made his way along the dusty track that linked the mess hall and the headquarters building. Saygen felt uneasy about the secret he had been let in on earlier that day. He enjoyed mixing it with the commando when the odds were even, but now that the deck was stacked against Rix, he couldn't help but feel the unfairness of the situation.

'Yeah – I certainly hope so,' Saygen said to himself.

. . .

Matt breathed in deeply. The late-afternoon air was clear and with the heat of the day now gone, so too was the stench from the open septic pits at the end of the airfield. It had been a long week for Yankee Platoon. The defence of the base followed by an ADFIS investigation and now rushing to prepare the vehicles for a mobility operation had worn Matt out. He was looking forward to getting out in the dasht. At least there he would be in charge of the operational tempo.

Matt looked down the road that ran out of the camp and all the way off across the airfield and up into the hills. He could see every-thing out in the landscape in sharp focus. He had noticed a few days before that at this time of the year the wind stopped at around three in the afternoon, and not long after that the dust would settle.

Walking past the kitchen he could hear the sounds of pots and pans being bashed around the sinks. The locally employed contractors were rushing to complete their day's work. They always worked faster at the end of the day. Matt assumed it was because they were keen to get to the front of the long line for the security check before being allowed to exit the base. They were all keen to get back to Tarin Kowt before sunset. The sprawling township would soon come alive with the evening call for prayer.

Matt continued past the door to the headquarters and followed the winding path down to the intelligence cell's small offices. Overhead, two giant CH-47 Chinooks thundered in, their twin blades snapping through the wind as they landed at the airstrip on the other side of Camp Russell. The helicopters were part of an intricate resupply system that maintained the utility of the outposts. They would fly in fast and low, always mixing up their routes to avoid sporadic ground fire. Not ten seconds behind, the two Apache escorts screamed in, their sensors scanning for threats. The Apaches circled overhead as the Chinooks settled down on the landing pads.

Matt stood there for a moment, watching. The commandos had done months of build-up work with the Chinooks and the Black Hawks at their base back in Holsworthy. They had rehearsed loading drills, exiting the aircraft at speed while simulating being under fire, and practised fast roping onto target roofs all under covering fire from the snipers restrained in other circling helicopters. Prior to their deployment, the training had been tortuous and yet they had not been given any firm indication of when they might actually get to use the Black Hawks. Matt found his frustration growing as he watched the aircraft land.

The intelligence cell was deliberately located separate to the main buildings so that the most sensitive information and capabilities could be housed there. Pushing open the wooden door, Matt stepped inside; the aroma of apple cider muffins, microwaved just minutes before, filled the air. From the small foyer he could go in one of two directions. To the left was the intelligence briefing room, the den, and multiple offices for the staff; to the right was the common room where the analysts spent their downtime. From this room, Matt could hear the sounds of an Aussie Rules football game blaring.

'Can I help you, mate?'

Matt turned to see a scraggly-haired corporal. Straight away Matt profiled him as a support guy. He was wearing the largest dive watch Matt had ever seen and had grown his bleached hair to the point where he could have stepped straight off a surf beach in Hawaii. Probably great at his job, but subconsciously he had a complex that he was not an operator.

'G'day, is Sam around?'

'No, he left.' The corporal went to skirt around Matt but Matt took a step to the left, blocking his exit.

'Where to?'

'Kandahar. He left with the CO an hour ago or something like that. I dunno, to be honest.'

'Right, so will he be back tonight?' Matt could feel his patience wearing thin.

'Nah. Maybe late tomorrow. Now, if you don't mind, mate . . .' The young corporal motioned to move past Matt.

Matt grabbed the corporal's arm, his frustration mounting. 'Listen, mate, I know that you can read the rank I'm wearing and I suggest that at some point you find a certain level of professionalism. I'm not here on a social call so let's start this conversation again, shall we? Where's Sam?' Matt released his arm and the corporal took a quick step backwards.

'Like I said, he's in Kandahar – *sir*,' the corporal responded, the emphasis on the 'sir' bordering dangerously close to insolence. He rubbed his forearm where Matt had sunk his thumb in.

'Careful, champ, it's a long tour and I have an even longer memory,' said Matt. 'Sam told me earlier today to come here for an update briefing regarding Yankee Platoon's next mission. Did he say anything about it, or is there someone else here I can see?'

'Oh, you're Yankee's commander? Right, right – sorry, I didn't realise. Nice work the other night, man. Jesus, I can't believe you smashed the Bushmasters through our own gates. Fucking awesome, bro!' The young signal corporal stuck out his hand.

Matt briefly shook it, inwardly shaking his head. He didn't like this new type of support guy. On what planet does a corporal call a captain mate, especially on their first encounter? It was the lack of respect that this new breed of soldier displayed that amazed him.

'Oh yeah, that's right, Sam left a target pack and some maps and an area overview for you. It's in the briefing room. I'll just go get it, mate,' the corporal said, as if to reinforce Matt's already low opinion of him. He turned and jogged off to the sound of cheers from the common room; someone must have scored a goal, thought Matt.

Standing there waiting, Matt considered the corporal's response when he realised that Matt was Yankee Alpha. He wondered what everyone else made of the counterattack that Yankee Platoon had conducted. The contractors had worked feverishly all week to fix the barracks and gates and now there was no sign of what had occurred; it was as though the whole thing had been nothing more than a hellish nightmare.

The corporal returned and presented Matt with a map and a large yellow envelope. 'Here you go then, sir.' Matt noticed that this time the 'sir' was uttered with genuine respect. 'This should do the trick. If there's anything else I can help you with, just drop by anytime. The name's Jarrod – though my mates call me J-dog.'

'Of course they do, Jarrod. Are you going to explain any of this to me?' Matt said as he opened the yellow envelope and began flicking through the sheets of paper.

'Well, no, Sam didn't actually tell us anything about it – he just told me to get it to you today. Oh, he did say to pass on that the Taliban have an IED campaign going on, so you should keep off the tracks where possible.'

Another cheer erupted from the common room.

'Did it ever cross your mind to maybe come find me?' Matt demanded.

'Sam said *you'd* find *me*,' the corporal countered. 'Can I go now, sir?' He gestured in the direction of the common room. 'I really want to watch this and it's actually my day off.'

'Oh, I see, it's your day off,' Matt said sarcastically.

The corporal shrugged and smiled.

As he left the intelligence cell, Matt considered going to the platoon office, but then thought better of it. He had spent too many hours in there over the last month, jumping through all the admin hoops required when a unit arrived in Afghanistan. The Yankee Platoon common room was also not an option as the guys would undoubtedly be Skyping wives or girlfriends. Even worse would be if the lads had networked their computers across the barracks and were now screaming insults at each other across the hall as their avatars fought it out in *Call of Duty 2*. The mess hall would be free, though, and there Matt could spread the maps and reports out across one of the long tables and study them in silence.

• • •

Matt had delivered his platoon preliminary orders earlier in the evening, setting the wheels in motion for JJ to organise the feverish packing and repacking required to get outside the wire. While the men packed Bushmasters, changed batteries, printed maps and loaded global positioning systems with waypoints, Matt worked on his final orders. He would deliver these early the next day, prior to setting off on their first vehicle patrol of the tour. Sometimes the best thing to do with these types of operations was to just to get out of the base and onto the dasht. Out there they could set up and conduct an even more detailed analysis, safe in the knowledge that in the middle of the desert plains nothing the enemy had could reach them. Well almost nothing, save for IEDs and the occasional 107mm rocket. The great thing with a disrupt mission was that just being out there was disruptive to the enemy and provided most of the stimulus needed to draw them in.

Matt stared into his cup of black coffee, wishing it was half as good as the coffee he'd enjoyed in Italy on his last leave. And thinking of Italy inevitably led to thoughts of Rachel. Matt had really enjoyed her company in the Dolomites. They had been friends for a while, and had started a long distance relationship some months before when she had arrived from London to see friends in Australia. Matt had suggested they meet next in Italy, in a little place that his family went to every few years for holidays. The meeting had coincided with his leave before his next deployment and she had seemed very keen to see more of him.

After the skiing holiday, Rachel had come back to Dubai where Matt joined the rest of his platoon at the Al Minhad air base prior to entering Afghanistan. From there Rachel had gone on to India on a writing assignment. The last time he had seen her was when they parted at the airport. She had told him that their lives were going in different directions and that there was probably no point in continuing with their relationship. He'd begged her to reconsider, promising that they would talk again soon. That had been eight weeks ago. It was the same old story; he had never been able to maintain a relationship for more than a couple of months. It always came down to a choice between the girl and the army. Work had always won in the past – and he had a feeling it always would.

Yawning, Matt gathered up the papers and maps and stuffed them back into the envelope.

Making his way back to his room, he looked at his watch. It was already past midnight and with the promise of only four hours sleep to come before he was to prepare for the final orders, he dropped the maps and his notebook on his bedside table and lay down on his bed, boots and all, and was asleep in seconds.

10

MIRABAD VALLEY

'How much further, Ahmed?' Dahwood Wardak had volunteered to carry the heaviest of the equipment. At six feet two inches, he was a lot taller than Ahmed, and very strong as a result of years tending his opium crops. One of Dahwood's talents was to blend in with the locals. He looked like a poor simple farmer, but he could pull out a PKM machine gun that had been hidden in a bush, fire off a long burst, and then be ploughing the field again in the space of a minute. He was very handy and Ahmed was glad for his help.

Dahwood tried to adjust the heavy load on his back; the evening's work had taken its toll, even on someone with his strength. The two twenty-kilo containers of homemade explosives shifted awkwardly, forcing him down onto one knee. 'I'm not sure I can carry these much further,' he said. 'It feels like we have been out here all night.'

'See that tree, Dahwood – the one on the edge of the small creek bed? We will put the surprise in there. These are the last two, and then we are done. My family has a small farm not far from here; we can rest there and then walk back to the car in the morning.'

'How do you know where to put these, Ahmed?' Dahwood asked. 'We have been all over the dasht and placed these containers everywhere, but not one of them is buried on a road.' Dahwood resumed walking, focusing on where to place his feet.

'Brother Dahwood, you must be blind – the infidel don't use the roads anymore, my friend. Not unless they are hard black roads. It would be a waste of our time to put these on dirt tracks.'

'That's true. I noticed they don't use the tracks much these days. Sometimes they even drive through my new fields.'

'Yes, and digging under a real road is dangerous.' Ahmed dropped down into the creek line and started to count out his paces. 'Fifteen, sixteen, seventeen, eighteen – this is it.' Ahmed dropped to his knees and scraped at the ground with his small shovel.

'How can you be so sure?' Dahwood lowered the yellow water containers full of the explosive.

'I have seen them walk through here. There's no track but they all come together from the open to cross this small wadi at this narrow place. If we bury the explosives here, I can use that tree to judge when the right person is down near the surprise then use my phone to activate it. Now, let's dig this hole. Both of these containers need to be completely hidden, so it might take a while.'

The two men continued to dig the hole in complete darkness.

'Ahmed, I have another question,' Dahwood said eventually.

'Yes, brother, what is it?'

'Why did you choose tonight to do this?'

Ahmed gave a little laugh and stopped digging. He looked over at his friend. Dahwood had never been that bright but he was very loyal. In the infidel's lair he had given a particularly good account of himself. He was one of the last to climb the ladder out of the vehicle yard. He had stood at the bottom and fought till the last minute, encouraging the others to escape before him.

'Do you hear that, Dahwood?'

'Hear what?'

'The helicopters?'

'No, I can't hear anything at all – it's very quiet tonight.'

'Hmm, well, can you see the moon?' Ahmed went back to his digging while waiting for his friend's response.

'Yes.' Standing up, Dahwood looked at the horizon. 'It is almost down now. It was full earlier tonight, I could see a long way.'

'That's right, Dahwood. The infidel doesn't seem to come out when the moon is this bright. No helicopters or planes. They like to move when it is down or when it is not there at all. I'm not sure why, but there is a pattern. When the moon has fully disappeared our targets will come.'

'I think they might fit now, Ahmed.' Dahwood took the first container, placed it in the hole at his feet, then put the second one next to it.

'So what now? I know how to do the pressure plate but not this.'

Ahmed emptied the sack he had been carrying and arranged the various parts next to the hole in the order that they would be connected.

'Place these two squibs into each container, Dahwood. These will set off the explosives. You see the wires coming out of the back of the squibs?'

'Yes, I see them.'

'Good, braid them together.'

Ahmed watched as Dahwood deftly braided the four wires.

'Now we connect them to these two spikes in the receiving box. It turns this into an electrical firing circuit. This motorbike battery is the power source: it goes into the hole and we connect the receiving box to the battery.'

'Ah, I see.' Dahwood squatted by the containers. He was enjoying the lesson.

'This wire is the antenna for the remote control. Connect it to the box and then it is live.'

'Where is the remote?' Dahwood's face reflected the immediate concern he felt for his own safety.

'It's my phone, brother. But do not worry; the phone has no battery yet. It's completely pulled apart in my pocket. Once charged I will be able to send an SMS to a special number and it will set off this surprise. Boom!' Ahmed smiled at Dahwood.

'It's time to run the signal wire out. Take this and wind it up the tree. Try and hide it as much as you are able to,' said Ahmed, handing Dahwood the thin green wire.

'Yesterday, Faisal and I dug in another three of these into the ground. That vehicle patrol that you warned Faisal about, well, a friend told me where the infidel were going the day before they left. They went up to the Chora Valley and they are slowly making their way back to Tarin Kowt.'

Ahmed got down and laid on the ground watching a faint outline of Dahwood deftly climbing the tree with the wire. He sat back up and looked at his fingers, he could barely make out his hand in the darkness. 'A few years ago another of the infidel patrols

74

went up that same way. When they came back they crossed into this valley at the bottom. I watched them. They drive up and clear the tracks of mines and then when they come back they are more confident and take less time. That's when I will arm the mines. There's an area not very far from here where they drop down into a creek line. They set their tanks up on either side to cover the movement across. Then when it's clear they line up their tanks on the left of the road to organise themselves. All it takes is one wheel out of many to run over the mine. They're predictable, Dahwood.'

While Dahwood climbed down Ahmed put all the leftover bits and pieces, including the sack, into the hole then proceeded to shovel dirt back in.

'Now, let's finish off. If we walk over the hole and then brush these branches over it, the area will look untouched. Then the locals will start to use the track again. Tomorrow I will instruct Abdullah Afzal Aman to bring the goats through here for a few hours to disguise it even further. If the infidel happen to travel this way, which they will, they won't see it. It will just look like any creek crossing point.'

'But how do you know they will ever come out this way? They haven't been here for many months.'

'When I am ready, I will send someone to that building back there with one of our Thurayas.'

Dahwood gave Ahmed a confused look.

'It's a satellite phone. We have some that we know the infidel like to listen to. Once it's turned on it won't take long before they come looking for the phone and we will be watching them. Even if they miss all the bombs out there,' Ahmed pointed out into the dasht, where the two men had spent the evening placing pressure-plate IEDs, 'they will come through here, then I will give them a surprise myself.'

'You are much smarter than they are, brother. Allah will reward you with many infidel deaths, I think.'

'They believe we are stupid, but what they don't realise is that they wear the watches, but we have all the time in the world. I sit back and look at them and learn.'

The moon disappeared below the horizon and the valley was plunged into darkness.

'Do you hear that, Dahwood?' As if on cue a low hum started far out over the horizon. Slowly the low humming noise increased. 'Hurry now, Dahwood, we must be inside before they come overhead.'

The two Afghans reached the farm just as the low hum turned into the distinctive roar of four Black Hawk helicopters.

• • •

The helicopters sped across the desert plain, twenty metres above the ground.

Australian SAS troops sat on the edge of the birds, held in by retaining straps as they scanned the dasht with their NVGs. Unseen by the Afghans, giant infrared searchlights lit up the area. The birds dropped down to just ten metres above the desert floor and vectored in towards their target at a hundred and forty knots.

'Two minutes!' the loadmaster yelled inside the back of the first aircraft. He held up two Cyalume sticks to ensure the message was seen as well as heard.

'Two minutes!' the troops replied in unison as they unfastened their retaining straps, stowing them away in their left-hand cargo pockets. Weapons were checked and NVGs adjusted, last-minute checks of equipment and radios all carried out in grey and green darkness as the wind battered the men in the back of the aircraft.

. . .

The birds screamed across the top of the compound where Ahmed and Dahwood were hiding, four giant grey shapes flashing across the black sky.

'I wonder where they are going?' Dahwood asked.

'It doesn't really matter, brother – we're not there, but I suspect it's your compound in Sorhk Lez, Dahwood.' Ahmed smiled at his old friend.

'Huh, I don't understand?'

'Where was that vehicle patrol that went past this afternoon?'

'It was on the next ridgeline from my farm.'

'That's right, and where did you call Faisal Khan from to inform him of their movements?'

'From my compound, Ahmed?' Dahwood looked down at his feet and screwed up his brow.

'And where is your phone now? Is it still on? Oh, and how many times have I told you not to call anyone from your home, you silly old fool.'

11

CHORA VALLEY

'So that's it, boss – our first two-week vehicle operation done and dusted.'

Matt shook his head. 'Not so fast, JJ; the mission's finished when the last vehicle rolls through the front gate tomorrow. How about you guys: any questions, lads?'

Matt looked at each of the four team commanders huddled in the back of the locked-down command vehicle. The command vehicle was one of twelve operated by Yankee Platoon. Two vehicles faced out at every cardinal point, making a ring of steel that could be covered by the vehicle's weapon systems. The command vehicle sat protected in the centre of the ring with the two mortar vehicles directly opposite. Matt had just given the platoon commanders convoy orders for the next day and they had war-gamed events that could reasonably occur on the trip back to Tarin Kowt.

'No questions from me, boss,' Ben Braithwaite, the Team One commander said. The other team commanders followed suit.

They continued to pore over the maps in the dim red light illuminating the back of the Bushmaster. The tactical red lighting ensured that the vehicles remained hidden from any spotters sitting out on the mountains. It also reduced everything in the back of the vehicle to every shade of red. With the orders complete, Matt switched off the tactical lights, plunging the vehicle into darkness. The team commanders exited the vehicle one by one, returning to their team positions on the perimeter. JJ stayed sitting in the vehicle eating a cup of noodles.

For the past two weeks Yankee Platoon had been tasked with destroying the Taliban's spotter network throughout the Chora Valley. The Taliban had mistaken it for an Australian Infantry platoon operating away from company support. An important distinction not known to the Taliban was Yankee Platoon's will to take the fight right up to the enemy and the sophisticated targeting and optical systems fitted to its platoon's vehicles.

From the first day, the spotters had tried to organise resistance to the platoon's movements north. Matt's men had sat in the relative safety of the dasht and triangulated the spotters' locations using feeds from drones, sensors and optics. Once all the positions had been registered, Matt's mortars would engage the targets and the .50-cal machine guns and the MK19 40mm grenade launchers would take on those stupid enough to come down the mountains for a closer look. In some of the break-neck cuttings where there was only the one way to go through, Matt's men dismounted in front of the cars and fought their way through the clumsy ambushes that the enemy had set up to try and delay their movement. Conducting this type of disruption operation and taking the fight to the spotter network assisted the Americans in the area, who were conducting village security operations, and also the Australian infantry who had been having trouble moving along the main service road between Chora and Uruzghan.

In the last few days of their patrol Matt had taken the vehicles higher still up into the mountains and along the roads and passes north of the Chora Valley. The route deserved respect and careful navigation. The area itself was breathtaking; the lush green valleys became gigantic rock escarpments that soared into the blue sky. As their vehicles wound further up the tracks the landscape became more inhospitable and the air thinner, making the sky an even darker blue. Massive open areas of rocky desert plateaus overlooked the deep valleys far below. It was like being on top of the world. The time away from the base had been hectic and the men had inflicted heavy losses on the Taliban, but they had been left to their own devices. Far from the flagpole, they managed their own destiny.

'Boss, I know you've received orders from the CO to conduct another operation after we get back, and orders are orders, but don't they know we've been fighting here solid for a fortnight and need some downtime?' JJ leaned forward; reaching under the black steel cage that protected the radio stack, he fished around for another pre-packaged instant noodle cup. 'Can't you call the CO and let him know the guys are trashed and need a break? I mean, you have a duty to let him know that too, right?'

Matt stared at the sergeant thoughtfully for a moment. The CO would hardly be likely to view such a call favourably. It wasn't unusual, though, for a commando sergeant to give such frank, unsolicited advice – especially when it wasn't him who would have to do the asking. Matt considered JJ's protestation.

The light from the laptop reflected on Matt's face. 'It's all good, JJ,' he said finally, despite the fact that he shared the sergeant's concerns. 'It's a helicopter insertion and a roll-up of some small compound; it will be over in hours. It's a time-sensitive target, what we trained for back in Holsworthy.' Matt closed the lid of the computer, effectively putting an end to the conversation. A lack of food and a week of exhausting combat coupled with subordinates who wanted to question every decision had worn on Matt's patience.

'Yeah, right. Well, we both know that the reason we've been stuffing around up here in Chora is so that the cats don't have to justify their use of the helicopters or share them with anyone. Why are we getting them now anyway? It doesn't make any sense to me. It's probably some shit target that they didn't want.' JJ always referred to SAS as 'the cats', especially when he was pissed off at them. Matt knew that the truth was SAS were kicking goals with the helicopters at the moment. They were on a good run and he couldn't blame the CO for continuing to use them up until now, but they probably needed a break to refit their own gear. Matt knew that he had been penalised by his command, rightly or wrongly, for his role in the defence of the compound against the Taliban attack, which was why they were out here rather than jumping from target to target on two-hour missions and then spending the remainder of the day back in the gym at Camp Russell. But now it was his turn to prove they were up to the even faster-paced helicopter operations.

'JJ, don't be concerned with what *they* are doing, mate. You just worry about us. There's no point losing sleep over things you can't change or influence.' Matt sighed internally. It wasn't the first time that he and JJ had been down this path.

'Sure, let's just hope that the pricks don't take the birds while we're out there, leaving us to walk home.' Snorting, JJ shoved another spoon of noodles into his mouth, but missed. The noodles dribbled down his cheek.

'I'm sure it'll be fine. Let's concentrate on what we can control, like getting out of here tomorrow morning. Six hours of driving back to TK and then a full planning cycle. It's gonna be a busy day and I'm gonna need you on my side with this.'

JJ grunted his acknowledgment. Matt wasn't convinced of his agreement though. JJ felt hard done by when it came to SAS and headquarters and it had a negative impact on the platoon. He'd have to address the sergeant's attitude sooner or later, but for now he just wanted to focus on the task at hand and make sure the platoon survived it.

Matt opened the door of the heavy-armoured vehicle and stepped outside. The black of night was in complete contrast to the red lights of the command vehicle interior. He stood there for a moment and let his eyes slowly adjust to the night sky and the billions of stars above. A cool breeze whipped up and then disappeared back off into the quiet night.

Matt took off his combat body armour and placed it neatly on the ground, leaving the arm straps open in case he needed to pull it back on in a hurry. He placed his helmet next to the armour with the NVGs set up ready to be switched on, and put the M4 rifle just inside his swag, that was attached by a rope to the command vehicle.

Matt crawled into the small space. He was exhausted. The thin foam mattress and the old summer-weight army blanket did little to soften the rocks protruding from the harsh ground.

He could hear the muffled snickers of the commandos who were pulling security duties around the perimeter. One Bushmaster in every pair had a soldier manning a weapon system. The commandos were probably looking at each other through NVGs and talking over their patrol radios. Occasionally there was the distinctive sound of metal clicking or the whirr of thermal sites changing focus. Such noises could be fatal in the close quarters of the jungle, or even in a semi-rural environment, but out here on the open desert plateau it was different. They had three-sixty-degree views and the approaches were all covered by the .50-cal machine guns and the MK19 40mm grenade launchers. In the dark the platoon had technical overmatch against any weapon the enemy had, and for this reason the noises were comforting.

Overhead the dullest hum of a tactical drone, controlled somewhere out of Kandahar, provided another layer of safety and reassurance. The drone could see for miles all around the platoon's vehicles. Sleep came over Matt in a wave, the type of unconsciousness only known by those who have pushed both body and mind well past their breaking point. It was akin to going under a general anaesthetic. Matt's body instantly responded and started to repair. The sleep ensured that tired and sore muscles regenerated and energy levels rejuvenated.

. . .

High up the mountainside, a young Taliban spotter moved his position in order to get a better vantage point on the Australian forces. He had been walking for hours after seeing the vehicles earlier in the day. After talking to some goatherds, he had worked out the direction that the Australians would take and where he would be most likely to intercept them.

He concealed himself behind a rocky outcrop only a few kilometres away from the Australians. Cupping his hands, he lit a cigarette and peered down into the darkness of the valley below. His vigilance was rewarded as he spotted the faintest sliver of white light in an area that was familiar to him. It lasted a few seconds and then it was gone. He dragged deeply on the cigarette, little knowing that in doing so he was alerting the ever-watchful drone far above him to his presence.

The spotter sent an SMS to Faisal Khan, notifying him of the platoon's location and anticipated driving route for the next morning. This message sealed his fate: it gave the drone the confirmation of hostile intent that it legally required.

Two minutes later, a nearby AC-130 Spectre gunship was vectored onto the target by the drone. The Spectre crew worked silently and methodically on the information. They unleashed the 105mm gun of destruction on the lonely dark figure below. Through the gun-sight the crew watched the Taliban sitting there. The thermal digital optics showed the moment that the Taliban's body warmth spread across the ground like jam on toast. Somewhere down the valley yet another family had just lost a son.

The Spectre itself never felt remorse; it was a highly efficient killing machine devoid of emotion. This crew had spent hundreds of hours peering through green–black optics, securing their targets and eliminating them. They no longer even thought of the forms that they engaged with as people; the crew was merely a biological attachment to the war machine: a well-trained and tight unit in their electronic battle.

Matt slept through it all. Sometimes sleep like this is earned; to be dead to the world but still alive is a feeling only some people will ever know.

The Spectre continued its deathly flight home, deviating here and there to take more sons from their families. Judge, jury and executioner.

The circle of Australian Special Forces vehicles sat in the dark. The security piquet silently monitored the surroundings. So secure was the position that in the back of one of the vehicles the men were sufficiently relaxed to be playing cards in the red light. The next day, however, would be a different story. The next day, Yankee Platoon would receive a violent introduction to Objective Rapier. This meeting would have a profound impact on all their lives.

12

CHORA VALLEY

Crawling out of his swag Matt looked around the perimeter. Another cool dawn that would soon give way to a sweltering day. The sky was light blue with bright orange traces just starting to emerge on the horizon. The surrounding mountains kept the plateau in shadow.

Matt grabbed his body armour and his M4, ready to go patrol the perimeter.

The rest of Matt's six-man command team had slept on the other side of the vehicle. Daniel Barnsley, Matt's signaller, was sitting up in his sleeping bag. Looking off into space and scratching his head, Barnsley looked like he had not slept in a month.

'What are you doing, Barns?' Matt asked as he walked past.

'Nuthin', boss, just waking up,' replied Barnsley, his sandy-coloured hair matted in the shape of a witch's hat.

'Mate, why didn't you get your swag down last night?' said Matt, not at all surprised to find Barnsley, yet again, roughing it on the hard ground in only his sleeping bag.

'Dunno.' Barnsley yawned.

Matt continued walking. Lying next to Barnsley in their swags were the command vehicle driver and the Air Force JTAC, who talked to coalition aircraft and vectored them in to dump thousands of pound of munitions onto targets. Matt's JTAC had been so successful that there were times he truly felt sorry for the Taliban sitting up in the rocky escarpments. The next vehicle along was JJ's, and he was already up. JJ had the Jetboil on and was making his morning coffee, as was his ritual.

'Want one, boss?'

'Yeah, go on then. All quiet last night?' Matt asked.

'Yep, all quiet – other than the Spectre dropping bombs up and down the valley for an hour. I got some sleep and then woke up at about two and checked the security piquet. Cinzano's guys were still up playing poker in the back of their gun car.'

'What, the guys on piquet?'

'No, boss – the whole team.'

'Seriously? Did you kick their arses? We have a big drive today and I need them on their A game.'

'Yeah, boss, I rolled the lot of them. Rennie led the last hand with a pair of aces and I had a full house, took the whole kitty. You should have seen Cinzano's face when I collected.'

'That's not what I meant.' Matt slung his rifle and took the coffee from JJ.

Walking around the perimeter in the morning helped Matt to collect his thoughts. He would visit each team in turn and talk with the guys while they cleaned their weapons or sat around having breakfast. It was a good chance to make sure that everyone knew the plan for the coming day and their part in it. Matt believed that this was the type of discipline that won wars. No matter how tired or stressed he was, Matt made the conscious decision to see every guy every time they had a halt of more than an hour.

When he reached Cinzano's team they were all crashed out next to the vehicle.

'Rob,' Matt called, kicking Cinzano's feet. 'Get up, mate. Get your guys up and get your vehicles ready.'

A mumble came from within the swag and Cinzano unzipped the outer vestibule. Around him, his team started to stir and unzip their swags.

'On it, boss.' Cinzano sprung out and started to hurry his men. His show of enthusiasm did not fool Matt.

'Come and see me when we get back, Rob, I think we need to have a chat. It's twenty past six and you guys are still holed up in your swags.' Matt walked away before Cinzano could respond in earnest. Things had always been strained between them. Cinzano had the type of personality that irritated Matt: he had no ability to self-reflect and did not learn from his mistakes, both major weaknesses in Matt's books. Matt decided that he would have it out with him when they were back in TK. This past year Cinzano had actually got worse, not better. It was beginning to become apparent that Rob's future with the platoon was in doubt.

• • •

An hour later and they were ready to go. Matt's driver kicked the Bushmaster into action and they set off behind the lead cars.

Matt sat in the left passenger seat with his Toughbook computer and a small whiteboard that he used to keep track of information. Matt wrote down the order of vehicles in his platoon as they headed off. He turned on his GPS and noted their platoon patrol base grid reference. He had already selected a rendezvous point that they would use should they come under attack and he was now looking at his map to analyse the route home. The Toughbook contained aerial mapping and Matt had a digital overlay of concentric range rings for different weapons that he would superimpose over the lead vehicle. This was so that he could assess where the enemy might place an ambush.

Matt looked around. His platoon was strung out over a kilometre and they moved cautiously forward along the desert plateau. They had to cover fifteen kilometres before they were required to drop down into the green belt for a few kilometres. The lead vehicle carried the engineers. They stopped at every crossing point to check the area with metal detectors and the military working dog.

Cinzano's Team Two vehicle was directly behind it and then Ben Braithwaite's Team One vehicle behind that. Matt's command vehicle was fourth in the order of march, followed by Eddie Butcher and Joseph Hammond, leaders of Teams Three and Four. The last two cars were JJ's gun car and the snipers' Bushmaster. Matt had lead sniper Jensen Pharris's vehicle last as they had done the bulk of the navigating over the last two weeks and deserved an easy ride home. Jensen was Maori. He talked very little but heard everything. Matt was never sure if the other man actually liked him or barely tolerated him; either way he was happy to have him in his platoon. The guy was a jet and his snipers were often the deciding factor in combat.

Up ahead, the lead vehicle drew to a halt.

'Boss, we have something here.' The engineer warrant officer's voice sounded nervous over the radio.

'Roger – how long?' Matt enquired while looking down at his map and making note of the location.

'I'm not sure, it looks complicated. Maybe an hour?' This was delivered as more of a question than an answer. Matt hated that about these guys. While the engineers had more than proven their worth, the fact that they didn't have a robust selection course was always clearly evident to him. Matt felt they were softer than his guys, more easily rattled and concerned for their own welfare rather than the team's mission.

'Okay, Greg – do what you need to do.' Matt looked in his side mirror; he could already see JJ storming his way down the side of the parked vehicles.

Oh God, what now? thought Matt.

JJ stopped at the vehicle behind his and started to talk to the driver. Matt could see he was becoming animated.

Matt got out of his seat and moved through the back of the Bushmaster. He leaped out the back door and closed it behind him.

'JJ, what's doing, mate?' Matt asked.

'Nothing, boss – just pointing out to this dickhead that he isn't following your tracks and that he's going to get himself and everyone else killed.'

This seemed a bit dramatic to Matt. Looking up at the Bushmaster driver he could see that he was upset. JJ was terrifying when he decided to take someone to task.

'He gets the point, mate,' said Matt. He turned and headed towards the front vehicles. Greg was another hundred metres forward, lying on his stomach and, presumably, dismantling an IED. Matt decided not to distract him and returned to his own vehicle.

An hour passed and then word came from Greg that it was safe to continue. The vehicles started forward again at a slow pace. Losing an hour was all par for the course in Afghanistan and was already factored into the overall plan.

'Yankee Alpha, are you there, boss?' Greg's voice came over Matt's headset.

Seriously, what is it now? Matt grumbled to himself. *Another IED?* 'Yes, mate,' he said aloud, 'I'm here. What have you got now?'

'Nothing, boss, I just wanted to let you know about that last IED.'

'Go on – what about it?'

'Well, it had no metal in it. We only found it because of the dog. It was mega sophisticated and there was also a tamper switch inside the bucket with the homemade explosives.' Greg paused and then continued. 'Boss, the battery was flat, otherwise it would have blown me apart.' Greg sounded upset now; he was only alive due to the hinge factor, pure luck: a battery that was flat on its insertion into the device or that had just died after being left in the ground in the heat. Either way, it wasn't Greg's skill that saw him live to fight another day and he knew it.

'Okay, understood, mate – let's just move on and learn from it.' Matt looked off into the distance, waiting for the response. Nothing came. Matt knew he would need to talk to Greg on their return. Some things did not need to be said for everyone on the radio to hear. Greg's confidence had taken a huge blow and Matt would need to counsel him, showing him that everyone survived Afghanistan by a small amount of luck. Greg could get over this.

The vehicles continued on and came to the edge of the high desert area where the track they were following dropped down into the valley and out the other side. Matt positioned the Bushmasters to provide fire support across the ravine and, after a quick check by the dog, they crossed the bottom of the valley and rumbled through the shallow creek. This was a narrow piece of green belt, about three hundred metres wide, and had been the site of many an IED discovery. Today, to Matt's relief, there was nothing.

The vehicles reverted back into their order and edged forwards, except for Cinzano's vehicle, which swapped places with Braithwaite's to provide fire support as the other vehicles crossed. Cinzano's Team Two Bushmaster was now directly in front of the command vehicle. One by one they moved up into the wide-open desert. They were now on track to reach Tarin Kowt in the next hour. Matt unbuckled his harness and crawled through the roof hatch. His driver was used to him riding on the roof through town. Matt liked to look at everyone as they drove through. Looking through the windscreen didn't offer the same perspective as being on top of the vehicle and eyeballing the locals.

It was the sudden change in air pressure that hit him first, even before the almighty BOOM! registered in his mind.

The noise of the blast was huge, the sound deafening. No one could have survived it if you based survivability on the sheer violence of the explosion. A huge amount of earth was dislodged and sent skywards. Cinzano's vehicle was picked up and spun one hundred and eighty degrees. The front wheel zipped past Matt's head and straight over the next car.

'Shit!' Matt ducked.

The Bushmaster disappeared in a cloud of dark brown dirt. The vehicle came to rest, minus its side storage bins and front wheels, facing back in the direction it had come, a fine layer of dirt settling on it.

Matt could see through the front windscreen that the Team Two driver was screaming, his mouth opening and closing like a fish out of water trying to take a gulp, but there was no noise as the vehicle was locked down.

Behind Matt the platoon quickly conducted their IED drills and Matt dragged his eyes away from the incident itself to focus on the security of the platoon. JJ and Matt had talked at length about this very situation and they knew what to do. This was administration not tactics. He had to make sure the platoon was ready for combat if it was a complex ambush. The most important thing now was not to be caught up in the emotion of the event.

Matt jumped out from the top of his vehicle and started to direct cars into their positions to ensure they had all-around defence. There was a small mound that overlooked their position to the east and Matt ordered the snipers to move off and set up their positions on top of it so they could scan for threats. JJ was down at the IED site and Cinzano's own guys were dealing with the casualties.

'Yankee Alpha, this is Yankee Bravo, request CASEVAC – over,' JJ mic'd.

'Ack, no worries. Barnsley is already on it and there is a bird in bound.' Matt had foreseen that there would be casualties and Barnsley had likewise foreseen that Matt would request it. The platoon HQ was working as it should.

'What's the SITREP, mate?' Matt asked.

'Boss, wait out!' Over the radio, JJ sounded stressed – not annoyed or angry, but under stress. Matt didn't like whatever that meant.

'Boss, we have one KIA and at least a priority two.'

Silence followed. Matt stood with the handset for his radio pressed hard against his forehead. He finally sat down on the back step of his vehicle.

'Matt,' said JJ, 'it's Johnno. There's nothing we can do for him. He was standing in the back and he wasn't strapped in; his head was split in two.'

Matt heard JJ let go of the handset. He chewed on his thumb and thought for a second. 'JJ, stop talking, mate.'

The whole platoon had fallen quiet around the perimeter and was looking towards his Bushmaster.

Matt cleared his throat and put the handset to his lips. 'All call signs, this is Yankee Alpha. We have one confirmed KIA and one confirmed priority two. Maintain the security, let's get them evacuated and then let's get out of here. Yankee Alpha out.'

• • •

The CASEVAC helicopter arrived twenty minutes later. JJ had organised the work party and Johnno was loaded into the back of the bird inside a green rubber body bag. The RSM was with the medics. Matt looked up at him as the bird took off with Johnno's body and the other critically injured commando on board. The RSM supported the green body bag in his arms. His face was serious and he gave Matt the thumbs-up as the bird took off.

Everyone there saw the RSM holding Johnno the way a father holds a small child. Seeing this helped them all. It humanised the inhumane green bag. It was if someone was now caring for him.

Matt felt a heavy weight descend upon his shoulders. Johnno was Lance Corporal John Lewis, a commando who had been in the unit for six years. Quiet and competent, he had already completed four tours of Afghanistan as a sniper and had just been moved back to a commando team; he was about to be promoted to full corporal. He was only twenty-four.

Matt watched the bird lift off. He walked slowly out right into the middle of the landing zone. The dust engulfed him as he took off his helmet and squinted up into the brown sky, gazing in silence as the helicopter disappeared from view. The other commandos all sat in silence, watching from their vehicles. They had made a protective ring around the LZ. As the dust lifted Matt turned back towards his vehicle.

'Okay, let's get going,' he ordered. The crippled Bushmaster was already hooked up behind another vehicle. They had hit that IED way off the marked tracks, out in the open desert, and now one of the key guys in Matt's platoon, someone he had completed selection with and whom he considered a friend, was dead. How many more of those were out there? The whole area had to be riddled with them, Matt figured. For the first time in his life, he resorted to prayer. *I've never asked for anything before, but God, if you're there, please let me get the rest of these guys safely back to base.*

13

CAMP RUSSELL, TARIN KOWT

Yankee Platoon had arrived back late the previous afternoon to a sombre base. Now Matt sat on the edge of his bed, shaking. Although he was exhausted, sleep wouldn't come. At the time, he hadn't thought that the IED had affected him; he had just got on with business. Now, though, he couldn't stop replaying the scene in his mind. Matt realised that he was not just shaking but also tapping a fist against his thigh. His foot was tapping too. He looked down at his feet and stopped them from moving and then also forced his hand to stop. This set off a series of convulsions deep in his stomach. Usually after an intense patrol the guys would get together and go to the gym, throw some weights around and decompress, maybe even do some unarmed combat or BJJ. Matt couldn't even stand at this point.

A wave of emotion and nausea came over him until he was throwing up in the wastepaper bin next to his bed. Matt wiped his mouth and let out an inadvertent sob.

There was a knock at the door. Matt sat quietly back down on the bed and held himself still, not responding.

'Boss? Boss, are you in there?' It was JJ. Matt saw the handle move as the sergeant tried the door only to find it was locked.

Another voice came from the hallway. Someone was telling JJ that he had seen the boss in the dining hall not long ago. It sounded like Johnno's voice.

Matt lay back on the bed, unable to move, feeling broken in body and spirit. He lay there for what felt like an eternity just staring at the ceiling. There was a black mark on the ceiling. He wondered how it got there. He wondered if all the other platoon commanders had stared at it at some point. For a moment he allowed himself to consider if he was truly any good at this or if he had just been faking it the whole time.

Abruptly, he sat up. Enough. He had suffered a shock and now it was time to move on, move past it. His men would need him now. Matt rose from the bed with renewed focus. It was time now to be a leader.

• • •

After showering and changing, Matt went to sit at his desk in the small platoon office inside the headquarters building. He would be expected to speak to the lads about Johnno, but he didn't know where to begin. For a moment he contemplated calling his older sister Gwen in Melbourne – she could usually provide a good perspective on things. They had been great friends growing up in Bendigo where their parents owned the local hotel in the main street. Their mum and dad had been so busy trying to repair the family business from the shambles it was when Matt's dad had taken it over from his drunken father that Gwen and he had grown to rely on each other. Three years older, Gwen had been his most important relationship. She had encouraged him to go to the Royal Military College after finishing high school, the same year that she left home to study law in the city. He picked up his phone, then put it down again, thinking better of disturbing his sister as he looked up at the clock on the wall. Opening a new document, he stared at the screen, struggling to formulate some thoughts.

The SOTG medical officer, Captain Fiona Blake, knocked on the door then stuck her head in. 'Matt, are you there?' Seeing him at the desk, she entered, pulling the door half closed behind her. 'How are you?' she asked. 'You okay?'

'Yeah, I'm fine. It's been a hard few days but I think we'll pull through.'

Fiona gave Matt a concerned look. 'You know we can chat about what happened if you need to?'

Matt looked down again at the desk, struggling with what to say. He liked Fiona, she mixed easily with the Special Forces guys. Back at the 2nd Commando Regiment base in Holsworthy she would often personally oversee the Patrol Medic's training. Before the deployment, she had stressed to Matt the importance of every guy carrying an easily accessible tourniquet at the centre of his body armour. She told Matt how Israeli soldier's lives could have been saved in Gaza if they'd only positioned their tourniquets in such a way. The Israelis had learned the hard way. This had reinforced to Matt the importance of a fresh set of eyes over their procedures, as well as giving him an understanding of the passion Fiona had for her own role.

'When are you guys heading out again, Matt?' Fiona asked.

'Not sure. Sam said the RSM told him that we might be training the Afghan police for the rest of the month.'

'Hmm, I see. What do you think of that?'

'Ahh, it is what it is I guess.'

'Ah, there you are, boss. I've been looking everywhere for you.' JJ pushed the door open. 'Oh, g'day, ma'am. Sorry, I didn't know that you were here.'

'That's okay, Sergeant, I was just leaving. See you later, Matt. Let me know if you want to chat.' Fiona smiled at Matt and nodded at JJ as she left the room.

'You okay, boss?'

'I think so, mate. I just needed a few minutes to get myself in order and rehearse what I'm going to say, that's all.'

'Sure, of course, that's understandable.' JJ fidgeted awkwardly for a few moments. 'Well, the lads are going to be in the outside barbecue area in about ten minutes. Are you ready? Do you need me to do anything?'

'Do you have Johnno's beret?'

'Yeah, it's on a cushion sitting up on the pedestal next to his photo. The chaplain and I have set it all up and the RSM provided the final check. He's happy with it as well.' JJ looked up at the ceiling and Matt had the impression he was blinking back tears. Matt guessed he was remembering how he had teased Johnno about that very same photo. It was the only photo taken of Johnno since he'd joined the army – the one he had to have taken by the unit photographer. JJ had joked that anyone with only one military photo, and that being in their polyester uniform, would surely be KIA because it was their fate to have that photo used. The quip didn't seem so funny now.

'Okay, JJ, no worries – I'll be there in a few minutes.'

JJ nodded and stepped back out the door.

Matt sat staring at the screen for a moment longer. The words that he had just typed melted into a wet blur. Matt pressed the enter key and the printer came to life. Standing from his seat he walked towards the door, grabbing the sheet of paper from the printer as he walked past. He wanted another coffee but he knew that too much caffeine would make him even more emotional, and he didn't need that.

Was this my fault? he asked himself as he walked down the hallway. *Was there something I could have done differently, could have done better?* He shook his head. There was no use thinking like that. Nothing could change the outcome now.

Matt exited the headquarters building, leaving the air-conditioned interior for the harsh heat of the outside. He squinted as he placed his Oakley M Frame sunglasses over his eyes against the dazzling sunshine. The warmth felt energising but the task ahead of him felt anything but.

Making his way along the loose stone path he rounded a corner into the shaded open barbecue area. As he walked he placed his Sherwood green beret on his head. It was an old friend, comfortable, and embodied everything he had believed in these past six years.

Yankee Platoon was already assembled. They stood in silence, forming a U shape around the lectern and the framed picture of Lance Corporal John Lewis. Their heads were lowered. The SAS troops started to arrive in twos and threes, hovering at a respectful distance from Johnno's platoon, save for a couple who approached Johnno's closest mates to offer words of support.

Matt looked around. He saw Saygen standing and talking with some of the guys from his troop. The CO and RSM had also arrived. The CO gave Matt a nod. That was Matt's cue, and so he walked over and positioned himself next to the army chaplain. The chaplain was in his camouflage uniform with a white gown draped over his shoulders. He offered Matt his hand, which Matt shook.

Softly clearing his throat, the chaplain began. 'Very often, we observe that men are seemingly taken from the earth before they reach their potential. One of the many travesties of war is that young men are killed while still in their prime. We then, who are left behind as observers, wonder at the workings of the Lord. How can someone who in the morning was so vibrant and full of life be taken from the earth before the sun has set?'

The chaplain's voice became a dull hum in the background as Matt let his mind wander back to the previous day.

He recalled watching from the roof of his own car as JJ ran to the damaged Bushmaster. Saw once again the wheel that had barely missed his head, heard again the deafening boom. Just before these events he'd had a gut feeling about the area, he remembered. It was a foreboding that he had ignored; he'd been thinking about Cinzano and his team, and how they seemed to be going out of their way to create friction. Was it unreasonable to expect his men to man their guns, maintain security, pick up their rubbish? He just wanted Cinzano to hold his men to account. That was what he had been thinking when Team Two's vehicle was picked up and turned around in front of his eyes.

'Matt?' The chaplain's hand was on Matt's forearm. He motioned Matt to the lectern to deliver his eulogy.

'Thanks, Padre.'

Matt moved to the lectern. Looking out at the men, he could see that the SAS guys had their heads held high. They looked dignified and strong. This was in stark contrast to the men of his own platoon. Their faces were screwed up with emotion, fighting back the welling tears.

Matt felt a surge of emotion come over him, too – not emotion that crippled, but emotion that empowered. The type of feeling that coursed through you when it was time to be tested. Matt's men needed him now even more than they did in combat.

'Everyone gathered here knew Johnno in a slightly different way,' Matt began. 'The men of Yankee Platoon knew him as dependable and professional. He was well known across the wider unit as someone who actively pursued knowledge. Anything John became interested in, he would quickly become an expert about. Chances were that even if you were already an expert in that area yourself, he would still school you in it.'

A gentle laugh rose from the crowd.

'I knew John in a different way. It wouldn't be a stretch to say that he was a scared boy when I first met him. That was on our selection course, six years ago. He was only eighteen at the time, and he found the whole process overwhelming. I remember him wanting to quit on a couple of occasions. But he made it through. And that transformed him. He grew in confidence as he realised what he could endure, what he could push his body and mind to achieve. That's when he started to push all of us as well. He expected of us what he expected from himself: perfection.' Matt took a deep breath.

'Johnno continued to look for challenges. Mountaineering, adventure racing – it was as though he deliberately chose those pursuits that would turn him back into that scared boy, just so he could rise above the fear every time. In the end, he came across a challenge that he couldn't surmount, as we all will eventually. This time, though, Johnno didn't choose the challenge – someone else chose it for him.'

Matt turned the paper over and looked down for a moment. Then, raising his head, he looked out at his men. Thirty sets of eyes were locked on him, anticipating his next words.

Matt narrowed his eyes and lowered his voice. 'Someone took the time to put that IED in the ground. That person knew that we were coming – and they should know that we are coming still.'

Matt looked across at his CO and then back at his men. They seemed to be standing a foot taller now, their heads up and shoulders back, exuding pride and determination.

'John Lewis was the much-loved son of Harold and Deirdre.' Matt paused to acknowledge their loss before continuing. 'He is the brother of Emily and a brother of the 2nd Commando Regiment – he shall not be forgotten.'

He let go of the lectern and turned to the photo of John Lewis. 'Lest we forget.'

The men repeated this in unison and stood in silence as the bugler played the last post.

At the conclusion of the ceremony, the men moved out of the barbecue area and started to wander down towards the dusty airfield. The Special Operations Task Group formed an honour guard, starting at the open doors of the waiting Boeing C-17 Globemaster. As they stood there in the heat, the infantry battalion of the Mentoring and Reconstruction Task Force took up positions, lining the road all the way back to the base.

'That's an incredible sight, boss,' said Ben Braithwaite, who stood at the front of his section.

'There must be close to a thousand men and women here,' said JJ. 'I'd be surprised if there's anyone left in the camp, boss.'

Matt nodded.

'The Dutch and American Special Forces detachments are here too,' he said, tilting his head down the line towards the two different units.

Johnno's section appeared at the gates. The men of Team Two had ensured that someone was with the body at all times. Forming an honour guard around the Long Range Patrol Vehicle, they accompanied the casket from the hospital to the waiting aircraft.

The crowd went silent. At first, the only noise was the low hum of the Land Rover, then, as the honour guard approached, their footsteps could be heard.

The makeshift hearse arrived at the giant cargo plane and the honour guard removed the casket. Slow marching, arm in arm, they moved it inside.

Minutes later, the honour guard reappeared from the belly of the plane and stood in a line at the aircraft's back. Then the tail door of the plane closed. Inside was Johnno's casket, accompanied by his closest mate, who would stay with him until he was back with his family. The huge jet engines started and minutes later it was taxiing down the runway. The men and women of Camp Russell continued watching in silence until the aircraft was just a speck on the horizon.

Matt and JJ turned and walked back towards the base. For some time, neither of them said a word.

Finally, Matt said softly, 'JJ, we need to get after this guy, mate.'

'I know, boss – I was thinking the same thing.'

Matt beat a fist into the palm of his other hand. 'I want to find out who did this and I want to turn their whole world upside down.'

JJ nodded. 'Agreed, boss. Let me make a recommendation though: we need to get the guys out on the range – tomorrow. A hard day's training is in order, especially since the CO saw it fit to can the helicopters and cancel our time-sensitive targeting mission.'

'Yeah, in his defence, though, I understand why he had Saygen keep up the TSTs. But you're right, JJ, we have to shake them out of feeling sorry for themselves and we need to build their confidence so that they know we can take this fight right to the Taliban.'

'There's a rumour going around that we might spend the next three weeks helping to train the Afghan police force in building searches. That could slow things down a bit. I'd much rather jump straight back on the horse, so to speak.'

'I heard that too. I'll ask the CO this arvo. If it's true at least it will give the intel guys some time to get us a solid lead.'

'Right, shall I make the bookings then, get the compound target and the 25m range sorted?'

'Good plan, bro.'

They walked the rest of the way to the camp in complete silence.

14

MAIN STREET, TARIN KOWT

'I know she tells you things, Faisal, but she's also been asking lots of questions of other people; I think she may start to figure things out.' Ahmed Defari picked up a handful of dates and shoved them into the small plastic bag being held open by the elderly shopkeeper.

'It's not just that she tells me things; it's *what* she tells me, Ahmed. She lets me know whenever the devils are moving, reveals details of their plans that we wouldn't otherwise know.' Faisal pulled out a plastic bag from his pocket and emptied out old orange peel onto the ground. He picked a pomegranate out of a small bucket on the stall and placed it in the bag then handed the old shopkeeper a handful of coins.

'Faisal, this foreigner has become a problem – you must see that. There is nothing she tells us that we couldn't find out from our own people. They see everything; when a plane lands or takes off,

106

when a gate opens or closes, vehicles coming and going. We have eyes everywhere, Faisal, even in their camps and even working for the infidel. We don't need her anymore.'

'Ahmed, I know this – but to kill her might deprive us of a useful source of important information.' He picked up a bag of goat hoofs and leg flesh and presented it to the shopkeeper. 'How much?'

'Two hundred and fifty-six Afghani,' said the old man with a toothless smile. The deep lines on his face gave away his advancing years. 'Did you men hear that the foreigners lost another tank a few nights ago?' the shopkeeper asked, thankful to have someone to gossip with.

Ahmed looked at the old man, weighing him up. 'No, I didn't hear that,' he lied. 'What can you tell me about it?'

The old man cleared his throat, seeming excited to have an audience. 'Many young infidel killed – burned alive in their war machine. Just like we used to kill the Russians when I was young.' He blew his nose into his hands then wiped the mucus down the front of his trousers. Receiving the money from Faisal, he continued, 'It was a buried bomb and it must have been big, because it picked up the tank and spun it around like a child's toy.'

'Do you know who was responsible, grandfather?' Ahmed picked up a small cucumber and bit the top off it, watching the old man as he chewed.

'It's said there is a new shadow governor – that he has taken over from Mullah Ghal. The tribes are coming together for him and many of Ghal's men have moved across to this younger warrior.' The old man placed a small twig in his mouth and swirled it around with his tongue while he watched the reaction of Ahmed and Faisal.

'I see. This is good news then.' Ahmed paid the old man for his bag of food, giving him a little extra for his performance, and the two Taliban walked off into the busy street.

The morning was already hot and locals moved up and down the dusty main thoroughfare shopping for bits and pieces of food. Some were conducting business over sweet glasses of chai or black coffee at one of the many makeshift coffee shops on the porches of the houses lining the street. Old chairs and tables adorned with plastic tablecloths hinted that the black-market economy was flourishing.

Ahmed adjusted the small Makarov pistol in the belt of his trousers.

'We will receive the new weapons soon, Faisal. Abdul will hide them and then we will carry out our plan. It is going to be expensive, but I have already organised the finance from last year's crops. Men came from the north and paid for the resin blocks like you said they would and they also delivered new seeds. We have lived in poverty to be able to inflict this pain on the infidel.'

'That is good news, Ahmed – you must be pleased.'

'I tried to explain to my brother Omar that there is no money in pomegranates. As you said, opium is how we are going to win this war and regain control of our lands. I don't like that it is such a vile poison, but these are desperate times.' Ahmed stroked his black beard. 'The men who are going to wear the uniforms are nearly all in place. Once we have the weapons we need to make sure they get to these men and that they understand how they are to be used. Then they must study their targets and learn the plan. They must all strike around the same time to make sure we have the biggest effect.'

'I understand, Ahmed. God willing this will break the puppet government and we will take back our homes.'

'This is why we must kill the American girl. We must leave nothing to chance. There are other infidel you can play with, Faisal. This one has asked too many questions of you. She has asked about me and that is worrying; she mustn't find out who I am or where I am from. Send her off to be judged by Allah, Faisal, so that she knows once and for all that her God never existed.'

Ahmed passed his bag of food to Faisal. 'Here, hold this and meet me around the back of this shop.'

Faisal watched Ahmed slowly climb the steps of the small electronics shop. A flashing sign indicated that they sold Nokias and repaired phones. Making his way around to the back of the shop, Faisal could hear two men yelling inside. The exchange was becoming heated.

What's going on here? Faisal wondered. The yelling got louder and then there was a woman's scream, followed by a single gunshot.

Faisal ran to open the back door, but before he could get a hand to it, Ahmed calmly walked out, wiping blood from his cheek with the back of his hand. He placed the Makarov back into his belt.

'Let's go, Faisal.' As they walked away, Faisal could hear a woman sobbing and praying to Allah for mercy.

'What happened, Ahmed? Whose blood is that?'

Ahmed said nothing for a brief moment, just put his hand out for the plastic bag. When Faisal handed it to him he pulled out another cucumber. 'A few nights ago Dahwood's home was raided by the infidel and his son was taken away. He was returned the very next day, not a mark on him.'

The two men walked a while longer in silence, past a group of skinny young men loitering around their motorbikes. They were gathered around a street vendor's stall laden with bottles of all sizes; each bottle was filled with petrol.

'And since that time, Faisal, that son has spent money on a new bike and it was rumoured he loaned a friend money to buy a gun.' Ahmed bit into the cucumber.

'Who did you just kill, Ahmed?' Faisal asked, concerned but already knowing the answer.

'Dahwood's son – just like I would have killed any of my own sons if I discovered they were providing information to the foreigners. We are at war, brother, and only the strong will survive this.' Ahmed grasped Faisal's elbow as they continued walking. 'My brother Omar, he's old now, troublesome. He himself would die if he thought that he could make a real difference, avenge our father, but instead he sends these Pakistanis.'

'I see,' said Faisal.

'Convince him that he *can* make a difference, Faisal. If he was to go and talk to the American girl . . .' Ahmed's voice trailed off. 'I think that you could persuade him to give himself to a greater cause, Faisal.'

'I understand, Ahmed.' Faisal could feel his own heart grow heavy at this request.

'Make the preparations, Faisal: talk to the Egyptian, too. We will need to buy someone's help on the inside, not one of the Pakistanis that we already have, but someone who is already in uniform. Kill the American girl, Faisal.'

15

CAMP RUSSELL, TARIN KOWT

'Thanks for coming, gents,' said Sam. 'Can everyone see the screen?' He adjusted the projector's focus then sat down in his chair at the side of the table and flicked through his notebook to find the page that he had scribbled on recently. 'Well, the good news is that we have received some information over the last month, some from interrogations and some from bribes, and we've been able to tie that in with other evidence to indicate that it was this guy –' Sam clicked on the computer mouse to bring up a slide '– who was responsible for the IED that killed Lance Corporal Lewis.'

Matt stared intently at the slide headed OBJECTIVE RAPIER.

Sam clicked again and a fact sheet appeared.

'Not much is known about this objective, but we have a few working theories. They all revolve around how well he has been able to avoid detection and how effective his IEDs have been.

111

What we do know is that he has taken an interest in Matt's platoon.' Sam raised his eyebrows at Matt.

'Yeah, he can throw an IED together, I'll grant him that,' Matt conceded grudgingly.

'First theory, and the most plausible, is that he is a local disaffected Afghan citizen. Perhaps he is a soldier or police officer that we trained in the first few years of the campaign who has since gone back to herding goats. Evidence for this is in his familiarity with our tactics, his ability to gain information from within the Afghan security apparatus, and his extensive knowledge of the local area.' Sam took a sip of water and then clicked on the next slide.

'The second theory is that he is an ISI-trained agent – a Pakistani Special Forces officer sent to destabilise the area. There is no reliable evidence to back this up, but if we are talking about abilities, this guy is a rock star and at the top of his game. It would appear that he has had extensive and specialised explosive training. That means we can't rule out this theory.'

The CO, who had been silent as Sam spoke, turned to Matt. 'Sounds like we might have a serious player on our hands.'

Matt nodded in agreement.

'The third theory,' Sam continued, bringing up a new slide, 'is that Rapier is not one person but a complete network. We have never heard Rapier himself talk on any of the identified handsets associated with his profile so we can't even prove that Rapier's not a woman, for instance. Until we have a positive identification of Rapier the only way to discount the network theory is to ensure we follow every lead.'

Sam turned from the screen to face the men gathered in the intelligence cell briefing room.

'The point is, lads, we don't know squat about this guy.'

'Or girl,' said Barnsley, giving Matt the thumbs-up. Matt was regretting bring him to the intelligence briefing.

'Sure, or girl. But what we do know is that his –'

'Or hers,' Barnsley interjected.

'Cut it out, Barns,' said Matt, shooting him a death stare.

Ignoring the interruption, Sam went on: 'We do know that Rapier's reputation is starting to precede him, and this is becoming a self-generating intelligence source.'

'How's that, Sam?' asked the CO. 'Say it in English, mate.'

'Well, sir, we ask many questions of the human intelligence network based on our assumptions and theories and we get cyclic reporting back.'

'For example?' said the CO.

'We might ask: *Is this person's name Mullah Dawooral?* And we get back: *Yes, I heard only yesterday that it is Mullah Dawooral and he is an ISI officer who used to be an Afghan policeman in the National Army and is now a woman,*' Sam explained.

'Great, so now we are hunting a Pakistani-trained cross-dressing Afghan goatherd?' Matt said.

'Oh, fair go, boss, and you tell me to shut up?' said Barnsley.

'Yeah, well, it's ridiculous,' said Matt. 'This guy killed Johnno and we know nothing about him.'

'It's true we don't know much about the objective,' Sam agreed. 'We don't even have a name. The Taliban refer to Rapier only as "the dark shadow". He never personally uses a mobile phone that we know of; we suspect he uses an intermediary and so we monitor all those phones associated with him. What we do know is that these intermediaries use a complex code system to provide Quetta with updates. We also think that Rapier or someone in his group might be related to Mullah Omar, based on some emails we've had access to.'

'What, the head of the Taliban?' Saygen asked incredulously.

'Exactly, mate.' Sam let this bombshell sit for a moment and then continued. 'Last night we narrowed down a possible location for Rapier to this compound on the edge of the Mirabad Valley. It's a stone's throw from the dasht that separates here and the other arm of the Teri Rud.' Sam clicked on the screen and brought up a topographical map. An orange circle was drawn around a series of ten compounds on the edge of the green belt.

'We profiled all the calls that have been made in which the dark shadow is mentioned. Then we mapped them to this area and yesterday a mobile phone appeared right within this small area of compounds. I couldn't believe it at first, it shouldn't be that easy. I asked one of our spies to describe the buildings. The descriptions match some of the signals intelligence and in particular where to park cars or drop people off. We believe Rapier might be staying here.' Sam used the cursor to identify the primary target on the screen.

'Right, we're off then,' Saygen joked as he half stood up.

'Matt, do you want this one?' the CO asked, ignoring the SAS officer.

'Yes, sir!' Matt could feel the excitement building in his gut. The guys were going to go bananas when they heard this. The last month training the Afghani police force had been rewarding, but all the men knew they had unfinished business. It was time to get out there again.

'Good – it's yours, mate. Develop a plan, brief me in an hour, then go out there and get Rapier tomorrow morning.'

'No worries, sir. Er, obviously I am going to need the Black Hawks.'

The CO frowned. 'That's not going to happen Matt. Just think about it for a moment. Terence's men have just gone on line to support the Delta Force guys in Kandahar. We can't drop the ball on that mission because of a lower level punter like Objective Rapier. He might be important to us, but in the grand scheme of things ... Well, I'm not releasing the helicopters and SAS from their allocated mission and that's final.' The CO's voice was firm now and it was clear that there was to be no argument.

Matt looked down at his notebook, fuming, as he attempted to get his temper in control. Just as the silence was getting uncomfortable, he looked up. The CO was staring at him, waiting for a response.

'Of course, sir, understood.' Matt looked across at Saygen. The SAS commander was looking down at the table and would not make eye contact with Matt.

You prick, thought Matt. *You could've backed me on this – you know how dangerous it is out there.*

Saygen shifted uneasily in his seat, as if he could hear Matt's unspoken thoughts.

'That's it, gents,' Sam said. He looked across at the CO, who nodded. 'If you've got a few minutes, Matt, I'll give you what we have on the compound for your planning.' As the intel guy pulled out a briefing folder, the others got up and left.

Matt stared after them.

'That's a good outcome then, Matt, going after Rapier,' Sam said as he passed the folder across the table.

'Jesus, is it, Sam?' Matt ground his teeth together. 'Is it a good outcome? Taking vehicles across the dasht, without any solid planning, to the edge of the Mirabad Valley?'

Matt opened the folder to look at the grab sheet on Objective Rapier. 'God knows how many IEDs there are between here
and there. I'll be lucky to even get there, let alone not to be seen
coming from miles away.' Matt stood up to go. 'And you know
what, Sam? There's no bloody arguing with him, the CO, and I bet
you anything that SAS don't even fly out to support Delta Force,
not today or this week for that matter. This operation could have
been completed in an hour and now it's going to take all night, and
at what cost, Sam? At what bloody cost?'

16

KANDAHAR

Sweat beaded on Steph's forehead, partly from the humidity but mostly in anticipation of the conversation she was about to have. It had been only a few minutes since she had seen the Australians' concept of operations brief come across her desk and it had alarmed her.

Opening her desk drawer she removed her notebook, secured her paddle holster to her belt and picked up the phone containing only one saved number. She slipped quickly through the door of the oval room and out into the hallway. A few steps along the hallway, Steph exited the back door of the old demountable. Once out the back she quickly climbed the wooden stairs that had been built to give access to the roof. Steph looked out at the large satellite dishes and telecommunications towers that sat at the side of the building as she strode across a small walkway connecting the roof of the building to the top of a stack of Connex shipping containers.

The roof overlooked the Kandahar airfield. She breathed in deeply, composing herself. Steph had grown accustomed to the smell of aviation gas; in some ways she found it comforting. She dialled Faisal's number.

'Hello, sister.' His voice was relaxed.

'Faisal, they're coming for your brother, they're coming tonight.' Steph drew another deep breath, trying to calm herself further. 'They know the exact location of the house in Mirabad.' She hoped she didn't sound as panicky as she felt.

Faisal laughed softly. 'Don't worry, sister – he's not there. He left for Quetta last week.'

Faisal knew better than to let Steph have too much information when it came to the whereabouts of someone as important as Ahmed. It was true that he wasn't in Mirabad, but he wasn't far away. Faisal squatted down in the motorcycle yard. Holding the phone against his shoulder with his ear, he hitched his black and dark red robes around his waist and urinated into the dust between his feet.

'But I saw their plan, they think he *is* there – they asked specifically to go after him.' Steph was confused – surely if the target had left for Quetta Sam would know; he was usually so thorough when cross-checking intelligence sources.

'No, sister, he isn't there. He won't be back for a week.'

What are they playing at? Steph wondered. Sam wouldn't knee jerk to unreliable sources, he would have layered this with geospatial and signals intelligence.

'Don't think too hard about it, sister – we can have a surprise waiting for them when they come to slow them down.'

'Hold on a minute, Faisal,' Steph snapped. 'I'm just telling you what you need to know to keep you and your people safe. In return, you give me the information I need. You're not supposed to use the information I give you to harm anyone.'

'I think that maybe things have changed,' Faisal said, still in the same relaxed tone. 'Every day they leave their base another brother dies. Quetta are asking that we level the playing field.'

'That wasn't the deal, Faisal.' Her legs feeling weak all of a sudden, Steph sat down on a small seat behind the sandbag wall.

'Ah, but I have information that you will want. When you hear it you won't care about a few infidel.'

Steph pressed the phone to her ear. 'What are you saying, Faisal?'

'I can give you information about bigger fish.'

Her heart was beating faster now, Steph whispered, 'Mullah Omar?'

'No, sister, don't play games with me. We have discussed this already.'

'I'm not,' Steph protested. 'I mean, I don't know who the bigger fish could be then – tell me.'

'There is someone that you should meet – someone who has information . . .'

'Who?'

'A pomegranate farmer.'

A pomegranate farmer . . . was this the solid link to the Iranians Faisal had promised?

'But how can I meet him, Mohammed? You know I can't leave the base without an armed escort.'

'I mean that he should come to you.'

'Right, I see.' Steph paused to digest this. It *was* possible to get informants onto the base – it was highly dangerous but achievable. She had done it before.

'Faisal, I need a few days, maybe even weeks, to organise this properly, to ensure that he is protected. The information he has must be worth it.'

'Oh, it will be worth it, sister,' Faisal promised. 'Make the arrangements.'

'I'll see what I can do. Let's speak again in a couple of days.'

Steph ended the call and looked off into the distance. What information did this farmer have, she wondered. She was intrigued by this turn of events. Faisal had been quick to snap at the mention of Mullah Omar, she noted. It was always said that the Taliban leader remained in Afghanistan, somewhere in the border regions, and the recent frictions within the Taliban leadership might be the catalyst for someone to offer him up. No that wasn't it, but Steph sensed that Faisal probably would have access to Mullah Omar and that she should tread lightly around the subject in future. This time it was about the Iranians and that in itself was an exciting prospect.

• • •

Mohammed Faisal opened the back of the small phone. He levered out the SIM card and held it between his teeth. From his waistcoat pocket he took another card and slipped it into the phone. He rang the only number on the card; it was picked up within seconds.

'Hello there, Mohammed, it's great to hear from you. How are you?'

Faisal loved the sound of her Dutch accent.

17

CAMP RUSSELL, TARIN KOWT

'Hey man, can I come in?' asked Terence, who had moments before seen Sam walking to his accommodation block and followed him over.

'Sure, what's up?' asked Sam. He hadn't even closed the door fully when Terence had knocked.

Sam's room was like all the other single rooms at either end of the corridors, designated specially for the officers and senior NCOs, except that he had no pictures or posters on the wall. Nor were there any magazines or books. It was like a prison cell. The room contained only a bed, with a single blanket, a wooden wardrobe and a small table.

Terence sat on the edge of the table facing Sam. 'I heard that Matt is going after Rapier on foot.'

'Yeah, that's what I heard, too.' Sam opened the wardrobe, taking out a PT shirt, ready to get changed.

'Well, that's just stupid. I mean, that's close to a thirty kilometre round trip. You know it's fifteen kilometres to the Mirabad Valley from here?' Terence shook his head to reinforce the idiocy of it all.

'Well, that's not exactly correct, mate. It's twelve k to his target, as I recall,' Sam replied as he undid his boots and placed them square against the wall.

'Either way, Sam, he'll be a sitting duck out there.' Terence watched as Sam folded the laces inside his boots and then placed a curled up sock into each boot in turn.

'I think he's taken that into consideration. His deception plan has him going out to the Teri Rud after they make it look like they are on their way to Patrol Base Wali. I've seen the plan, he's breaking up into teams and coming at the compound from all directions and then the ANA are going to do a soft knock on the compound, so no forced entry.'

'Sam, that might sound like a good plan, but they're going after a known IED specialist. They will have no fire support from their vehicles and with their force broken into parts they won't be able to sustain any injuries, let alone a guy stepping on an IED!'

'I wouldn't worry about that too much, Terence. We don't even think that he is using that compound. It's probably just a come on.'

'A what?'

'A come on. You know, a compound that they want us to hit so they can organise a counterattack, and remember, that's what the CO actually wants.'

'Jesus man, that's just insane! Are you listening to yourself?'

Sam thought about what he was saying and felt the guilt wash over him. 'Shit, you're right,' groaned Sam. 'With Matt now walking out there, they might be gone for ages, with no protection.'

Terence watched as Sam put his socks and boots back on and then bloused his trousers over them.

'Why can't they just drop in there with the birds, get it over and done with? I can react from here in Bushmasters if something pops up, or the birds can come back and get me – we can be there in twenty minutes. There are so many other ways to do this than those guys strolling around IED Alley,' said Terence. He stood up and took Sam's shirt out of the wardrobe and handed it to him.

'Maybe we should go and see the CO, outline a case,' said Sam, taking the shirt and putting it on.

'I think that's best, Sam, I really do. He's a reasonable man, right?'

'Ah, no, Terence, no, he's not.'

18

CAMP RUSSELL, TARIN KOWT

'Come in, guys, don't just hover around the door. What is it?'

With Terence Saygen right on his heels, Sam peered around the door of the CO's office to ensure that he was alone.

The CO leaned back in his large leather chair and looked up from his computer monitor as the two walked in. CNN silently played on the large-screen TV mounted on the wall to his right. On the other wall an equally large screen showed live footage from a drone, an MQ-9 Reaper. Somewhere in Afghanistan, a Tier 1 Special Forces unit, probably Delta Force, was prosecuting a raid on a high-value target. Sam watched as the breacher blew in the front doors and his assault team entered the bottom storey of the target. Far above, the drone relayed images of six little bird helicopters swarming like bees to their rooftop landing points. Four seemingly superhuman athletes sprinted from each of the birds, pulverising the light resistance before them.

'Sit down, gents,' the CO said, pointing towards the empty lounge against the back wall. 'Help yourself to coffee, it's freshly made.' He waved a hand towards a coffee pot that looked like a genie's lamp from *Aladdin*. Sam suspected that the pot and the small gold cups had been liberated by the CO on one of his dangerous missions to the Tarin Kowt markets.

The two officers settled themselves back on the Chesterfield sofa and exchanged a glance. Sam nodded at the SAS troop commander to begin.

Saygen cleared his throat. 'Boss, I was just in talking with Sam about the commando's next mission and he said there's a chance that Rapier might not even be in Mirabad at the moment. He might in fact be in Sorhk Lez. Given that could be the case, I'm just wondering if maybe we should rethink sending them out there.'

The CO shot Sam a quizzical look, perhaps wondering why the intel officer had deemed it necessary to reveal any of this. 'Yes, that's correct, Terence, but it has no bearing on your mission.' The CO rose from his desk chair and moved around to sit on the other Chesterfield. 'It's true, perhaps Rapier is not on the target at all, but you and your men will be ready to launch on him should he present himself. I'm of the opinion that he will try and organise fighters from Sorhk Lez and if he does, if he tries to coordinate resistance against Rix's platoon from out there, then that's when you and your troop strike! We've discussed this, Terence. Your troop vectoring onto him in helicopters will offer you the element of surprise and the highest chance of success.'

'Sir, what do we do if he doesn't pop up at all? In Mirabad or Sorhk Lez for that matter?' Sam asked. 'It seems that we only have

125

a small window for this, and if Matt's guys aren't detected they might be in and out in less than a couple of hours.'

Sam had harboured reservations about this plan from the very start, especially now that Matt had put so much thought into his own deception plan, but it was Saygen who had put the final element of doubt in his mind.

'Well, that's pretty simple, Sam – we just keep Matt out there for a while. They will hit his guys sooner or later, right?' The CO drained the coffee from his cup. As he did, Sam noticed the words *Made in China* stamped on the bottom. *Was nothing over here what it seemed?* he wondered.

Saygen was looking troubled. 'I think they'd be sitting ducks, boss, if you left them out there past first light. They're not actually deploying for a protracted action.'

The CO laughed easily. 'Terence, this is a platoon of commandos you're talking about. C'mon, mate, you know what these guys are like. They'll be spoiling for a fight – it's what they live for. They want to take it to the enemy to avenge Lance Corporal Lewis's death, don't they? So let's help them find some peace.'

'Boss, I have the same reservations about this,' Sam chimed in. 'It seems like it could be organised better. If we just explained the plan to Matt, he could –'

The CO held up a hand to silence him. 'We've been through this already. Matt and his team won't be in any real danger; Saygen and his team will have their backs. Look, someone is leaking our plans, that much we know. Obviously that's not ideal, but let's use it to our advantage just this once. As soon as we've neutralised Objective Rapier, then you can put some pressure on the network, Sam, and sniff out this rat.'

'Sir, there's another possibility: what if Rapier *is on or in vicinity of the target*?'

'You told me he wasn't.' The CO gave Sam an unblinking stare. '"All the indications were," you said.'

Sam shifted uncomfortably. 'But we've been fooled by him before, sir. What if he sent someone else to Sorhk Lez with his handset and then started the rumour that he was gone? It's possible – and think what it would mean for Matt.' Sam was clutching at straws now.

'That would be the best-case scenario for Matt, wouldn't you say?' the CO countered. 'Think about it, Sam – it means he's on the target and Rix will get his man.' He nodded with grim satisfaction as he looked back at the SAS troop commander. 'See, Saygen? It's win–win.'

The CO rose from the sofa to stand in front of the TV. CNN was on the scene of another school shooting in the United States. 'Nasty business, this,' he said, shaking his head. 'What will it take for America to understand the need for tighter gun control?' It was clear that, as far as he was concerned, the discussion was over.

But Sam wasn't ready to let the subject go. 'That's not Rapier's MO though, sir, to just be sitting at a compound. I guess I didn't really explain myself properly. What I mean is, if he is in Mirabad, and he knows Matt and his guys are coming, he'll IED the shit out of them – either on the actual target or almost definitely on the way out from it. This could be a set-up. Rapier tries to make us think he's not there, our source tells us there's a compound he uses in Mirabad and Sorhk Lez, we send our guys there to check them out and – boom!'

'And without the Black Hawks, Jesus – they'll be carved up,' Saygen added.

A frown settled on the CO's face. He walked back to his position behind his desk, his eyes fixed on the other screen now. On Kill TV, the illuminated green figures of Special Forces operators paced silently around the roof of the target compound. Four men came up the stairs with two detainees shuffling along between them. Even on the black-and-green screen it was clear they had been hooded and tied together. A Black Hawk dropped into view, its rotors making green circles in the dust as it landed on the roof.

The CO grunted in appreciation of the pantomime playing out on the screen and it seemed to strengthen his resolve. 'Gentlemen, I understand that you have some reservations.' His voice was cold. 'But I have made my decision. The mission will go ahead as planned. This is war, men; to make an omelette, sometimes you have to break a few eggs. Now, let's get this thing done.'

19

MIRABAD VALLEY

Nine hours later, Yankee Platoon lined up in the shadows against the Hesco wall that surrounded the base. Pointing their barrels into the wall, the men placed their magazines on and then cocked their weapons. Their NVGs were turned on and the focus adjusted and the MBITR radios, preferred by most of the world's Special Forces units, were checked. The plan was simple: walk out into the night, skirt around the heavily popu-lated centre of TK, conduct a deception plan to shield the true intention of the platoon, isolate the target from any reinforce-ments and then send in a small team from the Afghan National Army to detain all those inside. Simple. It had taken Matt about two hours to write the orders, forty-five minutes to deliver them to his platoon and then a further five hours to explain to the ANA what they were required to do. This explanation involved them running through continuous rehearsal, of concept drills on an exact replica of the target floor plan made out of mine-marking tape.

'All call signs, this is Yankee Alpha. Move now – out.'

And with that, Team One led the platoon out the gate.

Moving onto the road, the men took up staggered positions ten metres apart. They patrolled out towards the first roundabout, six hundred metres from the gate itself. Matt noted the energy in the night air. The call to prayer echoed loudly across the valley from speakers high up in every minaret.

• • •

From windows and roofs, the darting yellow eyes of the Afghan spotter network watched Yankee Platoon's progress intently. Mobile phones sent frantic messages outlining the platoon's most current position, but it was their weapons and tactics that were of most concern to the spotters. These were Special Forces on the move, that much was certain. M4 rifles, high-tech scopes, disciplined movement – and the main giveaway was that each man patrolled wherever he wanted, rather than sticking to rigid formations or spacing as dictated to him by a commander. It was true, the Taliban had reason to be worried. Yankee Platoon's average age was thirty-four years old, as opposed to the infantry's average age of twenty-three. In Matt's platoon everyone had deployed at least twice before, and most guys had around four tours under their belts already.

The silent observers paid particular attention to the six ANA soldiers and their interpreter moving in the middle of the column of troops. The thing they hated more than the infidel was a traitor.

• • •

The target was around twelve kilometres away from the front gate, a nondescript compound of three rooms contained within a square wall set among a thin area of the green belt. It was flanked on two sides by a deep man-made irrigation ditch. Matt had initially ruled out vehicles, mainly due to the complex nature of the terrain leading to the village, but also to lower the signature of the platoon in the hope that they might confuse the enemy as to the intended target location. The platoon moved through a force separation point, the predetermined location where it would break off and go in different directions to further lower its signature. The entire move into the target would take around four hours, patrolling at three kilometres an hour. The intended H-hour was at 0200 hours.

Matt felt pleased with the platoon's progress. They came back in together at creek line on the edge of the dasht, a few hundred metres from the target. Matt guided his team around and switched their axis to the east. Teams One and Two moved ahead on the opposite side of another deep creek that ran down the valley and curled around to approach the target from the right. They took up their positions on the other side of the target. Matt's team and Teams Three and Four came in from the left and the team being run by JJ brought the ANA straight up to the target compound.

All going to plan, Matt thought to himself.

He watched the infrared target designator beam down from the sky, invisible to anyone not wearing NVGs. It was illuminating the front gate. Its source was the silent MQ-9 Reaper thousands of feet above that had been following their progress since they set off.

Somewhere inside the compound a dog barked, setting off a rooster. A noise came from the roof – it sounded like a hacking cough – and then the compound lapsed into silence.

Matt looked across at his signaller, Barnsley, who was crouching down under the weight of his radio next to the track. The two of them both shook their heads.

'That's compromised, boss,' whispered Barnsley.

'I know, mate, standard early warning signal.'

Matt looked across at JJ. He was too far away to hear Matt's whisper so Matt used the radio to order the sergeant to send in the ANA.

'Roger that, boss,' JJ said. 'Do you want me to go in with them?'

Matt was quiet for a moment.

'Boss, do you want me to go?' JJ enquired again softly over the radio. 'These guys are shitting bricks, boss.'

Matt considered the consequences of sending JJ in with no support. In recent months pressure had been put on the Special Forces units in Afghanistan to make the ANA the face and voice of military operations wherever possible, especially if a night raid was required. As it was, they should have been carrying out a cordon and call out rather than making entry.

'No, let them roll with it – no point changing the plan on them now.'

Matt watched through his NVGs as, a minute later, the green ghostly figures approached the compound. A creaking sound interrupted the silence as an iron gate was forced open. The ANA entered with the first three guys jogging in; the fourth guy tripped over the doorframe making a hell of a racket as the fifth and sixth ANA piled into him on the floor. More dogs barked, some inaudible yelling came from within a room – then silence again.

'Boss, they're in,' JJ whispered.

Matt could see his sergeant standing at the entrance to the compound, just outside the door, talking into his radio. Nadeem, Matt's Afghan interpreter, had accompanied JJ and was now standing a few metres to JJ's left. Matt watched as Nadeem lit a cigarette, the small flame an indelible pointer for the surrounding compounds. *That's loose*, thought Matt. Some shouting started up again in the compound and Matt knew that it was the ANA yelling at the locals to get up. They would be separating the women and children, and getting all the men of fighting age together.

The rooster wasn't to be outdone by the commotion and started his morning call again. Then there was a loud squawk as an ANA must have kicked the rooster up the arse.

Finally, the ANA commander came to the front gates and motioned for Matt and his team to move in. It had all gone as they had rehearsed, more or less.

This is going to be a breeze, thought Matt, *not even a shot fired*. 'Come on, Barnsley – let's get in and see what we've got.' Matt found it hard to contain his excitement. If they had Rapier now it would be a great outcome. Matt moved inside at the same time as JJ arrived at the gate. He had with him the two engineers who would take the biometric data with the SEEK system.

The ANA commander was smiling from ear to ear, clearly counting his team's efforts as a huge success. Looking at him, Matt realised that his metric for success might be a bit different to Matt's own. As Matt moved inside the compound he saw the other five ANA soldiers sitting around the fire pit scooping stew from a pot with pieces of bread. In one corner four men sat cross-legged, facing the wall. Two looked to be in their early seventies while the others were barely in their teens.

'Where's everyone else?' Matt asked of no one in particular. He looked around the almost-deserted courtyard. 'Shit, seriously, is this it?'

JJ, who was taking photos of the area and writing down corresponding notes, replied: 'There're some women down the other end. They have babies too.'

Matt gestured to the ten or more plastic cuffs hanging from JJ's body armour. 'Didn't need those,' he said as he kicked a pile of dirt with his boots.

'I'm just relieved we got it done, boss. It won't be the last dry hole we hit in Afghanistan.'

'I know.' Matt undid his helmet and scratched his head.

'Did you see that room entry? At least we have the ANA to the point where they can almost *all* get into a room at speed,' JJ said.

Matt looked at JJ and realised he was talking sense. It was time to wrap this up and he would need to keep the guys focused. They would all be disappointed and there was no point in Matt dropping the ball. He sighed deeply and then turned his mouth to his radio, sending a message out to shrink their perimeter positions into the compound and to pull it apart. They were to look for anything incriminating, in particular evidence that IEDs had been made there.

'Lads, turn this place over. Rip it apart and do it quick. I want to know the instant you find anything that even looks like it could be used in an IED.' He wanted an excuse to level the place but they were running out of time.

'One more thing, guys,' he added. 'I don't want to be out here when the sun comes up. Let's do this with a sense of urgency.'

If they were late getting out they would be in danger of being caught moving on the edges of TK in the heat of the day and in full view of anyone who wanted to cause them some trouble. Matt knew that with no vehicles or heavy weapons they were an easy target for an ambush.

The teams went through each room in turn and then swapped rooms to double-check. Eddie Butcher's Team Three even removed all the coals from the fire and then dug up the earth underneath it. Butcher had read about another platoon's success with this in an old patrol report and was now sure that every fireplace was the hiding place for Taliban weapons. He was yet to find any. He stood over the hole that his team had dug under the remnants of the fire with a look of utter disappointment on his face.

'Don't worry, mate, I have a feeling that if anyone was here, they left as soon as Team One took their first step out of the base this evening.' Then Matt had a thought. 'Hey, have you got someone to go and poke around in their shit pit yet? There could be something in there, right?'

'That's genius, boss!' Eddie almost tripped over himself as he took off to brief his men on the new opportunity.

Matt watched their excited reaction to the unsavoury order and slowly shook his head. 'Seriously,' he muttered under his breath, 'sometimes I don't understand these guys at all. They won't pick up their own rubbish, but they jump at the chance to dig up an Afghan's shit.'

Matt adjusted his body armour and lifted the NVGs on his helmet. They made an audible click. Dawn was approaching fast.

'Boss,' Barnsley called from the edge of the first room. He had been sending updates back on their progress and receiving further orders. 'HQ wants you to send a route report for the walk we did out here last night.' Clearly the signaller hadn't fully thought about what he was saying.

'What are you talking about, Barns? Didn't you tell them I'll do it when we get back?' Matt shook his head and returned his attention to Butcher's guys, who were on their hands and knees excavating the putrid hole in the corner of the compound.

Barnsley finished speaking into the digital radio and then looked up at Matt. 'Boss, it was actually the CO on the radio; he said he needs you personally to send that report ASAP because the SAS guys are driving out that way later this morning on an escort job for Mutallah Khan.'

Matt stared back at him, furious, but before he could respond JJ arrived at his side.

'Finished, boss – let's get the hell out of Dodge, I say.' His smile faded as he looked from Matt to Barnsley. 'What's going on? Who's nicked your cupcake, Barns?'

'HQ wants the boss to write a report before we leave here this morning.'

'What?' JJ turned to Matt. 'That's bullshit, boss. You need to jump all over that – get on the blower and tell the CO he's a fucking retard. Does he have any idea what's going to happen to us if we're stuck out here after sunrise?' Now it was Matt's turn to keep JJ's morale from crashing.

'Mate, there's nothing I can do about this, surely you can see that. It'll take an hour – two, tops.'

But this fell on deaf ears. 'We're not set up for this. We rolled out in light combat order.' JJ pointed to Barnsley's small daypack. 'If we get stuck out here during the day, it could end up being another night. Then what? We have hardly any water, no food, no spare ammo, limited radio batteries. For Christ's sake, boss, call the CO!'

'JJ, you're not helping, mate. The longer we argue about it the longer we will be sitting here. It wouldn't matter if I *did* call the CO – we both know I'm writing that report before we leave here. I suggest your time now would be better spent organising the lads.'

The awkward silence was broken by the sudden arrival of Eddie.

'Hey, get a load of this, boss – turns out the Taliban are shitting Thuraya phones.' Eddie was panting and nearly dry retching, but he wore a huge grin. He was holding up two clear plastic bags containing the expensive satellite communication devices.

'Seems that someone's been using this compound after all,' Matt observed.

Eddie's arms were covered in brown waste. 'Best day EVER!'

Matt looked at JJ and Barnsley, who were both covering their noses against Eddie's stench.

'I hope it's worth what's coming our way, boss,' JJ remarked. 'I truly hope it's bloody worth it.'

Despite JJ's gloomy tone, Matt felt his mood lift. Eddie had made a brilliant find and those devices would be particularly valuable for intelligence. The night had not been a complete waste of time after all.

'All right, guys, let's lock down these three compounds. I need about an hour to bang this report out.' Matt took off his small daypack and pulled out his Toughbook computer.

He looked over his shoulder. 'And, Eddie – for Christ's sake go and clean yourself up, mate. I can't concentrate with that smell hanging around.'

Eddie was sitting on the ground filling out evidence cards that would accompany the Thurayas back to TK. He was still grinning jubilantly, knowing the significance of the find. The satellite phones were used by the Taliban to talk to their senior leadership in Quetta.

Matt plonked himself down in the far corner of the compound as the lads started to move around, sorting out the post-raid admin.

'JJ, can you go and get the teams locked in place, mate? I don't want any movement after sunrise. When we do head off, I don't want the Taliban to be able to predict which way we are going to go.'

JJ nodded. 'No worries, I'm on it. This isn't cool though, boss. I mean, what the hell is the CO thinking?'

'We've discussed this, JJ – you know I can't fight it from here. I'll talk to the CO when we get back. Now let me get this done.' Matt started to fill out the report, thumbing through his small notebook and his GPS for clarification of grids and distances.

• • •

JJ returned twenty minutes later. 'Boss, all three compounds are secure. The ANA are with Team Three. They just need to pray before they take up their positions.'

'Okay,' Matt replied, still preoccupied with the finer details of the report.

JJ held an SD card between Matt's face and the computer screen. 'Here, boss – the team's patrol photos.' Matt looked up at JJ, surprised. He hadn't expected JJ to go around and download all the photos for the report – though it made sense: JJ wanted to get out of there too.

'Thanks,' he said. 'Good thinking.'

'I'm just trying to speed things up, boss.' JJ kicked at the dirt floor. 'Boss, this is just bullshit,' he said, his tone exasperated. 'Why are we doing this now? Is the CO trying to get us in a contact in the daylight? The guys are all asking me questions. They think you're daft for keeping us out here past dawn.'

'What?' Matt stared at JJ and then looked around at his guys. Most were sitting there in silence looking out of the compound and scanning for the enemy, except for Cinzano's men, who were talking among themselves. 'Pull your head in, mate! Go and tell the guys we'll leave the minute the message has been sent. Just remember, you're the senior soldier here. I don't need to be hearing this crap from you; if the men are grumbling, then you're not doing your job.'

'That's not right, boss; if the men are grumbling and I'm telling you about it, I'm exactly doing my job.'

JJ walked back to his own team. Matt looked over at one of the small rooms that opened onto the courtyard. Sitting there in silence were the four women, two of them cradling babies. They were all wearing black burqas that covered them from head to toe, leaving them with just a narrow slit through which to view the world. One of them stared back at Matt.

Matt looked back down at the SD card and inserted it into the computer. Scrolling through the photos on the screen, he started selecting which ones to insert into the brief.

Ten minutes later, he was done.

'Barns, here's the report, mate – it's filed as Route Recon 26P12. Send this through to HQ and let me know once it's gone.'

Matt passed the Toughbook to the signaller, who had already started setting up his digital radio.

Standing up, Matt moved over towards the women. One of Sam's theories was that Rapier might dress as a woman, but searching women would almost certainly be a career killer. Perhaps they would complain and it would get back to Mutallah Khan, the Uruzghan police chief, or the ANA would complain through their chain of command, or, worse still, one of his own men would file an official complaint that would have Matt instantly stood down pending an investigation.

There must be millions of women in the world living invisible lives just like this, thought Matt as he stood above them, his M4 held in a loose grip angled away from the women. Judging by their eyes, he guessed that three of them were old ladies and one of them was maybe middle-aged or even younger. As he stared at them, they huddled closer together. The youngest never took her eyes off Matt and her gaze was vicious. Matt shivered. He wondered if her husband had been killed by the coalition at some time – or even her kids.

'Boss, we might have a problem,' JJ called from behind him.

Matt turned to see the sergeant jogging back into the compound courtyard.

'What is it?'

'I was passing your message on and found the ANA leaving the other compound; they were going out to look for locals to bring them some more food. They wouldn't stop when I asked them. They said they have to eat.' The stress he was feeling was apparent in his voice. The ANA could be difficult to manage and Matt had given this responsibility to JJ and the interpreter.

'Alright, mate, tell Hammo to get his team ready to respond if they get into trouble. I'll go and get Kiwi to take the snipers out and bring them back.'

Matt glanced up at the sky; it was becoming light. Looking out the compound door he could tell that the area was the start of a larger village that followed the green belt. The villagers were already up and moving around out there, getting on with their daily routine.

He didn't have to wait long before Jensen Pharris, the Kiwi sniper, returned with the ANA soldiers in tow. The Afghans had bags of bread and pots of warm goat stew, all prepared for them by the locals. They sat down in the middle of the courtyard and unpacked their feast.

Nadeem Karne, the young interpreter from Kabul, approached Matt. 'The guys want you to sit with them and have some food, boss.' Nadeem said.

The Afghan soldiers looked up and gave Matt wide smiles. They enthusiastically motioned for him to sit, clearly excited by the prospect of him eating with them. They sat there in the dust, their ill-fitting green uniforms all in various states of disrepair; their boots were unlaced and their weapons had been flung aside.

'Okay, Nadeem. Can you ask them how long they need?' Matt sat down cross-legged and food was thrust into his hands. He knew that it was no use trying to rush them, even as keen as he was to get out of there. This was the thing that frustrated him the most about partner force operations. Afghans' sense of time was relative to their dress and bearing. For the ANA's part, they loved to host the Australians; Afghan culture was based on giving and supporting. Matt didn't really understand the Afghans and didn't give much thought to the development side of the coalition's mission. As far as he was concerned, the ANA continued to find new ways to disappoint him.

The Afghan soldiers, completely unaware of Matt's frustration, ate and chatted among themselves, smiling and laughing, seemingly oblivious to any concept of urgency.

'Nadeem, tell them to finish up, please, mate – we need to get going before it gets too hot.'

Matt stood up as Nadeem began to argue with the ANA. Moving away from the group, Matt approached his platoon: it was time to move and if they were lucky they might just get back unscathed.

20

THE DASHT

Thirty minutes later, Yankee Platoon was moving out of the three compounds. They set off in the opposite direction from the way they had come in. Only when they were several hundred metres from the compounds did they circle back towards their base.

As they emerged from the green belt, Matt looked across at the small villages that dotted the landscape and traced the edge of the open desert. He could see the perimeter of the military camp on the horizon. Behind Camp Russell was a mountain range that jutted out; it was an awe-inspiring sight.

The platoon was spread out in a giant wedge, with the lead team in a diamond formation three hundred metres ahead of the last team. They were choosing the route and clearing the choke points.

The platoon came across a deep sandy creek bed that should have been tackled as an obstacle crossing, with the requisite caution; instead Team Three moved across without stopping. Watching, Matt decided to let the rest of the platoon continue on. He could tell they were all buggered now. Guys were not patrolling their designated arcs of responsibility anymore. They were looking down at the rocks under their feet rather than scanning the terrain and the squad radios were silent. Matt turned to look behind him. The ANA were walking behind his team in single file. There was no more than two metres between each man and they all carried their weapons on their shoulders or by the barrels. Matt shook his head; time to take control: the platoon was becoming far too complacent.

'Lads, switch on,' he ordered over the radio.

Almost instantly, he could see a change in demeanour. Sometimes even the Special Forces guys needed a bit of a kick up the arse.

Another sandy creek bed and again Team Three moved straight across. *Jesus, these guys have completely thrown in the towel.* Matt gritted his teeth with frustration.

A hundred metres away he saw a couple of old farm compounds that overlooked the area. The sound of kids playing was evidence of occupation. Three young boys ran out of the closest compound chasing an old tyre across the jagged rocks and stones that they called a field. They were pushing it with big sticks and yelling at the top of their voices. Adjusting the weight of his daypack, Matt dropped down into the sandy creek bed and noticed the footprints and tyre tracks going in each direction. *This is a track crossing! What the bloody hell?* Matt could feel the anger rising in him. Crossing a creek or even a track at the crossing point was a big mistake and the commandos would never usually do this given the opportunity to pass anywhere else. The plateau was open and there were hundreds of places to cross that would be less dangerous. Eddie Butcher's guys had dropped the ball, and even though there were only four kilometres to go, those four kilometres were as dangerous as anywhere else in Uruzghan.

Matt emerged from the deep creek crossing with Barnsley at his side.

'Jesus, Barns. How many times do I have to tell you to put that bloody antenna down? And for Christ's sake, get away from me when we are crossing an obstacle.'

'C'mon, boss, who's the target, you or me? I'm just trying to hedge my bets a bit.' The signaller smiled at Matt.

'I think you're misjudging my mood right now,' Matt snapped. 'Any comms from headquarters?'

'No, it's been real quiet to be honest.' Barns hitched the heavy pack higher on his shoulders. 'Bloody hell, it's getting hot, boss. I'm glad we are heading back in. It must be over forty degrees now.'

Matt nodded as he increased his stride. Ahead of him, Team Three started to spread out into the desert.

Finally, Matt thought.

• • •

As the ANA dropped down into the creek behind the platoon commander and signaller, Rapier was watching from behind the compounds. There was a small tree that stuck out of the far bank. The creek bed was twenty metres across and when a person dropped down into it they disappeared. Rapier used the tree as a makeshift sight. When he could see a head in line with the bottom of the tree, it meant that the person behind was directly over the IED buried beneath the creek bed. Rapier had worked this out based on the spacing that the military units would use. The ANA, unlike their Australian counterparts, were all bunched up.

Moments before, Rapier had watched as the man in front of the platoon commander appeared at the base of the tree. That meant the commander was over the IED. Rapier quickly considered his options. The officer was an obvious target, and the impact of his loss would be profound, but Rapier had a better thought. One thing he hated even more than an infidel was a Muslim traitor. He watched one member of the platoon very closely. Wearing the same uniform as the Australians but was not carrying a weapon, he was about twenty kilograms lighter than the rest. It was obvious that he was their interpreter. As the interpreter crossed the IED, Rapier whispered 'boom', and gave a small chuckle. He let the interpreter climb the bank on the other side and refocussed on the men behind Nadeem. Waiting until the head of the first ANA soldier appeared level with the tree, Rapier then typed in the number on the mobile phone and hit send.

A thunderous explosion shook the earth. It vaporised three of those down in the creek and disorientated those within a radius of fifty metres. The noise was repeated across the valley as the sound waves bounced back off the mountain range in the distance. Rapier laughed as he saw Nadeem fall over and then get up and fall over again, obviously shocked as a result of the blast.

Smiling at his handiwork, Ahmed Defari melted into the crowd of women and children who were now streaming out from the farm compounds, rushing from the scene. In thirty minutes from now, the place would be crawling with medical response choppers and the Quick Reaction Force, including the dreaded Apache helicopters that could be so unpredictable. This was no time to hang around.

21

COMPANY OPERATIONS CENTRE, TARIN KOWT

Captain Craig Reilly strolled into the company operations centre. He walked past his own makeshift wooden desk located on a raised landing overlooking the operations floor down below. The carpenters had worked overtime getting the command centre together. All the tables looked like they had been made in a back shed, probably because they had. Descending the small flight of steps to the operations floor, Craig could see that the first three tables in the centre of the narrow, rectangular room were scattered with topographical maps. Computers lined the next three tables, with power cables and Ethernet cords connecting them from the ceiling above. At the end of this line of tables Craig's operations staff huddled around one of the terminals. A whiteboard on wheels had been rolled around behind them and it already had the urgent scribbles of a half completed contact report written on it in large blue letters.

'All right, Jerry?' Craig said as he approached the group. In an instant he could see that all was not right. Sergeant Jerry Dewhurst, the watch keeper, was staring at his computer screen. Notification clerk Corporal Phil Rennie and the Unit Medical Officer Fiona Blake were looking over his shoulder.

'Yankee Platoon has hit an IED, boss,' Jerry said. 'I was just about to page you.'

He was typing in synchronisation to a frantic message being sent by Corporal Barnsley, from out in the field, to the duty signaller, located just next door.

It felt like a lifetime ago that he had finished his selection for Special Forces. In truth, Craig had only completed the full rein-forcement cycle, including all of the specialist courses necessary to be deemed a qualified commando, seven months ago. Joining the team during its build-up training to deploy to Afghanistan, he had quickly established a good reputation among the other officers and soldiers alike.

'Fiona, can you send a message to Kandahar? Just a heads-up to the OC that there has been an incident and there'll be more infor-mation to follow.' His boss, Delta Company Officer in Command Major Heath McCaig, had no reservations about leaving the command centre under Craig's watchful eye. He would be gone for twelve weeks with his deployable HQ while X-Ray Platoon conducted operations on the northern approaches to Kandahar. Craig had worked out at the start of the tour that the more infor-mation he could send before being asked the better.

Corporal Barnsley's voice came over the radio again. It was clear and panicked all at once. 'Zero Alpha, this is Yankee Charlie, confirm receipt of nine-liner over!' he demanded. In the background the company command centre staff could hear yelling. Barnsley had started to send the NATO nine-liner, the official medevac request format, within seconds of the IED blast occurring. Even though he was himself dazed and in shock, the habit of establishing and maintaining communications was second nature to him.

As Barnsley sent the nine-liner to request immediate medical evacuation of the injured the whole scene unfolded right there, pouring out of a radio stack in one corner of that long dusty room inside the relative safety of Tarin Kowt. Craig could imagine men running in and out of the dusty creek line frantically trying to orientate themselves amongst the carnage. He could hear the screams of team commanders trying desperately to account for their men and the soldiers replying that they were still alive. JJ's voice came over and drowned out all the other sounds for a moment, as he tried to set up some type of defensive perimeter around the dead and injured. Then the voices of the patrol medics could be heard, complaining they'd run out of first aid dressings and tourniquets. '*This situation is hopeless without more tourniquets,*' one yelled, probably to Yankee Alpha. All the while, Barnsley continued to re-send the nine-liner. The pick-up site location, frequencies, equipment needed, the number of patients and security at the pick-up site. Barnsley was second-checking everything and leaving nothing to chance.

Having completed the transmission, the command post became silent once again; now they could only imagine what was happening out on that dusty plateau some six kilometres away. Jerry had been feverishly tapping at his keyboard while Barnsley was talking, using the chat program, Sametime chat, to send information straight down to the flight line.

'What have you got, Jerry?' asked Craig.

'It's not good, boss.' Jerry turned down the radio stack in their office as further information came in from Barnsley to the signal operators next door in the communications centre. The nine-liner brief was designed to speed up the casualty evacuation process and contained only the important details. Now that it had been passed along, Barnsley was following up with extra information about the incident itself. Dewhurst scribbled the information on a notepad next to his computer and was trying to make sense of the details.

'Wheels up from oscar one-one, boss,' called Corporal Jenkins, who had moved back to his computer opposite Jerry, his ear buried in the flight line radio handset. The American crews of the Black Hawk CASEVAC choppers down at the flight line had implemented a new process recently in response to constant reviews of their performance. They would also monitor the Special Operations Task Group's communications and, if there were no other priority missions, they would immediately launch and make their way towards the incident. The American CASEVAC crews had saved countless lives and they were always looking for ways to speed up their response time.

'Awesome, that was fast,' said Craig. 'So we have a CASEVAC chopper en route. Jerry, can you confirm that exact pick-up grid as well as the IED grids? Put a pin in the main map to show their locations. Let's get some information together to give to the CO.'

'Boss, I should tell you that Barnsley has asked for at least four body bags in this nine-liner,' said Dewhurst, looking at his screen.

Fiona gasped, dropping the plastic coffee cup that she had been drinking from on her desk.

'Shit!' Craig swore. 'Really?'

'Yeah, I'm afraid so.' Jerry adjusted his glasses and rose from his chair. The whole team stood around their workstations looking at each other. Craig thought about asking Jerry to request the names but decided against it. It didn't matter at this point in time. Nothing would change what had already happened. The command centre's task now was to track the information and be prepared to provide further resources should circumstances change on the ground. Craig's mind raced as he considered what to do next.

'God, I hope it's not JJ,' Jerry said under his breath.

Craig looked across at him. The two sergeants were close, he knew. For a moment his mind was blank, still in shock – then it came to him: *triage the stimulus*, he thought.

'Okay, team, listen up,' Craig said, moving to stand at the head of the long planning table. 'Yankee Platoon are in a bit of strife.'

'That's putting it mildly,' said Dewhurst.

'We need to start sorting out the administration and preparing the notifications, but we also need to be ready should they request ammunition resupply and fast air support. Jerry, I need you to build a PowerPoint presentation and record all the times of specific events and the grid references as well.'

Craig looked at the map and then down at his desk. He had written a list of steps on a cheat sheet to be followed for a CASEVAC. 'We have to assume that perhaps they will need some backup. The other platoon is away, operating north of Kandahar. What do SAS have on today, Jerry? Aren't they supposed to be escorting a convoy or something like that later in the morning?'

'They went on a job in birds about twenty minutes ago, boss.'

'What?' Craig looked across at Fiona and then back at Jerry. 'Where's the concept of operations brief? I haven't seen anything.'

'They didn't do one. The CO authorised them to go.'

'Without a CONOP? That's insane.' Craig thought about it for a moment. 'That's just ridiculous. Phil, I want you to get hold of the RSM and tell him I want to see him when he's free. I think we should stand up a reserve force. Losing four guys is a big hit.'

'On it, boss.' Phil grabbed his phone and dialled the RSM's extension.

'Also, we're going to need some help in here. Jerry, talk to the engineers. Ask them to come across and support us for the next few hours.'

The door to the command centre flew open and the CO stormed in.

'Who's dead, Reilly?' the CO demanded, his face bright red. 'What's going on? Why are you all just standing there?'

'Boss, we don't know the names yet. We're waiting for further information,' Craig replied in an even tone.

'Well, get on the radio and find out,' the CO ordered brusquely.

'Sir, with respect, that would probably confuse the issue further out on the ground.'

'We need to start the notification process as soon as we can – I need to know who has been killed to inform the special operations commander. News doesn't get better with age, Captain Reilly.'

'No, sir, but it does get more accurate.'

'Reilly, what's so hard about calling them and asking for the names?'

Craig struggled to keep his voice calm. Was the CO incapable of listening to reason?

'I'll get onto it in due course, sir,' he promised. 'I think maybe Matt has enough to worry about at the moment without me hounding him for names of guys that were just killed.' Craig was determined not to let the CO have his way; things would just become more convoluted if the correct process wasn't followed. They needed to focus on their priorities.

'Zero Alpha, this is Yankee Charlie.' Barnsley's voice filled the command post. 'The bird has arrived and all the KIA are now being loaded.'

'Yankee Alpha, this is Zero Alpha,' came the reply from the communications centre next door. 'Acknowledged – over.'

'Give me that handset.' The CO shouted, walking over to the radio stack.

Then the voice of Matt Rix came over the airwaves. 'This is Yankee Alpha, just confirming to you prior to the full report that all the deceased were ANA soldiers – over.'

At that the CO stopped dead in his tracks and slumped into the seat facing the whiteboard. Everyone else watched him in silence as he stared off into space.

After a few long seconds, he spoke. 'Thank God for that hey, Reilly?' He leaned back in the chair and clasped his hands behind his head. 'That's a relief.'

'Probably not for the Afghans' families, sir,' said Craig.

The CO got up and headed to the door. 'I'll be in my office, Captain Reilly.'

'No worries, sir. I'll be sure to get the dead soldiers' names to you as soon as I can.'

The CO left the room. The command centre staff looked at each other, bemused.

'Seriously, did that just happen?' said Fiona.

Craig shook his head. Turning to the whiteboard he started to write the after-action review headings.

'Listen, guys, go out and grab a brew and then come back in. I'll hold the fort here now that the Apaches are on station for Matt's guys. When you have had a rest let's go over what just happened and review our processes.' He was fuming inside but was desperately trying to conceal it from his team.

When the others left, Craig settled down into his chair to review the Sametime chat log. He stared at his own reflection in the computer screen. He had let his hair grow out so that it was now a blond curly mess. His beard was thick, with hints of red through it. He looked older than his twenty-seven years and older still than the reflection that had looked back at him from the mirror only this morning when he was brushing his teeth.

Thinking about the interaction with the CO, he realised that it had stressed him more than the critical incident itself. Jesus that guy is a dickhead, he thought to himself. Noticing an A4 pad of paper sitting next to the computer, Craig took a pen out of a glass jar on the desk and started to write. The words poured out. He might not be able to confront the CO about the way he handled the incident but he could sure as hell make sure that it was all recorded for future use.

22

CAMP RUSSELL, TARIN KOWT

As the platoon entered the outer perimeter of the base they moved into two files, one on either side of the road and staggered so that there was at least five metres between each man. They walked along in silence, each man lost in his own thoughts as he dealt with the abruptness of death. Trudging along in the ankle-high dust, they approached the gate that they had successfully defended in their first weeks in camp. The fine silt stirred up by their feet became the very air that they breathed. It hung around their heads like a light brown smokescreen. Above the dust the early-afternoon sky was clear and deep blue in colour, holding the promise of gentler days ahead, if they could just survive the next day, and the day after that. Already hours overdue, there was no longer any urgency in their movements. Only JJ quickened his pace as they arrived. He caught up to Matt as he was unloading his M4 rifle into the Hesco wall.

'What's the plan, boss? Do you want me to see if I can get the mess to do a late lunch for the guys?' JJ took the magazine off his rifle and cocked the working parts back. He watched the bullet that had just been seated in the chamber land in the dirt next to his foot. He stooped over and picked it up.

'No, it's all right,' Matt said, 'we're not rationed in. Let's just eat with everyone else tonight. It's only a few more hours. I don't need to see the guys until tomorrow morning. Get everyone together in the common room after breakfast and I'll let em know what's going on for the next few days.'

JJ nodded his head as he wiped the dust off the previously ejected round. He pulled the top bullet out of the magazine and replaced it with the one he had just unloaded, then put the fresh bullet back on top. 'You know, boss, I was thinking about this morning, I want you to know that the guys don't think it's your fault – I mean, the IED and all that. Because of that conversation we had back in the compound, you know?' The sergeant sounded wretched.

'It's okay, mate, I understand,' Matt reassured him. 'Afghanistan is a shit sandwich, JJ, and we had to take a big bite of it today. Sometimes things are said in the heat of the moment.' Matt placed the magazine from his weapon back into his combat rig and fastened the clip. He let the bolt fly forwards on his rifle and fired the action. He then cocked it again and put the weapon on safe, closing the dust cover in the process.

'I hope we're going to get some time inside the wire now, boss. We've been whipped like a stolen pony for the last month.' JJ placed the magazine into the open pouch on his body armour and fastened it shut.

'I'm sure we'll be here for the next week at least, unless something comes up. As it is, mate, I now need to go and see the ANA commander and explain to him why four of his guys are dead. And we need to do some movement training and talk about some basics again. The guys were sloppy today, JJ.'

Matt's mind drifted back to the breakfast he'd shared with the ANA guys only a few hours before, recalling how animated and happy they'd been.

He turned and walked off through the perimeter gate, looking up at the guard tower where, two months ago, his men had dragged out a young wounded kid. It felt like so long ago now.

JJ caught up with Matt and fell into step with him. 'Boss, is everything okay?'

Matt looked across at JJ and could see that he was genuinely worried. 'Yep. Wish I could go back in time and have breakfast with the ANA guys again is all. I would have liked to let them know that I appreciated them being with us.' Matt swallowed hard and unfastened his Kevlar helmet. 'JJ, go and find Nadeem – he'll probably be in the morgue. Get him to see the psych, mate. He escaped being killed in that blast by a bee's dick. Any of the other guys too, if they need it.'

'Understood. Do you want to give Nadeem some leave, boss? I think his parents live in Kabul.'

'No, we're going to need him over the next few weeks and there's just no one to replace him with,' said Matt.

'That's a shame.' JJ started to roll up the sleeves on his top, the heat was starting to really annoy him now.

'Why's that, JJ?' Matt thought JJ's response was a bit strange and wanted to get to the bottom of it.

'Ahh, I'm just sick of him asking everyone if they'll help him get citizenship in Oz after this, that's all. It's getting old.'

'Oh, right. Well, can you blame him? When we pull out of here in a few years he will have to fend for himself. They'll remember him. An American-schooled Afghan walking around Uruzghan with the Australian SF? His days are numbered, JJ.'

'Fair call.'

The two walked on. Matt wiped off some dust from the lenses of his Oakleys.

JJ looked across at Matt and could see that he was still annoyed. 'How about you, boss? Do you need to go see the psych?'

'What?' Matt thought about it a moment. 'No, mate, I'll just deal with this the way I always do.'

'Right, so I'll see you in the gym then.'

'Sounds like a plan. Let's go after dinner. How does eight pm sound?'

'Cool. I'll get the guys working on getting their weapons de-serviced and see you there.'

Matt nodded. He'd hit the pads for an hour and then he and JJ would wrestle it out. Most of the guys would probably gravitate towards the gym anyway. It always ended up being a good team-building session.

Matt broke lines from the front of the platoon and headed over to the HQ building. The CO was standing on the steps with a cup of coffee, watching Matt's platoon file past.

'How are the guys, Matt?' asked the CO as Matt approached.

'They're okay. Obviously the ANA didn't fare so well, they were vaporised. It was a shit day all round, to be honest.' Matt stood at the bottom of the steps as the rest of his platoon filed past behind him.

'IEDs, a nasty business – I'm glad you're all back safely, mate.'

Nasty, eh? I suppose you know this from your vast experience, thought Matt.

'G'day, Eddie, how're the lads?' the CO called as Eddie Butcher and Team Three filed through.

'Fine, sir.' Eddie didn't look up from the ground ahead of him as he continued walking.

'Nasty business, sir, that's true,' Matt interjected. 'However, Eddie's team found a couple of Thurayas today; I think we might have only missed Rapier by a few hours.'

'Yeah, bad luck that. Still, it was never concrete was it? On a positive note, though, Saygen hit a couple of targets a few kilometres to the west of you and had a pretty good result, so it wasn't all for naught.' The CO rocked back and forth on his heels, clearly pleased. 'They may not have found Rapier, but Saygen's guys dropped multiple fighters across a series of compounds. They were caught completely off guard.'

'Hang on – I thought Saygen and his lads were taking Mutallah Khan out on some vehicle patrol? I mean, isn't that why I stayed out there to do the route recon report?'

'You just have to be flexible in this game, mate,' the CO replied. 'Things change; some targets popped up so we launched on them.'

'No, no, no, just hold on a second. What do you mean they "popped up"? They popped up because we remained in our location after sun-up. Every fucking Taliban in the valley would have been talking about us. You know that. They popped up because you left me out there as a tethered goat. For Christ's sake, sir, there are four dead ANA because you had me write a fucking bullshit report in the field.' Matt's voice had risen to a yell and he could see the last teams of his platoon looking over at him curiously.

'I suggest you keep yourself in check, Rix,' hissed the CO as he stepped forward so that he and Matt were standing toe to toe. 'You need to remember your place, Captain. Circumstances change, and we need to respond to them accordingly. I suggest that if you want a future in Special Forces, you'll remember that.'

The CO flicked his wrist and tipped the remains of his coffee onto the ground at the base of the steps.

'You're doing a good job here, Matt,' he continued. 'But don't you *ever* yell at me again, or I will have you on a plane back to Sydney faster than you can even spell Rapier.' The CO glared at Matt. 'Do I make myself clear?'

At that moment Sam came jogging out of the building and almost ran headlong into Matt and the CO on the steps.

'G'day, Matt,' he said. 'I'm sorry to hear about this morning, mate. How are the lads – are they okay?' Sam looked from Matt to the CO, as if suddenly sensing the tension in the atmosphere.

'My guys are fine, Sam – I just wish I could say the same for the ANA,' Matt told him. He looked around the camp, considering how to respond to the CO, then realised he had no option but to defer to his superior officer. 'As to your previous comment, sir,' he said, looking at the CO now, 'I take your point.'

'Good lad,' said the CO. 'Now, I know you're probably tired and could do with some rest. Why don't you go get yourself cleaned up and enjoy some downtime while you can. I have another task for you in a couple of days.'

'What?!' Matt couldn't believe his ears.

'That's right. I've had X-Ray platoon released back to us for a few weeks. They're going to help us clear a valley to the south. It's been a Taliban stronghold for some time. I want to get your guys up one end and X-Ray down the other and see what comes of it. Saygen's guys have done the planning on this. He'll be ready to launch on any targets who might show their heads. The American Special Forces are going to be involved as well.'

'Right, of course they will. And how long do you expect we will be gone for?' Matt felt broken. He knew there was no point arguing, especially since Saygen had already developed the concept.

'It will be a four-day operation; X-Ray has submitted their insertion grids, so you can get them from Sam. You'll be pleased to hear that Saygen has organised for Black Hawks to insert you. It promises to be eventful, that's for damn sure.'

'Eventful ... That's one way of putting it.' Matt raised his eyebrows. 'I'll go give my guys a heads-up and come back after dinner to see Sam. I'm sure the guys will be thrilled.'

Matt looked at Sam, but the intel guy was oblivious to his sarcasm. He was studying some papers intently and it was obvious to Matt that Sam was waiting for him to leave.

'Right, I'll be back soon then.' Matt jogged down the steps and set off in the direction of the Yankee Platoon accommodation.

• • •

The barracks were silent when Matt entered. Most of the guys were either lying in their bunks or in the showers. Matt knocked on JJ's door.

'Yo?' JJ answered the door dressed just in MultiCam shorts and holding a strip of cleaning cloth. His rifle lay in parts on the floor of his room and *Kick-Ass* was playing on his computer.

'It's just me, mate.' Matt turned and opened his own door on the opposite side of the hallway.

'What's going on, boss? How was the CO?'

Matt ignored the question. 'I need you to get the guys together in the common room. We're off again for a few days.'

'Huh? You're joking, right?'

Matt turned to face JJ. 'No, I'm afraid not. Just get them together, mate – I'll explain it all then.'

'Alright. Can you give me half an hour? Some of the guys went across to that Dutch café, Echos, and I'll have to send someone to go get them.'

'Sure, that's fine; I need some time to sort my shit out anyway.'

'Are we going in Bushmasters?' enquired JJ.

'No, we're flying, believe it or not.' Matt wondered how far south they would be going if they needed to be choppered in.

'Well, at least we can't hit an IED in a chopper.' JJ laughed at his own black humour.

'Yeah, that's right – except with my luck we'll land on one in the middle of the landing zone,' Matt smirked at JJ and then entered his own room. Sleep was calling him, if only for twenty minutes.

23

Omar Defari fumbled in his pocket for the source of the vibration. Dropping the bag of fertiliser he had just hauled up the creek bank, he pressed the green answer button.

'Omar Defari?' a female American voice enquired.

'Yes. Who's this?'

'My name is Steph. Faisal Khan gave me your number. I really hope that you are well and that your family are healthy and well too?' Her fake courtesy grated on Omar.

'I'm in good health, thanks be to God. Faisal told me that you would call someday.'

Steph explained to Omar how she might be able to help him and his family. Omar listened to her speak; although her arrogant American drawl irritated him, her naivety regarding the complex situation in Afghanistan actually amused him. But when she started to explain that she would pay for the information he provided,

Omar took more notice. Perhaps, he thought, she could help him after all.

'I was told that you'd like to meet to give me the information in person,' the American said.

'Are you able to send money first?' Omar asked. 'So we know that we can trust each other?'

'I could give you half upfront and half after you have delivered the information,' she offered, then named a sum that was more than Omar could ever have dared to imagine.

'But, Omar, the information must be worth it,' the American cautioned as they concluded their conversation.

'It will be,' he assured her.

Ending the call, Omar shouldered the twenty-kilo bag once again and walked slowly through the archway leading to the pomegranate orchard. He strolled along the narrow gravel path. On either side were the new pomegranate saplings, planted just last spring. He entered his family's compound to the sound of children playing happily in the courtyard – just as children had done in Zabul for as long as he could remember. This area of the province had been left mostly untouched by the last ten years of war, and in the twenty years before that the Soviets had dared not venture too far up into these higher areas. It was peaceful here: the perfect spot for his younger brother to command a powerful legion that was determined to rule the surrounding valleys and beyond.

'Mouza, how are you on this day?' Omar asked the eldest of his brother's wives. She was sitting on a stone step watching the children playing in the yard. She looked up at him through the narrow slit in her veil.

'I'm well, Omar, thanks be to God. What have you here?'

'This is for the orchard – it's food to help with the new plants. Fasili in Arghandab brought it for me. You remember: he is the cousin of Faisal Khan. He dropped me off and has just left now.' Omar settled down next to her, stroking his grey beard.

'Oh, I should have liked to have seen him. His family, are they fine? Did you ask if they are in good health?' She coughed gently into a piece of white embroidered cloth and then passed him the plate of dates that she had been picking at.

'God has seen to it that they are all well,' said Omar, selecting a few dates and then settling back against the cool wall. The shade of the larger trees gave much-needed shade in the height of summer and kept the compound wall surprisingly cool. Omar had sat on this step for more than fifty summers and knew the seasons from the shadows of the trees. He was already conscious of the cooler months now approaching.

'Faisal also saw Ahmed last week, Mouza.' Omar looked down at the cracks in the ground and watched a trail of small ants scurrying towards their nest. He picked up a stick and scraped it across the line of insects. 'Ahmed gave him this bag to give to you.' He put down the stick and, picking up a small bag, handed it to Mouza. 'He wants you to keep it safe for him.'

Mouza took the bag and held it against her chest. Omar could tell that she missed her husband. In his absence, she was required to maintain his part of the family. This included organising the two other wives, managing their part of the plantation and keeping their young sons from taking off into Kandahar. Ahmed's remaining six boys were almost teenagers and, with the loss of their brother as a martyr, they needed their father here now more than ever.

'On Friday, while we prayed together in the Arghandab mosque, Faisal told me of an American woman who was going to help stop the foreigners from taking our fruit. She called to talk to me just now. I don't know what she thinks she can do. She talks of markets, new roads to Kandahar and new machinery. She asked me to go to Kandahar to see her – she had many questions. She says she will pay me a thousand US dollars just to meet with her. We could use that money, Mouza – it's more than the Iranians will pay and more than Ahmed can hope to make fighting.'

'Well, you must tell Ahmed,' she counselled. 'He would want to know all about this. Perhaps it's a trick. Remember, brother: Ahmed is in charge of this whole tribal area now. He knows what he's doing. Soon enough he could go to Quetta. Imagine then! Imagine the wealth he will send back, the future that the children might have.'

'Future? What about the past? I remember when our fathers' fathers owned all these orchards, Mouza, peace be upon them. Our families were rich and had all they could need. I went to school in Kabul. We learned the language of the West. Now we give these other foreigners the fruit for our own protection, they pay but a fraction of its true worth and leave us with hardly enough to survive. Their protection from God should not be so assured, I feel.' Omar picked up the stick again and smashed it into the hole the ants had been disappearing down.

'Be careful, Omar,' Mouza cautioned. 'God knows what is best for all of us. Anyway, Mullah Ghazi has never raised these issues that you speak of.'

'Hmph, Mullah Ghazi! Who is he? A foreigner, that's who. What would he know of our troubles? My father was the mullah here when I was a boy, not some teacher from the madrasas in Pakistan.

He brings me these sickly creatures. They can't even tend to the trees let alone fight. They sit in the mosque and eat our food then when I send them with a vest to take a message to the Americans they can't even stand up long enough to get close and kill them.' Mouza ignored the reference to the Pakistani suicide bombers. Ahmed would not approve of her taking an interest in the suicide bombings. Ahmed and Omar kept these things between themselves. It wasn't her place to think about such things.

'They disappear, Mouza, one by one only to be replaced by others. And all the while Mullah Ghazi poisons our own boys' minds and they leave us for Quetta. Your boys will be next, Mouza, wait and see.'

'Your father is gone now, Omar. You need to talk to Ahmed before you speak to any other foreigners, be they Muslim or infidel.' Mouza's tone was firm and it unsettled Omar; he decided to change tack.

'You are wise beyond your years and station, Mouza. Perhaps you're right, sister. But I cannot tell Ahmed – he will not be back from Tarin Kowt until the end of the summer and I promised not to contact him; he worries about the ears of the West, you know.' Omar looked back out along the path and up into the mountains at the end of their valley.

'He is safe enough, Omar. Abdul Rahman is a good host. I suspect they are very busy there.' Mouza opened the bag to look at the contents.

'And not just fixing motorcycles in Rahman's shop, either,' said Omar.

Mouza glanced across at him and then started to unpack the contents of the bag; she was becoming annoyed by the old fool.

'Look at these things: old broken watches, all these phone parts, hair dye, black eyeliner, an oven timer and these – what are these? They look like the eyes of a giant bug.' Mouza held up the strange goggles to examine them. They had long black lenses with rubber caps on each end and were held on a frame that was made of grey aluminium. An American flag was stamped on the left and dried blood covered the right tube. She dropped them back in the bag, not wanting even to speculate how her husband had chanced on these.

'Ahmed has vowed revenge for your father's death at the hands of the Americans. Why have you stayed here instead of helping him?' she demanded.

'I do what I can, sister, but I am growing old.'

'Dropping a suicide bomber on the side of the road and then blowing him up in the name of Allah is not going to avenge him, brother Omar,' she said.

Omar looked up at the trees and slowly shook his head. 'I am old, Mouza, and I have been waiting for Allah to show me how I can right those wrongs.' He coughed into his open hand, as if to further reinforce his aging years. 'Did you know that my father's father had enough money from these lands to open a cinema in Kabul some sixty years ago?' Omar missed his childhood; from having so much, they had to struggle now merely to survive.

'I know that, Omar, but is life really so much worse now?' his sister-in-law asked. 'At least this valley has seen no violence, no fighting.'

'I saw black-and-white photographs of my mother riding in a car. She wore modern clothes – a loose shirt, trousers, a colourful headscarf. She could have been mistaken for the wife of American

169

President Eisenhower, who visited Afghanistan that same year. Then the Soviets came, followed by the Mujahedeen and then the Taliban; and now the Americans are back to try to make it like it was supposed to be. They were here not even a month when my father was killed. His only crime was that he was sitting, talking to a man in a field at night. We had hoped for so much when I was a boy. All the men my age that lived in the city will remember what it was like. I was a friend to girls that were at the school next to mine. Girls at school, Mouza – can you believe it?' Omar sighed. He was worn out from the long trip and the conversation had now made him sad.

'You spoke of your mother, Omar, but I ask you: what happened to her? What did the Mujahedeen do to her because of her lack of faith? Tell me that.'

'I must go now, Mouza,' said Omar. 'The night approaches and the water pump won't turn itself on.' He sighed to himself as he got up, taking his fertiliser with him. 'See you later this evening for the meal.'

Omar walked away thinking of his youth. He was old now and knew that his years were coming to a close. Secretly he envied his brother. People respected and feared the name Ahmed Defari. This American woman might be the answer to his prayers. The money she would pay could help the family and make the coming winter more bearable and the money that his family would receive if he was to do the task that Faisal asked of him would see them through many more winters. But there was so much more to it than just money. This was how the aging Omar could be remembered, sung about and revered as the one who stood up when he was needed. Perhaps God was showing him how he should help, and perhaps Afghanistan just wasn't meant to be as it was when he was a child. Yes, this American woman was the answer.

• • •

Mouza sat for a while longer, and then headed inside to her family's room. The bag intrigued her. She sat on a red velvet cushion on the dusty floor and opened it again. She picked up the goggles once more, shivering at the sight of the blood. She felt sorry for the young infidel who must have once owned these. Mouza missed her own eldest son now. Initially his loss had been celebrated by the village, but now she questioned the cost.

Mouza recognised Ahmed's phone when she had looked in the bag before: a black Nokia he had bought when they were in Kandahar together, maybe four years ago. He never used his phone anymore. Perhaps he had a new one now. All the phones had been taken apart and the little cards that made them work were in the bottom of the bag. She hadn't been allowed to use a phone, and really had had no interest in them before now. As she looked at the pieces it became clear how they all fit together. *It must need one of these cards and a battery*, she thought. She slid the small card inside and looked at the parts on the floor for a battery. Finding one that fit the space, she slotted it in place. The phone screen came to life. She smiled. Her father had always said she was the smartest of the sisters.

There was a shout from the courtyard, startling her. She quickly put the contents back in the bag and slid it under a set of drawers in the corner of the room. It was time to go prepare the evening meal. Ahmed would be proud of her, she thought. Perhaps he would even call her one day; that would be a treat.

• • •

In Kandahar, a small red dot came alive on the computer screen of the signals intelligence analyst. An aircraft above the country had recognised the phone coming to life. Some thirty minutes later, a drone was on station high above the mountain passes that secured Zabul from the rest of Afghanistan. Its payload was generally lethal but also highly intelligent. The electronics on this drone interrogated the mobile phone sitting under the cupboard some four thousand metres below. A handshake was established and the cloning began. All the texts, call registers, photos and other data ever stored on the SIM card was sucked up by the National Security Agency. Within minutes the intelligence was shared across the task forces of the Americans, British, Canadians and Australians. Any Special Forces outfit that had made it their business to prosecute high value targets was notified.

Captain Sam Long, sitting behind his desk in Camp Russell, smiled and leaned back in his chair. *Now we know where you're from!* He looked at the images as they started to flash up onto his screen. *So which one of you is Rapier?* he wondered.

Usually information is gathered through diligent research and judicious use of intelligence resources, but sometimes, just sometimes, it falls straight into your lap.

24

CAMP RUSSELL, TARIN KOWT

Craig Reilly emerged from the headquarters building. He squinted to adjust to the morning light; the fresh warm air was a relief after the stale refrigerated air of the company operations room. He felt terrible, the result of a coffee every hour for the past six hours and further exacerbated by sitting in front of an iridescent screen in a darkened room for the whole of that time.

By placing himself on the midnight to 6 am shift he had given the rest of his team a much-needed rest. *They deserve a break*, he reasoned.

He walked towards the mess hall, keenly anticipating toast and eggs – a sure-fire remedy for a caffeine overload and sleep deprivation. As he pushed aside the plastic strips covering the doorway of the mess, he spotted Matt Rix sitting alone at one of the many wooden tables, surrounded by folders and paperwork. The platoon commander's head was leaning on his left hand;

his usually neat spiked hair was now an unruly mess and well past regulation length.

Craig and Matt had become good friends over the last half a year. They had instantly bonded when Craig first arrived in the unit and walked into the Officers' Mess with two other officers late one summer evening. The three of them had just completed their selection and reinforcement training and were wide-eyed at the circumstances they found themselves in. It was a tough time to begin. The 2nd Commando Regiment was preoccupied with all manner of courses and training. Matt's own platoon was conducting a handover with another platoon, but even with this busy schedule he had made time for the newbies.

During the next few weeks of physical training sessions, the two six footers sized one another up. Matt noticed how Craig was always quietly there; every run, pack march, obstacle course, swim circuit or gym session, he was never far behind. In turn, Craig watched how Matt controlled the captain's lunchroom and the conversations with seniors and peers alike. Banter between officers could be brutal, even in the opulent dining room of the Officer's Mess, and Matt always had the judicious last say. Craig was equally impressed with how Matt was able to draw the best out of his own commando platoon. When it was announced that Craig was to go to Delta Company, Matt gave him a wry smile in the Officer's Mess that evening. And now, in the sparse surrounds of a kitchen hall, and even though he had been up all night, Craig relished the chance to sit down and have a chat with the commando platoon commander over yet another brew.

'G'day, champ, what's doing?' said Craig as he walked past.

Matt looked up from the report he was holding. 'Ah, nothing. I couldn't sleep, so I thought I'd just finish off my orders for this next mission.'

Craig grabbed some styrofoam cups from next to the bubbling water urn. 'Want a coffee, bro?' He held up a cup.

'Yeah, why not.' Matt stretched and yawned.

'How d'ya have it?'

'Standard NATO,' said Matt.

Craig looked at him and laughed. 'What, weak and white?'

Matt laughed too. 'Funny. No, just white with a couple of sugars, thanks.'

'So, what are you actually working on? It looks like it has ya stumped. Anything I can help with?' Craig asked seriously.

'Well, I'm trying to understand why I keep getting rolled up at the end of all my missions. It's like there's a weakness in my extraction plans or something. I just can't put my finger on it.'

'Yeah, right, well, good luck with that; you're probably over-thinking it though. You just can't plan for every eventuality, Matt, you know that. Don't forget, the enemy gets a vote too.'

'That's for sure. How about you, mate, you must be going crazy in that command centre?'

'No, not really. I mean, it's okay when the CO leaves us alone. I've learnt a lot about planning commando operations and the chance to work with other nations. SF has been invaluable, reading their reports and stuff too.'

Craig handed Matt the coffee and sat down on a wooden bench across from him. In the background the TV fixed to the wall was playing MTV video music awards. Lady Gaga was parading around in a dress made entirely of meat. It held their attention for a moment.

Finally Matt looked away. 'I don't know, Craig, but looking through all of these patrol reports for the last few rotations, it's as if at the end of each patrol we take a casualty or have a critical incident – like it's almost guaranteed.'

'Yeah, it's been a messy month, mate, that's for sure.' Craig sipped on his coffee and then stood up to make some toast. 'Sometimes it's almost like the enemy are sitting in on the orders,' he joked.

Matt looked down at his last three patrol reports. 'You know what, mate, I was just thinking the same thing.' Matt ran a hand through his hair and sighed. 'I wish the OC was here, mate, and X-Ray Platoon as well. This deployment has been really tough, having the company split in two like this.'

'Well, there might be better days ahead, Matt. We're getting X-Ray Platoon back for five days and the CO told Major Heath McCaig that he wants us to conduct a large operation with the US Special Forces and the Dutch down in the Mirabad Valley. I think that will shake things up a bit.'

'That's good news – especially if we conduct an operation doing the tasks that we have been trained for.'

'You should have a chat with Todd, the commander of the US Special Forces. I usually try to catch up with him once or twice a week. He's a good dude. You think you have problems? You should hear what those guys have to go through. I was meant to meet him this morning at ten for a coffee over at Echos, but I was planning to cancel – I've been up all night doing the late shift. How about I give him a call and tell him you're going to be taking my place?'

'That's a good idea. Yeah, why not.'

'Okay, I'll let him know straight after breakfast.'

Craig sat in the mess with Matt for a while longer, talking about the last few months – in particular the loss of John Lewis and how it had affected Yankee Platoon's morale. The quiet of the mess was disturbed when a group of troopers from SAS strolled through the door. They were in sweaty PT gear and, although company rules forbade it, had obviously just come straight from the gym.

Matt shook his head. 'You know, the RSM just about blew his top when my guys did that a couple of weeks ago.'

Before Craig could respond, the RSM himself entered the mess.

'G'day, lads,' he said. 'How are you liking the new Pendlay weights and Crossfit racks?'

The troopers all voiced their appreciation to the RSM for the new gym gear, and he beamed.

Craig noticed that Matt was glowering. The Yankee commander got to his feet and began gathering his papers. 'Thanks for the chat, Craig, but I'd better get on with the day. I'll head over to Echos at ten unless I hear otherwise from you.'

'No worries, mate. Why don't we get together in a few days? Come watch *Californication* in the operations room.'

Matt snorted. 'You know what that show is, don't you? It's *Sex in the City* for men.' He lobbed the empty coffee cup towards the bin and looked over at the RSM talking with the SAS guys. The double standards infuriated him. 'Sure, I'm in. Catch you later, bro,' said Matt as he turned and left.

25

'JJ, are you in there, brother?' Matt said, knocking on JJ's door.

A banging came from inside the room, and then a crash as a wardrobe door was slammed shut and something heavy fell on the ground.

'Hang on, just a second.'

JJ opened the door about a minute later, dressed in nothing more than cut-off cargo pants. 'Sorry, I was playing chess online,' he said, wiping sweat from his forehead.

Matt took a step back from the door as the overpowering smell of something similar to old socks followed JJ out into the hallway. 'Shit, dude, turn on your air conditioner, it's like a bloody oven in there.' He smiled at JJ. 'Seriously, mate – chess? I don't even want to know what you were really doing.'

'Whatever are you implying, my good man,' said JJ in a mock upper-class British accent.

Matt pointed through the open door to the bottle of Nivea hand cream lying on the desk beside the computer.

JJ shrugged innocently.

'Anyway . . .' Matt said, remembering the reason he'd dropped by the sergeant's room in the first place. 'I'm off to go and see this American guy, the commander of the Green Berets – Todd someone.'

'You mean Todd Carson, boss?'

'Right, Carson, that's it. I was talking with Craig Reilly this morning and he told me we should expect to do some operations with the Green Berets in the next few months, so it's probably a good idea to get to know him. What have you heard about this guy? You've been training with his blokes, right?'

'Yeah, they've rocked up to a few of the sessions. Apparently he's a monster of a guy – some big square-jawed blond dude from Minnesota.'

'So, he's pretty much Canadian then,' said Matt, distracted by a low moaning coming from JJ's computer.

'I don't get the reference, boss,' JJ said as he slowly inched backwards into the room to close the lid on his laptop.

'It's just that Minnesota is a long way north – oh, forget it. Anything else?'

'His guys told me that he was selected to play professional hockey days before the 9/11 terrorist attacks. Instead he went to West Point, and a few years later he was in Iraq running a platoon. Pretty cool, don't you think?'

Matt laughed. 'Sounds like you have a bit of a man crush, JJ.'

'Whatever, boss – I just do my homework. Besides, he's a big dude and doesn't talk smack, unlike half the guys on this base, so it's easy to not be a hater.'

'All right, all right, I was just joking. Any idea about his combat credentials? I mean, is the guy the real deal?'

'How does Ranger Course, qualified Special Forces, three tours of Iraq and two tours of Afghanistan sound? I'd say he's legit!'

'You really did do your homework. You know about the restrictions that have been applied to the Green Berets? They can't actually target any individuals without gaining permission from the commander of Regional Command South, so I'm not sure what use they'll be to us anyway.'

'Shit, that's almost as bad as being forced to drive everywhere using our own tyres to search for IEDs. Oh, and boss, don't call them Green Berets. They're ODA guys now: it's short for Operational Detachment Alpha. No one calls them Green Berets anymore.'

'Yeah, right. Well, their missions are restricted to mentoring the Afghan partner force and conducting village security operations. It would be like being stuck in a remote village and getting attacked for nine months straight.'

'Poor pricks,' said JJ, kicking the Nivea bottle under his bed.

'The Taliban are actually winning the hearts and minds of the locals due mostly to targeting errors by the Afghan army, but they put all the blame on the US Special Forces. So the Green Berets have become risk adverse and we have the situation we have now. As I said, mate, I'm not sure we have much to gain from working with them on any operation. Perhaps we could use them as a blocking force or leverage their air assets. I don't know, to be honest.'

'We could always just send them out as bait and then when they get in a fight come in and thump the hell out of the Taliban,' said JJ.

'Ha – you're terrible, JJ.' Matt started to laugh then stopped abruptly as he was struck by something. It was like there was something teasing at the corner of his mind but he couldn't quite grasp it.

'Hey, I was only joking,' said JJ.

Matt waved a hand. 'Yeah, yeah, I know – it's just that at times I feel like that's exactly what's happening to us.'

'We've had a rough trot, boss, there's no denying that, but don't you become the pessimist – that's my job.' JJ picked his t-shirt up off the floor and pulled it on. 'Someone's gotta stay above that shit, boss.'

'Yeah, you're right, JJ.' Matt shook his head to dispel the strange feeling that had come over him. 'I'll drop in and see you when I get back from Echos, mate.'

Matt turned and walked down the hallway towards the exit.

JJ, the grand chess master – I'll have to remember that one, thought Matt with a chuckle.

26

ECHOS, TARIN KOWT

Matt walked to the back corner of the camp and punched the numerals 1957 – SAS's formation year – into the rear security gate combination lock. The push-button combination lock clicked open and the spring disengaged, allowing Matt to turn the awkward handle on the heavy gate.

'Operational security,' he grumbled to himself as he stepped through, leaving the Special Forces compound.

Walking along the dusty track that wound its way through the centre of the base, Matt passed a group of shipping containers that had been converted into small offices for the occupying Dutch forces. A group of five Australian infantry soldiers walked towards Matt and looked him up and down. They were in full battle rig, wearing long-sleeved shirts and weighed down with ridiculous old-fashioned body armour. They carried their Steyr rifles as if they were patrolling downtown Mogadishu. The infantry guys muttered something between themselves and then all stared at the ground as they passed Matt, who was wearing MultiCam pants and a faded brown t-shirt. His Heckler & Koch USP pistol sat on his hip secured by a paddle holster. Matt gave them a sideways glance and continued on his way to the cafe, Echos. This was the only place where the infantry troops could send and receive emails home, as the task force signallers had still not set up wi-fi in the soldiers' accommodation. In contrast, the Australian Special Forces guys had wi-fi connecting all their buildings, so visiting Echos was a novelty rather than a necessity. You could get a decent Italian coffee or a milkshake, depending on who was on shift.

Matt moved indoors, his eyes taking a moment to adjust to the soft lighting and the green and blue furnishings. Echos looked like a 1980s disco lounge. The old Italian lady who managed the place recognised Matt and gave him a sour nod from behind the main counter. She seldom smiled and made no exception for him. She barked some orders at the young Filipina serving the customers at the front of the queue. Matt took his place in the line and studied the menu board. Nothing had changed since his last visit and probably never would, he thought.

'Hey, man, how long have you been here?' Matt looked up at the guy who had joined the queue behind him and then back at the woman making the coffees. This was obviously Todd, but there were games yet to be played.

'Too long,' Matt said, somewhat dismissively.

The blond all-American sports star was not to be so easily ignored.

'Really? So since breakfast then?' he said in a teasing manner.

Matt frowned, partly at the theatrics of the young woman making the coffee. She was taking orders, frothing and spilling the milk and bashing the cups on the side of the machine, all the while shouting in Filipino at some either deaf or non-existent helper in the back room whose absence only served to frustrate her all the more.

'You probably *would* assume that, mate,' Matt said dryly, 'because we are always outside the wire in combat, while you guys –' he turned to face the American commando, needing to tilt his head back a little to take in the man's height '– are always in the gym or slapping each other's arses in the shower.' Matt turned back to the coffee pantomime.

Todd laughed raucously and slapped Matt forcefully on the back, giving Matt an immediate understanding of his strength.

Matt glanced at the American a little more cautiously now, wondering if his smart-arse response had perhaps overstepped the mark.

'When this broad finally gets her act together and actually makes us a coffee, let's sit and have a chat, you and me – what d'ya say, Matt?' Todd extended a huge hand for Matt to shake.

Matt nodded as he shook Todd's hand. 'I have nowhere else to be, mate,' he said. 'Besides, I'm hoping you can tell me how I can get those Black Hawks of yours to fly my platoon somewhere.'

'Flying is the only safe option, pal,' said Todd.

'Three lattes and two Americanos!' barked the barista as she spilled half the contents of the cups while pushing them across the counter.

Todd and Matt looked at each other. Matt shook his head.

'What are you having?'

'I'll take my chances with a black coffee, thanks, buddy,' said Todd.

'Two black coffees, keep the change. We're sitting over there.' Matt gestured towards a table in the corner of the dimly lit, blast-protected building. The walls were festooned with photos of the world's capital cities, all artificially faded to give the appearance that they had been there for a decade. The barista squinted towards the table.

'Okay, ma'am, sir,' said the barista. She always addressed everyone as ma'am and sir simultaneously – just to be on the safe side, Matt assumed.

At the corner table, Todd and Matt discussed the war, their soldiers and their countries' politics, and Matt felt himself relax. It had been a while since he had been able to talk openly and unguardedly with a peer. Command was a lonely business. Every action and word had to be considered. 'The men need leaders not friends!' This was the mantra he – and no doubt Todd – had heard repeatedly at officer academy and the principle was now ingrained.

Todd talked of the new restrictions applied to his operations. His platoon was comprised of only three teams of six, but these eighteen men were responsible for mentoring one hundred and twenty Afghan commandos. They trained them, equipped them and then led them right into the fight. Recently, however, they had been ordered to base themselves in outlying villages for six weeks at a time in a futile attempt to deny the Taliban a safe haven or area of respite. Of course, the Taliban just found other villages to go to. Todd's men were frustrated by this strategy of waiting out the enemy and dreamed of getting back into the fight.

Matt told Todd of his own frustrations, and how he felt he was always left out of the higher-level planning. As he was talking, he noticed Todd become distracted and he turned to see a woman entering though the air-lock doors. She waved at Todd and her white smile, made all the brighter by her tanned skin, illuminated the room.

'Allie, how's it going?' Todd called.

Matt watched as she approached. She was about his height, dressed in khaki combat trousers and a light brown t-shirt that clung to her generous curves. Her long brown hair was pulled back into a tight ponytail. She looked like the military equivalent of Xena, the Warrior Princess.

'Hello there, Todd, I haven't seen you around much. Isn't there any work for you guys to do?' Even in what was clearly her second language, the woman was cheeky. 'Who's your little friend then?'

'This is Matt, he's the commander of the Australian Special Forces platoon. Matt, this is Allie van Tanken.'

'Oh, right, I have heard a lot about you guys,' Allie said. 'The bearded devils! Lots of time playing in your cars, I think.'

Matt couldn't help but laugh. It was hard to be offended by her.

'Yeah, we've done our fair share of driving around the place. I've corrected a heap of map data in and around Chora, that's for sure'. Matt held her gaze as he spoke, wondering if she, too, felt a spark of attraction.

Her light green eyes narrowed as she said, 'Map data? What kind of map data?' She leaned in closer to Matt to hear his answer. He could smell the slightest hint of her deodorant and it immediately aroused his senses.

'Doesn't matter,' said Matt, embarrassed. 'So what's your role here, Allie?'

'I'm the intelligence officer for the Dutch Apaches,' she replied.

'Wow, that's a big job.'

'What, for a girl you mean?' She frowned.

'Huh? No, of course not – that's not what I meant.' Matt shifted awkwardly and looked across at Todd, who was laughing into his coffee.

'It's okay, Matt, I'm fucking you,' Allie said in her accented English.

At that Todd burst out laughing, spraying coffee onto the table.

'What's so funny, Todd?' Allie asked innocently.

Matt rose from his seat. 'Can I get you a coffee or something, Allie?'

'Yes, I would like a vanilla milkshake, please.' Allie pulled a chair across from a nearby table as Matt went to place the order and get another round of coffees.

When he returned, Allie and Todd were discussing the spotter network and how they could best be defeated.

'One interesting point, Todd, is that the network often tells each other not only the direction of the helicopters in flight, but also their projected arrival times. That's why it's so important to make sure that the route is varied and that the duration is deliberately extended or shortened. Usually they are more accurate in their calculations than our own air controllers.'

'We could help with that, I think, Allie. Maybe Matt and I could join together, conduct another operation after this one to dismantle their spotter network up and down the valley. I'm sure Matt would like a chance to get out in the helicopters for a few days.'

'That could work,' said Matt, passing Allie the milkshake and handing Todd his coffee. 'We just have to survive this next operation first. The rough plan is for the other commando platoon, X-Ray Platoon, to start at the bottom end of the Mirabad Valley and my platoon at the top. We'll lock the place down and then you guys will fly in with your Afghan commando company and clear the key compounds of interest.'

'That's hardly a challenge, Matt. Cordon and call out has become our main business of late,' replied Todd.

'Tell me, Matt,' said Allie, 'how is Operation Odin's Raven going?' She took a sip of her milkshake, watching Matt intently for his answer.

'I don't know what you're talking about.' Matt looked at Todd, who shrugged.

'Sure you do, Matt.' Allie laughed and shook her head. 'Seriously, though, I need to get access to a couple of my contacts out in Chora. Perhaps I could jump in on one of your vehicle patrols when you go out there next? It won't take long – I just need a few hours at the most once on the ground. I'm sure my commander won't have an issue with me going out with the bearded devils.'

Matt was still puzzling over her question. 'I honestly don't know what you're talking about.' He frowned at her. 'I'm lost, Allie – what's Operation Odin's Raven?'

Allie looked at Matt in disbelief. 'I like you Australians,' she said, 'but I can't get my head around the stupid politics you guys play against each other and with us. Surely the SOTG would be better off all working together.'

'I agree. But since I'm obviously out of the loop on this one, perhaps you could fill me in?' Matt was suspicious now; what did she know about the way the Australians were operating? More than he did, apparently.

'Odin's Raven is your SOTG operation to seal up the leaks in the human intelligence network in Uruzghan and Chora. I believe it's been going on for about four months now. I'm really surprised you haven't heard of it; I receive an unofficial update every week from Sam. There has to be some sharing of intelligence to ensure that it succeeds, right?' Allie put the aluminium milkshake container on the table and leaned back in her chair.

'Well, I think that sounds like an intelligence operation or maybe an SAS job.' Matt sipped on his coffee and looked around the room. Something just didn't make sense to him; how was it that Allie was able to know about an SOTG operation that he knew nothing about?

Matt took another swig of coffee, trying to maintain a calm demeanour. When Todd rose from the table to go and reprimand some engineers who had entered the cafe with loaded weapons, Allie put her hand on Matt's forearm.

'Matt, there's more,' she said seriously. 'I've seen your plans briefed as part of this operation. I mean, I see all the plans for this operation and your concept of operations briefs are all submitted under the title "Odin's Raven". So, you see, it doesn't make sense to me that you don't know about it, if you're not the one conducting the operation . . .'

Matt stared at her in disbelief. He struggled to make sense of it. *I take my guys out on patrol, and the enemy, they know my plans. The CO denies me helicopters in order to slow me down and then keeps me out there, giving me stupid tasks to complete to ensure I stay in position, route recons and reports and such. Then he sends the SAS out to target an enemy who are, not surprisingly, descending on my position.*

Matt's knuckles became white from the fists he was making. 'I'm the bait – my platoon is the bait and they're using the leak to make sure the Taliban know where I am going to be!'

'Perhaps, Matt,' Allie replied. 'And it probably affects you more than most, I would have thought, especially given where you are operating and because of who you are chasing.'

'This has got to be a fucking joke.' Matt could feel the rage mounting in his chest.

'I wouldn't joke about something like this,' she said. She removed her hand from his arm as Todd returned to the table and instantly resumed her light-hearted, flirtatious tone.

'So, boys, who's buying me pizza?'

Matt sat there fuming. He looked across at the far wall at a picture of the Sydney Harbour Bridge hanging next to a picture of a Dutch windmill. How ironic, he thought.

'I have to go, guys,' he said abruptly. 'I'll be in touch, Todd.' Matt got up out of his seat and rested his hands on the back of the chair. 'I think I need to go and have a word with our intelligence guy.'

'Matt,' Allie warned gently, 'tread carefully – and remember: this information didn't come from me, okay?'

'Yeah, of course, sure.' He stepped back. 'I'll see you both later then.' Matt wasn't sure what he felt. The death of John Lewis and the Afghan soldiers was on his mind. Someone was going to have a lot of explaining to do. Rapier was top of the target list in Matt's mind, but a few Australian officers might just be joining him there, depending on their answers over the next few hours. Target one – Sam Long!

27

The gate slammed behind Matt. He stood there for a moment inside Camp Russell and surveyed the area. Matt wasn't sure what to make of this new information. The short stroll had helped him put things into perspective. It was obvious that he wasn't briefed in on something going on, but was it truly as dire as he had first thought?

Looking around, he noticed that in the short time he'd been at Echos the ring road around the base perimeter had been covered with gravel. Things sure moved fast in Afghanistan and nothing is ever as it seems. One minute there's a dirt path and then blink and it becomes a gravel track, he thought.

As he passed the rear of the gym JJ emerged, carrying some boxes and a plastic bag. 'Hey there, boss, how'd the meeting go?'

Matt opened his mouth to reply but couldn't think of the words. 'It was okay, mate,' he said finally.

'Cool. Well, I took the Green Berets for a session – a couple of their lads are good grapplers.'

Matt looked down at JJ's cut-off camouflage shorts and brown desert boots. Those items, teamed with an orange Adidas running top, would probably not have looked out of place on a Mardi Gras float. He wondered if the Green Berets were suitably impressed by the big guy's fashion sense.

'Oh, this came for you,' said JJ, passing Matt a couple of boxes. 'The mail came in while you were gone.'

Matt looked down at the mail; there was a box from his mother back in Victoria and a smaller box from London. *Rachel?* he wondered.

'JJ, we might have a problem, mate,' said Matt, turning his attention back to the platoon sergeant. 'While I was in Echos I met this Dutch intelligence chick – she works for their Apaches. She told me about some operation that the SOTG have been conducting that I've never even heard of.'

JJ gave a laugh. 'Nothing unusual there. Compartmented grey operations are the new black where the SAS are concerned, apparently. Seriously, boss, what's so special about tooling around wearing dish-dash and speaking Pashtu? Commandos were doing the same type of operations sixty years ago in the Pacific. The SAS are a bunch of wankers.'

'Yeah, well, I think there's more to it than that. I need some time to put it all together in my head, to be honest. I have to be careful here because I think we're being played.' Matt walked on with JJ and watched as two of his platoon, Eddie and Kiwi, patiently stretched rolls of cling wrap across the door of the second accommodation block. They were taking extreme care to ensure that there were no visible lines.

'Can't you just ask the CO? If there's a problem, you should just raise it. I mean, what's stopping you?'

'Nothing,' said Matt. He thought for another moment. 'Other than the fact that we are being sent out on missions that the enemy probably already know about and that as a result one of my guys is dead – not to mention the Afghan National Army guys.'

'Yeah, I see your point.' JJ moved in front of Matt to block his view of the accommodation block.

'Right, so what's all that about then?' Matt pointed to the goings-on behind JJ.

'Not sure, boss. Do you want to come to mine for a brew?'

'No thanks – seriously, though, what are those dudes actually doing?'

'Those guys? Nothing. Just cleaning up, I guess. Sure you don't want a coffee? I've got a new blend; it's not the stuff that's been eaten and thrown up by cats that you officers prefer, but it's pretty damn good.'

Matt sighed. 'Nah, I just need to crash out for a bit and think some shit through.' He watched as the lads JJ was subtly trying to conceal from his view smoothed out the cling wrap. 'Let's get together later this afternoon, though. I think it would be a good idea to go over our old patrol reports and see if I can piece some of this together. After that I'll go see Sam.'

Matt looked again at Eddie, who was now squatting behind his quad bike ten metres from the accommodation door. Kiwi was slightly less visible around the corner of the building, a fire hose nozzle protruding about an inch and aimed at head height.

JJ stepped slightly to his left.

'I know what you're doing, JJ.' Matt moved to get a better view of the two men as they set themselves into position.

JJ laughed. 'It's just a bit of fun, blowing off some steam, you know.'

'Make sure these guys don't destroy the place, mate. Also, book the range for tomorrow afternoon – let's go and check zero all the weapons.'

'Sure thing, boss.' JJ was hiding a smirk. Matt looked back to the accommodation block just in time to see Cinzano in full flight trying to exit the building. He let out a scream of shock as his face was met with the giant strip of cling wrap.

Now Matt understood what was going on; he had heard some muttering about it in the common room. It had occurred to the lads that Cinzano had established a routine. He would go for a shower every day straight after returning from the gym. Right before his shower, he would go into the toilets and hang his towel over the toilet door. His team devised a plan that started with the removal of all the toilet paper from the cubicles and liberating his towel from the back of the door before he noticed that the toilet roll was missing.

Cinzano came out butt-naked in a desperate search for poo tickets. Then, realising his towel was gone, he sprinted towards his room, where his team were ready for him. They chased him back down the long white corridor, three of the guys spraying him with foam from fire extinguishers while the other two fired BB pellets from a gun they had bought at the markets.

Yelping at the impact of the pellets on his bare butt, Cinzano sprinted towards the exit at the other end of the hallway. Just as he thought he had escaped, his face hit the clear film, the plastic muffling his scream as it stretched across his mouth and around his head. He tripped and fell to the ground just outside the accommodation block. Kiwi calmly finished the job, spraying him from head to toe with water. Naked, soaked and covered in cling wrap, it surely couldn't get much worse for Cinzano ... Except it did, as the rest of the members of Yankee Platoon came out from their hiding spots, all armed with baby powder and flour bombs. Cinzano was peppered with the bombs as he lay writhing on the ground. He looked like a giant cannelloni. *Yankee Platoon has executed the perfect ambush*, thought Matt.

He turned to say something to JJ, but at that moment he saw in the distance Terence Saygen running up the steps of the headquarters building, his troops throwing stores into the back of their Bushmasters out the front. The place was a hive of activity.

'What's going on there, do you think?' said Matt, gesturing towards the scene.

JJ turned his attention from the antics of Yankee Platoon and watched as the SAS guys readied their weapons and carried out team kit inspections.

'Not sure, boss. What do you think?'

'Just something else I haven't been bloody briefed on, mate – but I think it's high time I go and find out. I'm going to drop these off in my room and then head over there.'

One way or another, Matt vowed as he walked away, *I'm getting to the bottom of this Operation Odin's Raven today.*

28

Saygen threw open the doors to the SAS command centre. The fluorescent-lit room was alive with operations staff and intelligence analysts. They were all hunched over stand-up desks, shouting information to each other with the clear belief that their information was more important than anyone else's. The CO stood at the head of the long line of tables watching the staff as they tracked information. Sam moved fast between stations, collating their findings.

'Troops are all packed and ready to go, boss. What's the target?' Saygen stopped in front of the CO, waiting for further directions. The radio in his body armour chattered away softly as his men conducted their checks out on the dirt road in front of the headquarters.

'Sam, fill him in, mate,' the CO called.

'No worries, sir.' Sam approached, his attention fixed on Saygen.

'Righto. We've had a major development. We now know who Rapier is.'

Sam passed an old Kodak-style photo to Saygen. The image was so blurred and grainy Saygen could barely make out a man's figure.

'This is him: Ahmed Defari.'

'We might have a name, Sam,' Saygen observed, 'but we don't have a picture; this is fucking useless.'

'Agreed, the photo itself is not much to go on.'

'How did you get this anyway?' Saygen tried in vain to make out the face in the photo.

'We've had a tip-off. But don't worry about the photo too much; not only do we have his name, we think we know where he is located. Also, we're pretty sure we have his fingerprints from an IED that Yankee Platoon brought back from their last operation.'

'How reliable is the information, Sam?' Saygen was all business, his black hair slicked back and the long sleeves of his MultiCam shirt rolled up two turns so that he could have a GPS on one wrist and a watch on the other.

'It's a trusted source – a paid, trusted source,' said Sam. 'Here's the grid reference; it's a motorcycle repair shop a few miles from here.' The intel officer handed Saygen a sheet of paper. 'The other grid references on there are known Taliban safe houses within the area. They might factor during your clearance.'

'Got it,' said Saygen, glancing at the paper. 'Anything else I should know?'

'Nope, that's about the sum of it. Get in, grab him and bring him back here.'

Saygen placed the sheet of paper inside his map cover with the ground reference guide that the geospatial cell had developed for him minutes before. The intel guys had numbered the buildings and entry points for the three buildings in the area as well as putting a grid system over the top of the map image so that the teams could use an alpha-numeric system to communicate with each other.

'Do you need anything else, Terence?' asked the CO.

'No, sir. We should be back in around an hour with our man.'

Saygen headed back to his troops at the vehicles. They gathered around and listened as he gave them their final instructions.

• • •

Walking towards the headquarters building after dropping the mail off in his room, Matt was just in time to see the SAS troop leaving in the opposite direction.

What on earth was going on? he wondered. *What the hell was Operation Odin's Raven?* He didn't want to drop Allie in it, but at the same time he couldn't let his platoon be used as bait. How many more of his guys would be killed if he didn't say something? Matt made the decision to confront Sam straight away. He went through the front doors and made a beeline for the command centre.

'Hey, there he is,' said Sam warmly, emerging from the kitchen with a cup of coffee in each hand as Matt walked in.

'You!' barked Matt, moving directly towards Sam, his teeth clenched in an effort to suppress the violent rage that was coming over him.

'Yeah, me,' said Sam with a laugh, clearly completely oblivious to Matt's fury. He used his back to open the door. 'Come on in, Matt. The CO and I are monitoring the SAS troop's progress – we've found Rapier and they're going after him now!'

Matt could not believe his ears. As much as he wanted to confront Sam, the mere mention of Rapier took the wind out of his sails. He followed Sam to join the CO standing in front of a large screen watching the feed from a Predator drone. Something about the sight of the CO standing there grated on Matt and he felt his anger rise again.

'Matt, you've heard the news then?' said the CO, without bothering to turn to acknowledge him. 'Saygen is off after Rapier. Finally we have some information that should lead us to him. I suspect that catching him should lead us straight to Objective Talon too.' The CO smiled to himself as he stared at the big screen.

'Talon, that's right,' said Matt. 'He's always been the real goal, hasn't he?'

'Of course. Cut the head off the snake . . .' The CO's gaze was fixed on the screen. He stroked his chin as he watched Saygen's vehicles going straight through the second roundabout outside the base.

'So what's Odin's Raven then?' Matt demanded.

There was a loaded pause, then the CO slowly turned his head. He looked at Sam first. Sam's eyes were wide open and his mouth moved like a goldfish gasping for breath outside its bowl.

'Ah, let's see,' said Sam awkwardly. 'It's, uh – actually that's classified, Matt.'

'Really, Sam?' said Matt, his tone curt. 'Well, I think it's about time you brief me in, don't you? Unless the two of you are hiding something from me, of course . . .'

'Now, Matt,' the CO blustered, 'I suggest you lose that tone and think about the bigger picture here.'

'That's a bit rich, sir,' Matt snapped. 'Perhaps you would like to explain that *big picture* to Johnno's family? I assume they would still have their son if I had been briefed in on this *big picture* of yours.'

'For the last time, Rix, you need to stop running your mouth off and do what you're goddamn told.' The CO moved in and closed the gap between them. Lowering his voice, he continued, 'There are some things you don't need to know, Rix – for your own fucking protection.'

'Oh, is that right? Would you mind explaining how concealing the fact there's a leak in the human intelligence network protects me?'

'Perhaps the leak is one of your own guys, Matt,' the CO thundered. 'Ever thought of that?'

'Sir,' Sam said, in protest to what information the CO might divulge in the heat of the moment.

'Fuck you,' said Matt.

'What did you just say?'

'You heard me. You've been sending me out there knowing full well that the enemy is tracking my movements. Actually, as I see it, you may have well been sending them my orders.'

'Matt, who told you about Odin's Raven?' Sam asked. 'Was it Allie van Tanken?'

'Shut your mouth, Sam.' Matt was furious now; the CO's responses were an admission of guilt as far as he was concerned.

He took a step towards the CO. 'You're not a real leader. You've never even been in combat. You stand here in front of your TV screens thinking you're this amazing commander, but I know the truth. I've seen guys like you before; you'd be a coward if you were out there among the enemy – and to top it off, you have the blood of Johnno and my ANA guys on your hands. Live with that!'

The CO's face was now purple with rage. 'And you're fucking finished, Rix!' he shouted, banging his fist hard on the table next to him. 'Get the hell out of here – get the hell out of my sight. Go pack your things. You're on the next transport back to Australia.'

Matt stared at the CO for a long moment, then took a step backwards.

'Whatever,' he said, shaking his head. He spun around and stalked towards the exit.

'You'll never serve in Special Forces again, Rix!' he heard the CO yell as he left the room.

29

TARIN KOWT

Mohammed Faisal Khan stood up from his prayer mat and rolled it up quietly. He didn't want to disturb the other worshippers. He left the small mosque and crossed the potholed road that ran behind the motorcycle repair shop.

The repair shop was large as far as workshops in Tarin Kowt went, though the building – which had been constructed in the 1960s – had seen better days. The double doors that had originally stood at the front of the shop had been removed years ago, during the Mujahedeen's reign, and it had been a long time since the windows had had complete glass in them. Bike parts were scattered all over the greasy floor and bags and pots full of leftover food lay everywhere, the aroma a mix of putrid meat and dried herbs. Against the wall, boxes of all shapes and sizes were stacked precariously; they contained parts for every make and model of bike that had ever been imported to Afghanistan.

As he entered, Faisal saw his old friend Abdul Rahman sitting on a wooden box, tinkering with a motorbike's engine. 'Afternoon, Abdul.'

Abdul looked up. His eyes went to the small plastic bag Faisal was holding in one hand.

'What have you got there, Faisal?' he asked.

'Just some dates. You're welcome to them.' Faisal passed him the bag and placed his hand on Abdul's shoulder.

'Thank you. How are you, brother?' Abdul put the dates down next to him and wiped the oil from his hands with an old cloth he pulled from his pocket. He smiled at his friend.

'Fine, fine, Abdul. Thanks be to God, I am in good health. Where's Ahmed?' Looking around the shop, Faisal realised that there was no one else around. Usually there were men sleeping hidden among the bikes and rubbish. It was a well-known drop-in centre and halfway house for Taliban fighters. The motorcycle repair shop was the perfect cover, being a mere two kilometres from the Tarin Kowt base and right under the noses of the International Security Assistance Force.

Their conversation was interrupted briefly as Faisal's phone rang once in his pocket and then went dead.

'Ahmed left at prayer time. He said he would go for a walk to the old cemetery. He wanted to find someone to send a message to Quetta. Did you know that this morning the bombs arrived? The men hid them downstairs.' Abdul motioned towards the secret trapdoor that was hidden under the front counter. Under the metal plate the stairs dropped down into a huge room that ran the length of the shop.

Faisal was busy looking for the number of the person who just hung up on him, but there was no missed call on the phone he had taken from his pocket. He slipped it back in his trousers and pulled out another phone, an old Nokia handset with only a handful of numbers on it; he always erased the numbers and messages from this particular phone.

Abdul continued. 'The others were here too but they went to get some meat and bread for tonight's meal.'

Faisal was barely listening as he stared down at the retrieved number. It was the American's number – and it was not her mobile. She had only ever rung him from that number once before and that was on his own phone, when she had first made contact with him. He had saved the number across to this phone after she had given it to him, in case of an emergency.

What does she want, and why is she ringing from this number? Faisal wondered, puzzled. She had never rung him since the first call without sending a coded message prior.

BOOM!

The first explosion knocked Faisal straight off his feet and sucked the air from his lungs.

The initial blast was followed by another huge shock wave, sending parts of the back door flying in all directions, small wooden splinters tearing at the skin on Faisal's neck and face. The phone he was carrying was ripped from his hand; it slid across the room, coming to rest in a pile of motorbike parts.

There was a blinding flash, then BANG! BANG! BANG!, followed by another flash and then another, coinciding with hundreds of smaller explosions that illuminated the inside of the building with tiny, dazzling balls of light. The workshop was filled with dust and debris and the light reflected off the dust, disorientating Faisal. His eyes burned from the smoke and tears streamed down his face. He lay on the ground choking, completely overwhelmed by the violence of the moment. Through the dust he could see a pair of brown boots glide into the room. Through the ringing in his ears, the muffled sounds of Western voices became audible.

• • •

The first SAS team entered through the back door, the only door to the shop. It had been blown to smithereens by the team breacher.

'Clear,' came the call as the team commander's area was secured. Saygen's was the second team inside, making entry through the window in the back corner. Now there were four teams in the shop. They came from all directions, flooding into the building; their compact M4 carbine rifle barrels covered every angle. They moved with precision through the smoke and dust. The troopers yelled to each other in code and reacted to the calls.

'Clear!'

'With me!'

'With you!'

'Covering!'

'Go!'

'Coming out!'

'Moving!'

They cleared their allocated areas and moved on to their secondaries. It was over in less than a minute, a highly sophisticated, rehearsed and deadly movement of men and weapons.

A hand grabbed the dazed Taliban from the floor by the collar and dragged him upright, till his feet were dangling below him. He was slammed forcefully onto a stool in the corner of the room.

His head smacked against the wall; a rifle barrel wedged in the centre of his forehead kept his head in place while his pockets were emptied.

'Grab all the shit out of this prick's pockets, Sledge,' Saygen ordered as he moved from team to team to check their areas.

'Already done, boss. He had this old phone on him and some little bits and pieces – other than the phone, nothing of interest.'

'Chuck these plastic cuffs on him, Sledge.' Saygen watched as Marty, Sledge's team commander, threw a set of plastic cuffs to Sledge and then covered the Taliban from a right angle, giving his subordinate room to get around and secure the enemy's hands.

'You got his stuff there, mate?' asked Marty. 'Pass it over. I want to check his card and phone for any messages.' Marty took the phone.

'Anything else, boss, or do you want me to go and help the others looking over this place?'

'Get his biometrics too,' said Saygen as he checked out some boxes stacked next to the door.

'Here's the SEEK, Sledge.' The team commander grabbed the secure electronic enrolment kit – a handheld biometrics recorder – from his camouflage backpack.

The SAS trooper took the Taliban's iris scan, his fingerprints and a facial scan. This information was instantly sent to the FBI database in West Virginia. He only had to wait a few seconds for the reply.

'It's a negative on this one.'

'Right. There's another one over there; he's still knocked out in the corner.'

'Weak prick. I'm on it.' It took Sledge a minute to verify that the second man wasn't the guy they were after either. He plasti-cuffed the still unconscious Afghan and left him lying on his back.

'These are the only guys here, boss. What now?' Marty looked around at the chaos they had just caused and then back to Saygen, who was standing in the doorway looking down the empty street.

'Yeah, of course they are – I'd hate for the intel guys to ever get something right. Okay, lads; we've had a quick look, now pull this place apart, look for anything out of the norm. If that's even a thing in this bloody place.' Saygen spoke into his radio, and moments later the SAS's vehicles arrived, smashing an old car out of the way and taking up their dominating positions in the once-quiet street.

The rooms were torn apart. Anything not nailed down was picked up and thrown across the room. If it was nailed down it was ripped up and then thrown. Nothing was left untouched.

Saygen looked at his watch and listened to the radio chatter from the vehicles outside. 'That's twenty minutes, lads – let's get out of here before the cars start drawing any more heat.' Saygen knew that the last thing he needed was for the Taliban to have time to get an RPG close enough to destroy a Bushmaster; that would keep them there for a long time, and the longer they were there and isolated, the less survivable the operation became. The idea was to get in and out in quick time, before the enemy had time to respond.

Saygen led the guys out of the building. They ran off to their team vehicles, a carefully rehearsed drill that they could replicate under fire, by day or night.

Sledge, running at the back of his team, spotted a phone sitting in a pile of rubbish and bike parts. The screen was illuminated as it had just received another call. Sledge picked it up and stuffed it into his cargo pants' leg pocket and then sprinted to catch up to the rest of his team. He dived through the back door of the Bushmaster.

'Jesus, Sledge, cutting it fine, mate.'

'It's all good – just testing myself.' He grinned at Marty and closed the back door. The vehicles took off, crashing through a fence, and made their way through the backyards in the direction of Camp Russell.

• • •

Faisal sat on the stool surveying the damage, bewildered. What on earth had just happened? The plastic handcuffs still secured his wrists and he winced at the pain.

Abdul started to come around and rolled onto his side. He looked at Faisal, smiled, then winced in pain.

'Good hiding place, isn't it, brother? They have no idea about the room downstairs.'

Faisal grinned back at him and then remembered his phone. Terror engulfed him and he jumped up, eyes darting around the room. 'This is not good, Abdul,' he said gravely. 'Not good at all.'

30

KANDAHAR

The joint intelligence fusion cell was abuzz with energy. Steph stood in a corner of the long rectangular room tapping her foot nervously as she surveyed the scene. An assortment of army intelligence officers, representatives of all the nations involved in Afghanistan, stood in front of the computer screens lining the long wooden table that ran the length of the room. Wires hung from the ceiling connecting the workstations, ensuring that connectivity was maintained across the different task forces. The officers watched the grainy black-and-white footage anxiously as their units began to withdraw from their targets. This had been a huge day of operations; in a modern adaptation of the German Blitzkrieg, a multitude of targets had been attacked simultaneously. This 'saturation', as it was referred to, was designed to keep the Taliban leadership from being able to mount any counterattacks or quick reprisals.

'Okay, gang, I think that's a wrap of this afternoon's targeting serials. Get your data together from this end and make sure that you contact your units and find out what they came up with.' The baby-faced lieutenant colonel from Delta Force was broad-shouldered, tall and handsome with a perpetual tan, his short, jet-black hair parted to one side. He looked around the room and smiled, and the room smiled back.

'We'll meet back in here at eighteen-thirty, folks, if no one has an issue with that?' Despite his pleasant tone, everyone recognised it for the order it was and made no objections. 'Good. We'll go round the grounds then and see if we've turned up anything interesting.' Since he had taken over the fusion cell they had become an efficient team. No stone was left unturned and all the information gathered from the assigned missions was captured, interpreted and used for future targeting.

Steph tucked in her brown t-shirt and tightened her ponytail before slowly walking across the room. She spotted her own reflection in a small window on one of the side office doors. In that second she noticed how bright red her face was. She felt like she was about to be sick.

Taking a deep breath, she approached Captain Geoff Langston, the Australian targeting officer for the Special Operations Task Group posted inside the targeting and fusion cell.

'Hey there, Geoff, how's it going?' Steph said, forcing herself to sound cheery.

'All good, thanks, ma'am.' Geoff looked up from a series of photos that he was poring over.

'Glad to hear it,' Steph said. 'So all the guys are back safely then, no issues?'

'Yep, they're all fine.' Geoff looked up at her. 'Can I help you with something, ma'am, do you need something?' Geoff switched off his monitor, rose from his chair and turned to face her. It was unusual for a senior CIA analyst to be interested in the SOTG's operations; that sort of interest was usually reserved for what Combat Applications Group, better known as Delta Force, were up to. This wasn't lost on Geoff. He noticed her face, too, as he turned off the monitor; there was the slightest indication that she was taken aback by this, a barely perceptible widening of the eyes. 'Oh, sorry, that's just an old habit that was beaten into us on the intelligence course.' He smiled at her.

'Oh, of course, yes, I do the same – an old habit. I didn't even notice really.' Steph looked around to see who was in earshot. 'So, I thought I should just tell you that I had a source in the area of your task group's raid this afternoon. I want to make sure that he wasn't lifted, you know?'

'I see.' Geoff watched as others around the room started to clear out to go and grab coffees and get prepared for the next couple of hours that would be spent analysing the data they'd collected. He turned his focus back to Steph, leaning forward so that the others around couldn't hear. 'Well, that's meant to be identified prior to our guys conducting their missions, Steph.' Geoff didn't like the way the CIA could pick and choose their operating procedures to suit themselves, and he enjoyed alternating between using her name and calling her 'ma'am', depending on the point he wanted to make with her.

'To be honest, I only found out that he was in the area after the raid went in. I thought he was in Pakistan, so I didn't bother raising it; he wasn't even meant to be in the country.'

'So I presume you filed an out-of-country report on him? If you did, I must have missed it – or maybe we didn't receive it. Could you get me a copy? That way I can make sure that, if we do have him, he isn't interrogated as part of the process. If you could get me that report, I'll pass it on to Sam Long down at the SOTG.'

Steph's pulse quickened. *Shit*, she thought. She hadn't expected that Geoff would know the procedures so thoroughly and the mention of Sam Long concerned her.

Geoff sensed that he had got the upper hand, but he couldn't be bothered taking it any further. 'I'm just joking, ma'am. Anyway, we didn't take anyone off the target today, so your man is safe.'

Steph bit her bottom lip and then nodded slowly at Geoff, realising how clumsy her approach had been. 'I see. Well, that's good news. Thanks.' Steph fought hard to contain her relief. 'You're right, though, Geoff – I should have completed an out-of-country report. I completely forgot about it.'

Geoff sat back down and turned on his computer screen. In one corner of the screen was the Sametime chat program used to pass real-time information between Kandahar and Camp Russell. Steph could see that Geoff was in a conversation with Sam and saw the words DRY HOLE, the term used to describe when there was no intelligence value on a target.

She turned and started to walk off, making a mental note to tread lightly around the Australian in the future.

'Oh, Steph, one more thing, now that I think of it,' Geoff called out just as she was making her way to a door being held open for her by one of the officers returning with a tray of coffees. She turned her head to look back at him. 'We picked up a couple of cell phones from the target. I'll let you know if there's anything significant on them.' Geoff nodded to her and turned back to his screen.

Steph walked out into the hallway half in a daze. The realisation that the cell phone she had given Faisal might be in the SOTG's possession was terrifying, especially as she had broken her own protocol and rung the number from her personal mobile to warn him rather than sending a coded message and using her drop phone. *Holy shit, this is bad*, she thought.

31

Matt closed the door to his room and slumped onto the bed.

Well, that's my career over, he said to himself. Replaying the last four months over and over in his mind, he felt a certain satisfaction at offloading on the CO. There was nothing like hitting rock bottom to help clarify one's thoughts. Allie knew what was going on, and so did the CO and Sam. He suspected that Saygen was also a part of it – of course he was. Everyone was in on it except him. How could he have been so stupid, letting himself get played like that? *Who else was in on it?* he wondered bitterly. Craig Reilly – was he in on it too? What about Chris Smith, the X-Ray Platoon commander? *No.* Matt pulled himself up short. This was the CO's doing; the others would have just been following orders. He couldn't blame them.

There was a knock at the door.

'Piss off!' he yelled. He was in no mood for visitors.

'It's me, boss.'

The door opened to reveal JJ as Matt cursed himself for forgetting to lock it. 'Hey, man, what the fuck? I just heard some guys talking smack in the mess hall.'

Matt didn't say anything, just put his hands behind his head and stretched out fully on the bed.

'The CO has told Craig Reilly that he's commanding Yankee Platoon now.'

Behind JJ, Matt could see some other guys starting to crowd around the doorway.

'Right, well, that makes sense I guess.' Matt sat up and swung his feet off the bed and onto the floor. 'They played me.' He stood up to face JJ. 'They knew there was a leak and they used me.' Matt dragged his black roller bag out from under the bed and started to empty his drawers into it.

'I don't get it. Who played who?' JJ looked dumbfounded.

'For Christ's sake, JJ! Are you walking around in a bubble? The CO has been sending us out there knowing full well that the Taliban have been told of our plans. They've been using *us* as the tethered goat, so that Saygen can target the senior leadership.'

'Bullshit! Really? So what now then, are you just giving up? If you go, what the hell happens to us? We're doomed.' JJ took Matt's clothes back out of the bag and placed them on his desk.

'You're joking, right? The CO just sacked me. My career is over. Maybe I could have handled it better, but to be honest it was about time that he heard exactly what I thought. The command climate in this place is toxic, and if they aren't going to include me then so be it.'

215

'Why don't you just call our CO back home, Mark Hoff? Surely he would just go and tell the Special Operations Commander.'

'Yeah right, it's that easy. Do you think that SOCAUST would care?' Matt picked up his GPS from the shelf next to the bed and threw it in the roller bag. 'Mark was a troop commander in the SAS before our unit was even raised, Jack. Do you think he would give two shits about me, or the platoon for that matter?'

'C'mon, boss, he's not like that, not at all – the guys rate him. He's one of us now.'

'Dude, you're delusional! I bet you any money he chucks the sandy beret back on when he goes to the Special Operations Headquarters for his next posting.'

Matt picked the clothes off the table and shoved them back into the bag, looking back up at JJ. He noticed that the big guy looked broken, defeated. Maybe he had run off at the mouth without considering the consequences.

'I don't agree,' JJ said quietly.

Matt sat himself on the bed. 'The problem, mate, is that we're living in their shadow and the more successful we are, the more the ex-SAS officers band together and protect the SAS brand.'

'Yeah, right. But couldn't you have handled it a little better? I mean, getting yourself sacked. Jesus, boss, and you have a go at me for losing my cool over shit,' JJ said nervously, wondering if he had overstepped the mark.

'Maybe you're right,' Matt said coolly. 'So you think I was out of line then?'

'That's not what I'm saying, but perhaps we should have handled this together. At least we could have come up with a plan.' JJ turned to the other guys who were milling in the hallway just outside Matt's room. 'Give us a minute, lads.'

He closed the door, then, turning back to Matt, put a hand on his shoulder. 'Listen, boss, we were screwed, there's no doubt about it – but if there *is* a leak, then our job isn't done yet, is it?'

'Ah, it's useless, JJ; I can't take back what's been said. I didn't just burn those bridges, I blew them apart. And to be honest, I'm not sure I could work for that asshole again anyway.'

There was a knock at the door.

'Tell the guys to leave me alone for a while, mate,' Matt said. 'I need to get my head together. I'll talk to them in the morning before I go.'

The knock came again, louder this time, and then the door was pushed open and Saygen walked into the room.

'Hey, Matt, JJ.' Saygen nodded to them both.

'What d'ya want?' Matt said coldly. The SAS commander was the last guy he wanted to deal with right now.

'I've just heard the news, Matt. My signaller was in the room when it all blew up, and he told me what was said. I just want to say that I'm sorry, mate.'

Matt eyeballed him suspiciously. Was Saygen here to gloat?

Saygen continued, 'I knew what was going on, but I didn't have the guts to say anything about it at the time. I wanted to; it just didn't seem right, what was going on.'

'No shit it wasn't right.' Matt couldn't be bothered to soothe the guy's feelings. If he felt guilty for not speaking up, too bad – he *should* feel guilty. 'Is that it?' Matt raised his eyebrows. 'Are you finished?'

'I understand,' Saygen said. 'I'm SAS and you're a commando, we should be rivals – but not like this.'

The two men stared at each other.

'We didn't get Rapier either – just thought you should know.' Saygen looked at Matt and then JJ. He handed the sergeant a sheet of paper. 'Here's the grid reference. Apparently it was a hot lead and he was meant to be there, but it was a dry hole, as usual.'

'You should go, Terence,' Matt said, picking up the last of the clothes that JJ had put on his desk and putting them in his bag.

'Sure, no worries. I'll look you up when I get back home, yeah?' Saygen backed out of the room.

Matt continued to pack his bag in silence. JJ stood there for a while and then pulled his map out of his pocket. He quickly plotted the grid that Saygen had given them. 'Hmm, that's interesting.' JJ looked at the map again. 'Boss, what would you do if you were a Taliban commander and your lair had just been rolled up?'

Matt sat back on his bed. 'Really, JJ? We're going to play that game?'

'No, seriously, boss – what would you do?'

'Shit, I don't know, mate. Run for the hills, I guess.' Matt couldn't be arsed giving it too much thought.

'You wouldn't go back there? Wouldn't you figure it would be the last place we would look again?'

Matt shifted his attention back to JJ and frowned. They stared at each other. Matt's expression changed.

'I see what you're getting at. Show me that grid.' Matt looked at the grid and checked JJ's map. 'Shit – that's close, right?' Matt could feel his adrenaline start to rise. This was dangerous territory. 'How long ago did Saygen hit it?'

'Must be over an hour ago.' JJ smiled and cracked his neck from side to side as if he meant business.

'It's close, isn't it, JJ?' Matt repeated, tapping the location with his finger.

'Yep, it's close alright.'

'Not even a ten-minute drive, I reckon.'

Matt cleared the top of his desk with a single swipe of his hand. He unfolded the map out all the way and looked at the route to and from the motorcycle repair shop.

'Not even, boss.' JJ rubbed his hands together. 'What are they going to do, sack you?'

Matt laughed. 'Yeah, I've got nothing to lose now. I suppose they could court-martial me. How long would it take to get the guys onto the vehicles and out the gate?'

'What, like a time-sensitive target job?'

'That's exactly what I was thinking.' Matt grabbed his body armour and rifle. 'Gather the guys in the common room, mate – I want to make them an offer!'

JJ stood in the doorway and started yelling down the hallway. 'Team commanders, stop what you're doing and get your blokes in the common room *now*.' He turned back and grinned at Matt. 'Let's have one more roll of the dice, boss.'

'Yep,' said Matt, with a grim smile. 'Let's do this!'

32

TARIN KOWT

Faisal was frantically pacing around the workshop when the boys arrived.

'We came as soon as we dared. Are you hurt?'

'No. Just get these cuffs off me!' The eldest of the four boys grabbed a box knife from the low workbench next to the door. He began to saw at the cuffs that held Faisal's wrists together and then set to work on Abdul. Faisal rubbed his wrists and looked at the deep bruises. The devils had locked his hands tight and torn his shirt from the shoulder to the waist in the process.

'Listen, this is very important: look everywhere for my phone. We have to find my phone.' Faisal was panicked.

The boys started to search the floor, turning over the already-messy workshop.

Abdul stood up and looked across at the workbenches and the tools scattered all over the shop. 'I have to get word to Ahmed,

Faisal. I have to tell him that the devils have been. He would want to know that the vests are still safe.' Ahmed Defari wouldn't carry a phone himself, so Abdul looked at the boys. 'You, Mohammed,' he said, pointing to the oldest boy. 'Do you know the orchard house? The one they call the little castle?'

'Yes, I know the place.' Mohammed straightened while answering Ahmed, like a soldier standing to attention.

'Go to the cemetery there. Go now. Take those three bikes out back. All of you go, find Ahmed Defari and tell him what happened here today. But most importantly, tell him his things are safe.'

The boys nodded in agreement and ran off to the three Helmand 175s sitting outside the shop.

Abdul surveyed the damage. 'Look at this place, Faisal. They've tipped up everything. This will take weeks to fix.' Abdul lifted up one of the turned-over bike engines, placing it back on the stand. 'At least they didn't get the prizes,' he consoled himself.

'It wasn't the vests they were after, Abdul. Are you that simple?' Faisal shook his head at the blank look on Abdul's face. 'They checked our hands and eyes – that means they were looking for someone. They are after Ahmed himself.' Faisal thought about what he had just said. 'My phone is gone, too; they must have found it.' Faisal rubbed his eyes and looked at where the back door had once been. He was amazed at how fast the devils had arrived. It had shaken him, leaving him unable to think clearly. One of them had been strutting around the room, the others all seemingly bringing him information. Faisal had seen tactical teams training when he was in Pakistan, but never anything like this.

'They won't come back here again, Faisal – not now that they know he isn't here.' Abdul picked up another bike.

'Of course they're coming back, Abdul – this won't be the last time we see them. If they know that he has been here before, they will never stop watching us. This isn't safe, and now they have recorded our fingers and eyes, and maybe they have my phone.' Faisal sat down. He needed to think through the ramifications. They had his fingerprints and they had scanned his eyes. If they had his phone they would link him back to Steph. Would she protect him? *Could* she protect him now, or would she also be a target? Would the devils realise that she had been sending him information about their plans? She had rung as they came through the door, they would work that out. He was going to be linked to Ahmed; that was a certainty. They must know that Ahmed was responsible for all those deaths over the last year. What did that mean for him and the Dutch girl? Her number was now lost forever, gone with his phone. Faisal was used to operating in confusing environments, but this situation was making his head spin.

'We have to leave this place, Abdul. We have to leave here now.'

'I can't go anywhere. The vests.' Abdul pointed at the floor.

'Damn the vests, brother! Don't you understand? They're going to come back. When they realise who we are, when they see inside my phone, they're coming back – and unless you're wearing one of those vests, they're going to take you with them.' Faisal took off his torn shirt and threw it on the ground. 'Do I need to tell you what happens if they take you with them?'

Abdul shook his head furiously.

Faisal continued anyway. 'They will sit you in a small cage with a big dog inches from your genitals. They will ask you questions, and if they don't like the answers, then they give the dog a command

and he takes a piece of you, one piece for every question they don't like your answer to.'

He walked over and pulled a Nike sports bag out from under one of the workbenches. It was ripped, stained with old oil and had no zip. Faisal fished inside the bag and conjured up a somewhat fresh long green shirt. He looked at it, amazed that it, and the bag, had somehow escaped the wrath of the SAS. 'Then, when the devils release you, they give you to the Americans – or, worse, our own secret police. Either way, they don't let you have a trial, they just shoot you dead in a taxi.'

He pulled the shirt over his head. 'So, Abdul, shall I put you in a vest?' asked Faisal.

Abdul looked around at the shop. It had never amounted to that much and, if he was honest, it had only ever been a front for the Taliban anyway. He had spent the past five years making IEDs, sending information and hiding weapons and equipment. As much as he loved bikes, this shop wasn't really about the bikes.

'You know my brother in Kabul?' Abdul said. 'He's a university teacher. Perhaps we could go and stay with him.'

'Yes, of course I know him; what do you mean, do I know him? I think that blast may have broken your brain, Abdul.'

'Let's go stay with him, Faisal, lay low for a while. We'll be safe there.'

'Yes, that's a good idea,' Faisal ran his fingers through his hair. It was gritty from all the dirt and dust kicked up by the explosives. He thought about what they would be leaving behind. 'The vests will be fine, Abdul. When the time comes they will be ready, and we will have the kids bring them, one at a time if we have to.'

'Maybe I could open another shop in Kabul – you know, a real repair shop.'

'Yes, I'm sure you could. Grab what you need and let's go.' Faisal picked up an old plastic bag from the floor. Into it he put some bread and a warm Pepsi he took from a bucket that had once been filled with ice. He sat down on a small wooden crate while he waited for Abdul to pack his things. Faisal's thoughts were focused on Steph. She knew his full name and his connection to Ahmed Defari. She would try to save her own skin, of that much he was sure. His training with ISI had taught him that much. It might be time to get on the front foot. He had done his job up until now. She had been sold the lines that he was required to sell to her. She had been kept off the scent for long enough now. Faisal was sure that the information must have made its way to the top. They would all be looking where the magician wanted them to look and now they could do their trick unseen by prying eyes. Defari was right: it was time to make Steph go away, complete the loop, before the Westerners realised what it was that they were actually doing.

Seeing Abdul's brother in Kabul again would be a bonus, thought Faisal. Abdul's brother was always able to help with these things. As well as being a university lecturer he was a very good accountant and managed the Taliban's finances like his life depended on it, as it most certainly did. Seeing him would help to ensure Steph gave him no more problems. The accountant would organise payment to the Egyptian. He felt a bit more relaxed now; perhaps he had the upper hand after all.

33

TARIN KOWT

Life was getting back to normal on the Tarin Kowt streets. The heat of the mid-afternoon sun was giving way to the promise of a cooler evening. The local children had come out of hiding and were making their way back to their houses after all the excitement of the SAS raid earlier in the day.

Aziz noticed the first Bushmaster as it rounded the corner. He couldn't believe his eyes. Even at twelve years of age he was smart enough to know that this was out of the ordinary for the foreigners. *They had just left, why were they back?* Now more cars arrived, and they were gathering speed; the deep groan of their engines was deafening and the dust kicked up by their tyres engulfed all that were brave enough to stand by the roadside and watch them go past.

Aziz grabbed his younger brother and dragged him back off the edge of the road. 'Quiet, Imari – just watch, don't talk.'

Imari watched in silence as the vehicles hurtled past. On top of the first car, his upper body emerging through the roof hatch, was a huge man, his shoulders seemingly as wide as the vehicle. It looked like he was screaming something into his own hand. He turned his head and looked straight at Imari; his eyes narrowed and then he smiled a big white smile. Imari smiled back nervously.

Aziz counted the trucks as they thundered past; four, five, six, eight, ten trucks – that was six more trucks than the first raid earlier today! The noise was deafening, and the trucks were now only metres apart. Earlier in the day there had been twenty metres or more between them. Aziz could sense the urgency. At the very last minute they headed off in different directions, and then all at once they screamed to a halt surrounding Abdul Rahman's motorcycle repair shop. The contents of the steel war machines spilled out into the street – huge bearded men carrying black machine guns and other equipment of death. This time there were no explosions though, just shouting and lots of it.

'Let's get out of here, Imari,' Aziz said, panicked.

Imari looked at the repair shop and then back at his big brother. 'What's Abdul done, Aziz?'

'I'm not sure, Imari. Father always tells me to not go over there. He says that Abdul's friends will send us to Pakistan if they get to know us. I guess the Americans don't like him either; after all, they came back to get him again.'

'They're not Americans, Aziz, they're Australians. Mullah Mutallah is a friend of theirs. I met them once when they spoke to Mutallah behind the mosque. They gave me a chocolate treat and told me they live down under the bottom of the world.'

'You're smart, Imari, but we should go now.'

Aziz took Imari's hand and led him down into a narrow lane that ran between two old buildings. One of the grey buildings had a perfect circle that had been blown into the wall on a winter's night five years ago. The older men told the boys that rockets had come from the sky and killed three foreigners from Pakistan who were sleeping on the other side of the wall. There wasn't even a sound before the explosions. They said that there were no planes at all – just a flash of light and then the building shook.

The boys cut back down into an old rubbish tip at the end of the lane. Scrambling and sliding down the dirt path, they could hear the foreigners shouting at the back at the shop.

'Don't look back, Imari, just run,' shouted Aziz.

The tip was full of all manner of refuse: plastic bags and bottles, rubble, concrete beams and a couple of dead animals; the smell that hung over the place was a reminder that death was never far away in Afghanistan. The boys would often fly kites there during the cooler months when the breeze would take the smells away, but in the summer the stench was unbearable.

The track came out at the other side of the creek and afforded them cover as they ran towards the shed at the back of the orchard they called home. As they made their way up the slippery embankment, the street behind them grew quiet again. The vehicles' engines were off now and it seemed that even the neighbourhood dogs knew better than to bark while the Australians were doing their business inside.

• • •

Inside the workshop, Matt shook his head and looked up at the ceiling of the small building. 'Are you sure, Ben? No one, not a soul?'

'We surprised a stray dog out the back – he pissed off straight away – but there's no one else here, boss. The place has been ransacked too. The cats did a good job of turning it over.'

Matt looked at his platoon sergeant. 'Jesus, JJ – what the fuck have I done?' Matt watched the guys as they went through the boxes that had already been searched. 'If Rapier was here, this might not have been such a stupid idea.' One of the commando teams left the building and then returned with metal detectors from their vehicle. 'I'm not even sure what the military charge is going to be. Fuck, I can only imagine that it might mean prison time.'

'Rubbish, boss, we'll talk our way out of it.' JJ took a slurp from his CamelBak and spat the water on the floor next to his feet. 'It was worth a try.'

'Was it? I've just taken thirty Special Forces out on an unsanctioned, unsupported operation. Basically, some type of rogue force or broken arrow or some shit.'

'You've hardly stolen a nuclear weapon, boss.' JJ undid his body armour to get access to his empty CamelBak. 'We'll find a way to justify this. No one probably even knows we're gone. For all we know, they might be in the mess eating dessert, all fat, dumb and happy.' Placing his vest on the low workbench he pulled out the bladder and laid it down next to his M4.

'Ah, not so much, JJ,' said Barnsley. 'The communications centre has been sending me messages every minute for the past ten minutes demanding to know where we are and what we're doing. I turned the radio off about two minutes ago.'

'Barns, go and get me a bottle of water from the back of the car, you fucking dickhead,' said JJ.

'Sure, Sarge.' Barnsley moseyed out the missing front doors to the admin vehicle.

Matt put his weapon on the bench next to JJ's. 'I forced you guys to come, or maybe I tricked you – either way, we need to think of something so that this doesn't blow back on the rest of you.'

The guys were running the metal detectors over the walls and floor now, inch by inch.

'Anything, lads?' Matt asked of one of the commandos as he walked past.

'Nothing, boss, the walls are clear; there's nothing metal in there. There are a few metal plates secured to the floor by DynaBolts, but that's just for the benches to be screwed to, so that they don't move while they're working on engines and shit.' As if to demonstrate, the commando pushed on the bench. It didn't budge. 'The place is just full of old bike parts and rubbish; there's nothing left here of intelligence value.' He undid the metal detector handle and rammed the head back into itself.

JJ turned one-eighty degrees from the table towards Matt and Barnsley, who had just arrived back in from the vehicles with the water bottle. 'You know what, boss? We could leave a team here – you know, overnight. They could hide in here when we leave, and then when the pricks come back – tap tap.' JJ made shooting signals with his fingers as he took the two-litre bottle of water from the signaller and unscrewed the cap. 'Cheers, Barns.'

The commandos in the room all stopped what they were doing and looked at Matt, waiting for his response.

Joseph Hammond moved from behind some of his team, who had been looking through toolboxes. 'Team Four's up for it, boss – we'll stay, not a drama at all.' Hammond's face was determined, his chin stuck out in defiance. He looked around the room of commandos and then added, 'Fuck the CO!'

Matt looked around at the guys that he had commanded for the past two years. After Johnno's death, they had looked beaten, but now they stood proud, like warriors ready to do battle – to the death, if necessary. But Matt had to end this; Craig Reilly would be taking over and the platoon would be left in good hands. They would move on and chase Rapier without him, and at least now they would not be the bait.

Matt cleared his throat. 'Joe, are you completely deranged? That would just be reinforcing failure! Thanks, but I can't ask anyone to do that.'

Hammond nodded his acceptance of this.

Matt turned to the centre of the room. 'This is it, lads. I need to go back and get what's coming to me. It would take an act of God to save me now; I'm done, I'm afraid.' Matt grabbed his rifle by the barrel and pulled it off the bench, knocking the two-litre bottle of water onto the floor.

'Shit, sorry, JJ.' The water poured out of the bottle and pooled at JJ's feet. 'Okay, lads, let's wrap this up. Moving in two minutes.' With that Matt headed towards the door.

JJ looked around at the guys. They looked lost. 'Come on, guys, you heard the boss – let's get out of this shithole.' He bent down to pick up the half-empty water bottle. 'What the hell?'

He looked again at where the bottle had fallen: there was no water on the floor. It didn't make sense. Peering closely, he saw that the water had seeped under the metal plate that the bench was screwed into. JJ stood back up and grabbed his radio fist mic off his body armour. 'Yankee Two, bring me a wrench and a crowbar.' He looked at the size of the dirty metal plate securing the bench into the floor. 'Actually, better make that two sets.'

34

HOLSWORTHY BARRACKS, AUSTRALIA

'Hey, boss, there's a visitor for you coming up the stairs just now.'

Lieutenant Colonel Mark Hoff, the Commanding Officer of the 2nd Commando Regiment, looked up from his desk. The young curly-haired adjutant had just run into his office and was now standing inside the doorway with a confused look on his face.

'I've got no appointments this afternoon, mate.' Mark glanced casually out the large tinted windows. The strong wind outside made the Australian flag and the 2nd Commando Regiment flag stand to attention. Looking out from his office on the second storey he could see out past the flagpoles, past the Commando Memorial Rock that seemed to shine after this morning's winter shower, all the way down towards the guardroom.

'Actually, I don't think this guy needs an appointment, boss – it's SOCAUST.' No sooner had the words left Joel's lips than the man himself appeared in the doorway. In his mid-forties, with thick salt-and-pepper hair and the exemplary level of fitness that often accompanies a severe case of short-man syndrome, the commander of the Australian Special Forces looked every inch the formidable leader he was.

'G'day, Mark – bet you didn't expect to see me today.' The commander strolled into the office with his hand outstretched. The understated greeting was typical; the commander wore his authority lightly.

Mark leaped up from behind his desk. 'Sir, I thought you were in Canberra today. I mean, I received an email from you not thirty minutes ago.' Mark reached over to shake the commander's hand.

'Secure BlackBerry, Mark – how did we ever operate without them?' The commander settled himself down on the leather sofa opposite Hoff's stately mahogany desk.

'Can I offer you a tea or coffee, sir?'

'Nope, I'm fine, thanks.'

'Something stronger perhaps, sir? It's past five and therefore past the Queen's time.'

'No thanks, I'm not staying that long. Let's just have a quick chat, shall we?'

'Right. Okay then. Joel, can you close the door behind you, please, mate?' Mark asked.

'Certainly, sir.' The adjutant left the room and stepped back into the open foyer. 'What the fuck?' he mouthed at Eric, the 2nd Commando Regiment RSM who had half stood up from his desk to get a better view. SOCAUST, the commander of all the Australian Special Forces units, never just arrived like this. The last time he had arrived without notice, the unit deployed to Timor the next day to hunt for Alfredo Reinado in the Timorese highlands.

Inside the office, the commander was characteristically blunt. 'Let me get straight to the point, Mark: I have a job for you, a sensitive job, and I need you to leave tonight.'

'I see, of course. Where to then?' Mark was used to going away at short notice from his days as a troop commander in the SAS, but a lieutenant colonel just disappearing on a mission, especially a regimental commander? That was unusual.

'I want you to go to Dubai and wait at Al Minhad air base. You will receive further instructions once you get there. Your point of contact is Major Paul Dewalt, an ADFIS investigator. Deployable light, Mark, but take your SORD Body Armour too; you may need it and that's the best stuff on the market.' The commander crossed one leg over the other. 'Any questions?'

'What about 2 Commando, boss?' Mark was thinking aloud rather than looking for any real answers.

'I'm sure the XO can handle it, mate. After all, that's why we have a succession plan.' The commander focused intently on Mark to ensure he was taking it all in. 'Use the unit Visa card, Mark, not the travel company or defence travel card. I want to keep this on the down low. The Special Forces liaison officer has already been warned that you are coming. He will meet you at Dubai International and get you set up in the office at Al Minhad.' With that the commander slapped his hands on his thighs and stood up. 'Right then, I'm off to Kirribilli for dinner with the PM.'

'Really, sir? Is that related to what I'll be doing in the Middle East?' Mark was fishing.

'No, just dinner, Mark.' The commander gave him a bland smile that revealed nothing. He placed his hand against the door and then turned around. 'Oh, and Mark? A word of advice for while you're away . . .'

'What's that, sir?'

'Don't ever forget where you came from. I find this whole SAS versus commando thing rather tiring – but you *were* an SAS troop commander, Mark.'

'I know where I've come from, sir; neither organisation would let me forget it in a hurry.'

'This task is sensitive, Mark, and you have a foot in each camp. Good luck with it and don't let me down.' With a last nod, the commander walked out the door and strode quickly through the commando headquarters to his staff car.

What in heaven's name was going on? Mark wondered.

'Joel!' he yelled out.

The adjutant appeared in the doorway. 'Yes, sir?'

'Cancel all my meetings, mate.'

'For how long, boss?'

'I'm not really sure – make it indefinitely, I suppose. Oh, and Joel – call in the executive officer, give him a quick heads-up, mate; he's in command.'

35

TARIN KOWT

Matt responded to the radio call and moved back into the motorcycle repair shop. The men of Yankee Platoon had gathered around the huge hole underneath the table and were busy discussing its possible contents. JJ came back out of the hole, his head wet with sweat and his camouflage uniform filthy from the dust.

'Jesus, boss, you won't believe it.'

Barnsley offered his hand to the big platoon sergeant and helped him up out of the entrance to the underground cache.

Matt peered down into the dark cavern. 'What the hell is down there, JJ?'

'Tonnes and tonnes of stuff – no shit, boss: *tonnes* of stuff.' JJ could hardly contain his excitement. 'I would say that the room under there is almost as wide as this building. It's full of medical supplies, weapons, explosives, clothing . . . God knows what else. Go down and have a gander – seriously, you won't believe your eyes.'

'Sounds like we might have a Taliban supply store.' *Well, this changes things a bit*, thought Matt. He grabbed his fist mic from his chest rig and pressed on the handset. 'Team commanders in to me.' Placing the handset back on its Velcro patch he pulled the Gerber torch out of one of his pockets and dropped down to the edge of the hole to have a look.

'HOLY SHIT! You weren't joking, JJ; it looks like Aladdin's cave in there.' Moving the powerful beam of light around, Matt could see all manner of boxes. There were ammunition crates, cardboard boxes, metal tins and, ominously, there were thirty yellow plastic water containers – the type favoured by Rapier himself when making IEDs. In one corner was a pile of neatly stacked rocket-propelled grenades and other weapon parts. *Jackpot*, thought Matt.

He stood up, brushed himself off and moved over to the team commanders who had all arrived while he was looking in the hole.

'Okay, lads, this is the deal. Barnsley, get onto HQ, mate, and let them know we have found a huge cache of weapons, pictures to follow in fifteen minutes.'

'On it.'

'Get down there, Joe, and video what's inside this pit. Once we have enough footage I want your guys to grab all the pressure plates and any other bits and pieces – basically anything that looks like it's of intelligence value – and chuck it all in plastic evidence bags.'

'No worries, boss, it's all coming with – understood.'

'Make sure they're wearing plastic gloves too, Joe, okay? I don't want to mix our biometrics with the Taliban.'

'Sure thing.' Joseph Hammond took off his helmet and smoothed back his sandy hair while connecting the Kevlar to his chest rig.

Matt looked to his left. 'Cinzano, get your guys up on the roof, please. We need to lock this place down and dominate it. The Taliban may want to bump us from here and we need to be ready to respond. Take Kiwi and the other snipers to assist your team. I know your guys are up for a good fight, so get them moving.'

'No worries, boss. How long do you think we'll need to lock this joint down for?'

'However long it takes – I'd reckon a few hours at least.'

Cinzano left at a fast trot, talking to his team through the bone mic inserted in his left ear as he went. On the perimeter, his men responded to the radio calls and started to proceed to their areas of responsibility.

'Nadeem,' said Matt, turning to face his interpreter who had been following him around. 'Get into the command vehicle, mate, and get on the loudspeaker. Send out some broadcasts telling the locals to keep their distance and that it is a military operation and it will be over in a few hours.'

'Sure thing, sir,' replied the Terp.

'Oh, and Nadeem, do it in Arabic,' said Matt, laughing.

'Where's JJ, guys?' Matt looked around at the remaining team commanders.

'I'm here, boss,' JJ said, walking back in through the front doors. 'That useless bloody explosive detection dog has shat in the back of my car again. I was just checking on the Bushmaster drivers to make sure they were informed of what's going on and I found it curled up in its own filth sitting in my bed roll.' JJ joined the small group.

'That's what you get for always feeding it your leftovers, mate,' said Joseph.

JJ ignored Joseph and moved to stand next to Matt. 'Boss, my close shave with a pile of dog shit made me think: perhaps we should send a combat engineer down there first to make sure it's safe to move around. I mean, I just dropped straight down the stairs and didn't move from the actual entrance, but there could be booby traps or anti-handling devices, who knows what else.'

'Yeah, that's a good point, JJ; I didn't even consider that.' Matt took a moment to contemplate what this would mean for their timeline. 'Go get Greg to do a proper assessment.' Matt looked around at the rest of the guys. 'Looks like we might just have broken the back of the network today, lads – good result. If there are no more questions, let's get this done.'

Matt sat on an old wooden crate just inside the front door. His body armour sat next to him on the ground, and his rifle and Kevlar helmet sat on top of it. Matt looked off into the distance, through the missing double doors and out past the vehicles. Large black thunderclouds were starting to gather on the ridgeline of mountains up the other side of the valley. He turned back to the entrance to the Taliban cache as Greg emerged from the hole. JJ helped him up out of the ground and the two of them had a discussion that Matt couldn't quite hear. The radio sitting next to Barnsley's leg squawked alive and Matt almost jumped at the sudden noise.

Barnsley picked up the handset and listened for a bit, finally replying in the affirmative.

'What was that, Barns?'

'That was the command centre just wanting to know if we'd be back before dark.'

Matt felt the dread wash over him. 'I wouldn't go back at all if I had my way, Barns. Still, it could be worse – at least we have a solid result to show for it.'

'That's me done, sir.' Greg stood in front of Matt, visibly shaken. 'It's dangerous down there, boss. There were a few traps set and a heap of suicide vests. I cleared a small area for the guys to bring some stuff out, but we are going to have to blow most of it in place. Actually, I think you should get the guys out of here, sir; if we trigger something down there it will drop this building.'

'You didn't think to tell me that before you went poking around down in there?' Matt didn't give him time to respond. 'Let's get out of here then. Are the photos and video complete?'

'Yeah, your boys are finishing that now. I have a heap of stuff in the back of my car that we took out; pressure plates and fuse switch assemblies, phones and stuff like that.'

'That's excellent, Greg – good work. I'll get the guys moving then. What do you need to bring this place down safely?'

'It won't take too much. Some detonation cord, an M60 igniter and a slab of PE will do the trick. Sir, there was one more thing.' He held up a hand, sneezed, then continued. 'Just to the left of the stairs down there are boxes with ANA and police uniforms. They're numbered one to a hundred and I noticed there was a single uniform missing out of each batch. I grabbed a box of each uniform so that we can check them to see where they were made.'

'Really? That's interesting.' Matt thought about what this might mean. 'It's good to get them off the streets, in any case.'

'Yes, sir.' Greg sneezed again. 'Sorry about that, I don't know what's wrong with me – I usually only react like that when I come into contact with Semtex.'

'You think there's Semtex down there?' Matt asked sharply.

'Huh? No, no – it's just the dust. What's down there is either homemade explosives or basic military munitions.'

'Alright, Greg, get yourself sorted and get ready to drop this place. I'll have Barns radio it in and in the meantime I'll get the guys clear. Cinzano's lads will come down off the roof and provide you with some protection until you get it sorted out and then we will head back to camp.'

'No worries, boss.'

'Good – and Greg?' Matt placed his hand on Greg's arm. 'Great job, mate.'

. . .

Forty-five minutes later, Yankee Platoon's vehicles were lined up four hundred metres down the street from the motorcycle repair shop. Cinzano's team sprinted from the shop towards the relative safety of their Bushmasters, with Greg lumbering behind, barely making it into the back of his vehicle before the huge explosion shook the entire town. Windows in the house opposite Matt's Bushmaster blew out into the street from the percussion.

'Holy shit, boss.' Barns laughed hard into his vehicle communications headset.

Matt was shocked. The blast was so massive it rocked the command vehicle from side to side. They both watched as a Volkswagen-sized piece of concrete from the shop was launched into the air and over their vehicles for another thirty metres, the impact as it landed shaking the earth for a second time.

Greg came up on the Yankee Platoon radio network. 'Jesus, sir, I didn't really expect that.' The radio went silent for a minute.

'Really?' JJ said sardonically. 'You're a bloody explosives expert and you didn't expect that? You didn't expect that it would blow up after you set off a kilogram of plastic explosives among a huge stockpile of fucking bombs and rockets?'

Over the dull hum of the Bushmasters' engines Matt could hear the platoon erupt in laughter over the radio.

'All call signs, this is Yankee Alpha. Move now – out.' Matt turned to look at Barnsley. 'Time to go face the music, Barns.'

'It'll be alright, I reckon, boss.'

'Really? What makes you think that then?' Matt turned his attention to the small whiteboard on which he tracked the platoon's order of march and recorded important grid references and events.

The signaller shrugged. 'When I requested permission to drop the building, I had a response only a few seconds later to say that we could. In fact, since we found the cache they have pretty much left us alone the whole time except for asking when we are going to be back.'

'I'm not really sure that you're reading that correctly, Barns.' Matt took off his headset to end the conversation and looked out the armoured-glass window. The big Bushmaster rolled effortlessly along the gravel track. Behind the line of vehicles, the locals were starting to come out of hiding and make their way to the burnt-out ruins of the motorcycle repair shop just as the first drops of rain started to fall on the scene. Without any context, Matt thought, it probably looked to them like just another example of the Australians destroying a business important to the local community.

36

BAGRAM AIR BASE, KABUL

'Is it just the two of you today, sir?' the Black Hawk pilot asked. Although she was standing outside the helicopter, she was still attached to the cockpit by the communications wire that ran from down beside the seat out to her helmet. Popping up the mirrored visor, she pulled her notebook from the leg pocket of her khaki green flight suit and wrote down some final numbers being displayed on the digital readout inside the cockpit. On the other side of the aircraft, the co-pilot was in his seat conducting the final pre-flight checks. He reached up to adjust some controls on the roof of the aircraft.

'Yes, it's just the two of us, thanks, Jody.'

General Towers, the Commander of Australian Forces in the Middle East, took the headset the pilot offered him and climbed into the middle row of seats in the back of the helicopter. The general looked every one of his fifty-five years. The stress of multiple tours in Iraq and Afghanistan, as well as the responsibility he bore for the thousands of Australian men and women who had served under him, had taken their toll. A man of average height but with snow-white hair, he held himself like a statesman – an occupation he would soon pursue, depending on the politics back home.

Placing the headset on, he could hear the pilots going through their familiar routine. General Tower's operations officer, Lieutenant Colonel Gavin Gray, picked up the other headset as he settled himself in the seat beside the general.

'All set, Sir?' Jody enquired as she climbed into the front of the Black Hawk.

'Yes, all set, thanks.' Towers checked that his rifle was secured between his knees with the barrel facing the floor and tightened the four-point harness.

'There's a bit of weather around Tarin Kowt today, so we'll track in from the south.' Jody adjusted some GPS waypoint coordinates.

'Roger that, skipper,' the co-pilot confirmed.

Jody powered up the big helicopter's engines. The rotors started to slice through the air until they morphed into a single disc, spinning with such speed that they threatened to separate from the airframe and launch off into the heavens by themselves.

'Gav, how long do you think it will be before Mark Hoff's in the country?'

'About four days, sir. The commander spoke to him this afternoon Australian time. He'll need to jump on a plane to the UAE, so that's a day gone, and then he needs to get all the in-country information briefs at Al Minhad, which'll take another couple of days. I suspect he'll also want a day in Dubai to go over the information that ADFIS already has. So, yeah, I would say about four days or so before we can get him in country.'

'Right.' The general thought for a moment. 'I see. Do you think we should suspend the SOTG operations until Mark's been briefed and is on the ground?'

The lieutenant colonel reflected for a moment and then said, 'Yes, sir – almost certainly, sir.'

'Well, I don't, Gav. I think it's important that the men continue to operate through this period. If anything, I think that perhaps we should increase their workload so they don't dwell on events. That was my experience in Iraq with the Americans.'

'Yes, sir. Good idea, sir.'

'Anyway, Gav, given what occurred this afternoon with Yankee Platoon out on the ground, I think it's time we stepped up some pressure out there in TK. By the sounds of it, we were lucky our man Rix chose to chase up on instinct.'

General Towers sighed and looked back out the window at some of the ground crew pottering around the outside of a maintenance hangar. Finding men with initiative and a capacity for original thought was almost impossible at this rank; just being offered an unsolicited opinion would be refreshing. He was looking forward to meeting up with the men of the SOTG; from them he could be sure of receiving a very honest assessment of the mission in Afghanistan.

The Black Hawk lurched up into the air and then began a steady ascent, rising above the airfield and slowly banking to the left and out across the sprawling air base. Towers watched as the Kabul base disappeared behind them and they headed towards the jagged mountain ranges ahead. He remembered how in the cooler months they had been covered in snow. Just like everything in Afghanistan, the mountains seemed to change from one minute to the next. A pair of Apache attack helicopters screamed past the Black Hawk and took up their positions in the lead, their avionics and ground sensor suites scanning for likely threats. The Black Hawk pilots talked casually over the radio to each other for some time, mostly recalling when they themselves were attack helicopter pilots and debating the pros and cons of the Super Warriors versus Marine Corp Cobras in a ground attack role. While the pilots conversed, the two loadmasters on either side of the aircraft were all nervous energy behind their M60 machine guns. They scanned above and below the aircraft, out to the sides and then back down at the ground again. Nothing was going to escape their careful scrutiny.

'Sir, we are going to put on some altitude and move into a holding pattern for a few minutes. Some Navy SEALs a few miles away have requested immediate air support, and our Apaches are going to go and provide them with some fire support until the Quick Reaction Force arrives.'

'Okay, Jody.' General Towers moved closer to the door of the airframe to get a better look below and spotted the two Apaches breaking formation. Far below he could see the cloud of a red smoke grenade and as he watched the first Apache lined up. The attack helicopter's tail came up and its speed increased. Towers could see the gun under the fuselage of the aircraft light up and then moments later the sound of the thirty-millimetre chain gun reached them. The Apache pulled up violently and banked hard to the right and the next helicopter moved in, its cannon raking the earth. Then it pulled up hard to the left to be replaced by the first helicopter again, and so they continued their large elliptical patterns of destruction. Towers could plainly see the Navy SEALs conducting a break contact through an open field below. They resembled tiny action figures in a kids' game, running for their lives. The group in the centre of the pack was dragging two prisoners with them. A small group of men at the front of the unit carried what looked like a casualty. On either flank, six men were laying down covering fire, the last man peeling from the back of the line when his magazine was empty so that the next man could take over the task. Towers could make out the whole scene; what he couldn't see was how the men's lungs screamed for oxygen, nor could he feel the stress of the situation and the stimulus assaulting their senses from every quarter, knowing that their casualty was one of their own and only moments from death. He couldn't see the precision with which the SEALs returned fire, nor the speed of the magazine changes, and he couldn't hear the Taliban yelling, screaming, urging each other forward as they sensed the Americans' imminent defeat.

A pair of Marine Corp Cobras arrived moments before the CH-47 Chinook that was sent to extract the Navy SEALs. It was a close-run thing. The Cobras hovered at the far end of the field and laid down a murderous barrage of covering fire. The Apaches came in again from another angle and released their rockets, stopping the Taliban's momentum. Then, no more than a few hundred metres in front of the Cobras, two huge explosions engulfed the Taliban positions. The blasts echoed down the deep valley. The F16 that had been vectored in to deliver the ordnance was already gone as fast as it had arrived.

'Okay, that's our bit of excitement for the day, sir,' Jody said nonchalantly. 'We should be in Tarin Kowt in about twenty minutes.'

'Thanks, Jody.' General Towers settled back in his seat, relieved that the SEALs were now on the CH-47 and out of harm's way. It wasn't every day that a general had a front-row seat at one of the many battles raging across the country.

After a moment, the general spoke again. 'Jody, pass on my compliments to the Apache pilots, would you, please? That was really very impressive.'

'Yes, sir, will do.'

37

KANDAHAR

'Fuck, fuck, FUCK!' Steph beat her fist against the side of the metal shipping container at the base of the stairs. Two Marine Corps guys heading back from Hungry Jack's to their unit billets rounded the corner at the same time that Steph was losing her mind.

'You alright, ma'am?' the bigger of the two jarheads enquired.

'Fuck off,' Steph snapped as she turned and walked back towards her office without so much as a glance at the marines.

How long could Faisal hold out if he's gone in the bag? she wondered as she climbed the last few stairs. *What will he say under interrogation, and why didn't I give him a better cover story? If he tells them I've been leaking information my life is over!*

She opened the airlock door and stepped into the oval room, which was buzzing with activity. Analysts yelled to each other and operations staff were busy monitoring video feeds and prioritising information.

'There you are, ma'am. The old man is looking for you.' Dawson was referring to Steph's boss, Mr Pritchard, the CIA Chief of Station in Afghanistan.

Steph was stunned. 'What's he doing here? He should be in Kabul. Did he say what it's about?' She looked nervously across the room. The Chief of Station wouldn't just drop in to *see* an analyst. A couple of American Delta Force guys, who were focused on the TV playing BBC on the end wall, looked at her for a moment then went back to their conversation about journalists and how much access was too much in Afghanistan.

Dawson's brow was furrowed. 'What? No, ma'am, he just said you should go in and see him – he's in the spare office.' He turned his attention back to the map and the common operating picture board that showed the blue force tracker, a GPS-based program that could identify friend from foe.

Steph swallowed hard, surreptitiously placing her hand on her pistol and feeling the magazine to make sure it was there and secure. Then she turned and walked towards Pritchard's office, contemplating her next move.

Pritchard was talking into his phone as Steph opened the door. He motioned for her to enter and to sit down. Pritchard looked like an older and shorter version of Morgan Freeman. His thirty-five years with the CIA could in fact have been made into a movie; his face was evidence that he had seen it all in his time.

Pritchard hung up the phone. 'Stephanie, it's been a long time. What are your sources up to?'

Steph recoiled in shock. What did the old man already know? She looked quickly around the room, scanning the whiteboard in hope of a clue. Steph's palms were sweating and she wiped them on the front of her cargo pants.

Pritchard continued, 'Task Force 42 were conducting a raid in Garesh and they triggered an IED. Two British Special Boat Service guys were killed in action and a few more were injured.' He paused, as if waiting for Steph to respond, but she was speechless. 'But that's not the worst of it, or maybe it is,' he went on. 'Two French journalists were snatched an hour ago on a road near Kapisa. The Taliban are trying to reinforce the area and the whole place is going crazy.'

Steph looked at him, unsure of what exactly he thought her role in this might be.

'Did you hear me, Stephanie?' the old man barked.

'Y-yes, sir, got it – French journalists,' Steph stuttered.

'Get onto your sources, Stephanie, and see if anyone knows where they have taken them.'

'Yes, sir.' Steph began to breathe more easily. It seemed she was off the hook.

'The commander of NATO Special Operations informed me that the Australian Special Air Service Regiment will be stood up to provide a quick response option once they have completed their current task. You need to go down to the joint intelligence fusion cell and see if any of the units have more information.'

'Okay, sir, I can do that.' Steph realised that this meant she also had a legitimate reason to check on Faisal's whereabouts.

'Get onto your contacts and find those journalists,' Pritchard urged. 'If we don't know their location within the hour, we probably never will – at least, not while they still have heads.'

'On it, sir.' Steph ran out of the room, pulling her cell phone out as she went. She clumsily thumbed Faisal's number. No response; his phone was either still switched off or dead.

38

DUTCH INTELLIGENCE COMPOUND, TARIN KOWT

Allie van Tanken adjusted her reading glasses so that she could better see the military symbols on the operations map. The map was stretched out over a large trestle table positioned in the centre of the square room.

'What do you make of this, Christopher?' Allie pointed to a series of red dots signifying the IED strikes within Uruzghan province over the past two years.

Christopher placed *The Devil's Guard*, the book that he was thumbing through, on top of the white book shelf. He looked over at where she was pointing. 'Why are you even looking there?' he said. 'Shouldn't we be searching for those French journalists? Anyway, it would seem that the strikes are mostly concentrated around the Mirabad Valley, with a few strikes further to the east as well – nothing special about that,' he said flippantly.

Allie could tell that he had lost interest in looking at the same map all morning. She looked at Christopher over the top of her glasses. At ten years her senior, he should have been a major by now, but he had been passed over because of his love of whisky. She pitied him; he had once been one of the sharpest analysts she had ever met, but now he was just marking time until retirement.

'No, Christopher, that's not all. Look closely at the dates. See? There's one in the east and then one in the west, then another in the east then another in the west. There's a pattern.'

'Yes, I see it.' Christopher was interested now. He looked at the map more closely. 'So the bomber must strike once in the east and then move to the west and set up another for the next day. Perhaps he's a creature of habit – or maybe it has to do with the supply location he's working from.'

'No, it can't be that – look at the distances. There must be two bombers working together, one in the east and one in the west. And look here: the pattern has definitely changed. The one in the east has continued his work, no change, targeting the entrances to bases or vehicle checkpoints – nearly all suicide bombings and probably detonated by someone watching. The one in the west has gone after the Australian commando platoon, just IEDs. Suddenly there is no pattern and they are attacks of circumstance and opportunity.'

'Maybe it's just a coincidence? Perhaps there's a third bomber who's working in the west against the commando platoon.'

'I already thought of that. But if you look at the Australians' missions in particular, they are getting hit on the last day of their patrol every time; sometimes the attacks are deadly and sometimes not, but they're always on the last day.'

'I'm not sure I follow.'

'Well, it seems to me that the bomber doesn't just know about their plan; Yankee Platoon is *part* of the plan.' Allie moved a strand of hair from her face and tied it back into her ponytail.

'Why do you even care about this Australian platoon? We really should be concentrating on the spotter network and their commentary on our Dutch air assets. What has this got to do with anything?'

'It's just that we know the Taliban have an informant. I think that what this means is that the information the informant is sending is about the Australian Yankee Platoon specifically. Now, everyone is looking that way, focusing on that – but what if there's more to it than that? What if they are showing us one thing and doing another?'

'That sounds complicated, Allie – too much so for the likes of some simple farmers.'

'You're a fool if you think we're dealing with simple farmers here, Christopher. This has all the trademarks of a planned operation – the type of operation that would have been conducted in a European war ...' She thought about this, tapping her upper lip with her index finger. 'Or perhaps in a time of supposed peace,' she said slowly. 'It's a Cold War tactic, which means we're dealing with a Cold War-trained operator. And if that's the case, the next time we hear from them it might be a spectacular attack.'

Allie showed Christopher the shared intelligence that had come across their system that morning, the photos from a handset in Zabul. 'Sam sent these across to me. He believes that these are the family members of Objective Rapier.' Allie watched as Christopher looked over the photos, stopping at Omar Defari.

'I see,' Christopher said. 'So you think that one of these guys could be the other bomber? Christopher moved the photo of Omar to one side. I take it that you also think that Quetta might be using Uruzghan as a central piece to their campaign planning this summer?'

'Yes, I do. I think that the focus on Yankee Platoon is a decoy, that there's something bigger going on. It might be time for me to talk to Matt Rix again.'

Allie was quietly pleased with this outcome; she had thought about Matt a lot since their first meeting. Perhaps this evening she would wander over to the Australian Special Forces compound . . .

39

CAMP RUSSELL, TARIN KOWT

'Captain Rix!' General Towers boomed. He stood atop the wooden steps of the Special Operations Task Group headquarters waiting for the platoon's arrival.

'What the – ? Stop the car, mate,' Matt said to the Bushmaster driver. Matt moved through the cupola and climbed down from the roof of the vehicle.

'Evening, sir.'

'Captain Rix,' the general repeated. 'That's quite a find Yankee Platoon made today. I was listening to the radio and Captain Long showed me the photos you sent through. Good work.'

'Thanks very much, sir. We brought back some of the components – those that were safe to handle. The rest of the equipment was destroyed.' Matt watched the general's face carefully, trying to detect any hint as to the type of conversation that was surely about to take place.

'How many suicide vests would you estimate were in the cache?'

There was nothing hostile in Towers's demeanour; as far as Matt could tell, the general's only interest was in what they had found.

'Not less than ten, I'd say.'

'Good God! All fitted with explosives?'

'Wired up and ready to blow. They didn't have any batteries attached, which is just as well.'

'How's that then? Were you worried the radios might trigger them or something of that nature?' Towers nodded a greeting to the rest of the platoon that had by now disembarked from the vehicles into the fading evening light. They slowly unpacked the Bushmasters and Matt knew they were trying to see what was happening between their commander and the general; no doubt they were as amazed as Matt to see General Towers here in person.

'No, sir, that's not the issue,' Matt explained, as the pair were joined by Terence Saygen. *Trust the SAS commander to want to get in on the act with the general*, Matt thought – though he had to admit he didn't think so badly of the guy after his apology earlier; that had taken guts.

'The thing is,' Matt continued, 'these were really sophisticated – every device was fitted with a chicken switch.'

'A chicken switch?' The general frowned. 'I don't follow, Captain Rix.'

Saygen chipped in. 'Devices that are designed so that someone watching the suicide bomber can set them off if the bomber fails to detonate himself – if he chickens out, that is.' Saygen looked at Matt and grinned.

'Or if the bomber is stopped – apprehended before he reaches the intended target,' Matt added.

'Yeah, it's sort of the next generation in suicide vests,' said Saygen.

The general was nodding. 'I see. So they could have been used as remote-controlled IEDs as well as suicide IEDs.'

'Yes, that's correct, sir,' said Saygen.

'Well, I'd hate to see the next generation after that,' added the general.

'Also, sir,' Matt chimed in, 'there were army and police uniforms down there, too. We brought a couple back but the rest were destroyed in place – and the other munitions down there, my god, the blast literally levelled the place. It was incredible.'

'Well, that'll be a huge blow to the Taliban – excuse the pun – getting those off the street. It will be interesting to see where those uniforms were stolen from.' The general lowered his voice. 'So, Rix, Captain Saygen has been telling me that you've had a rough time of it lately?'

'Yes, sir, it's been a difficult few months,' Matt said cautiously. *What was going on here? Was it possible the general hadn't had a chance to talk to the CO yet?*

'Yes, well, you've handled it all very well, Captain. I should think that the Distinguished Service Medal that I nominated you for in July will be some consolation. Suffice to say that your CO didn't move the nomination through like I asked him to, but that's taken care of now. I did come to thank you in person for your part in stopping the Taliban breaching the base, but you had been sent out on a mission.'

Matt's jaw dropped. 'Huh? I mean – excuse me, sir?'

'Fighting off the Taliban like that when they attacked the base was very inspiring, Rix – and in the finest traditions of the Australian army, I might add. My only criticism is that the infantry battalion CO won't stop complaining about the amount of applications for service in Special Forces he has had to sign since then.' The general gave a quick laugh and put his hand on Matt's shoulder.

'Sir, I have no idea what you are talking about.'

'No, no, of course you don't.' The general smiled across at Saygen. 'That figures, though. You can chalk it up to a growing list of things your CO didn't tell you about.'

Matt thought about this for a second. Then it occurred to him what must have happened; Sam must have gone over the CO's head to report the leak and the use of Yankee Platoon as bait.

'Well, sir, I'm just relieved that Captain Long saw fit to report it up the chain of command before anyone else was killed.'

Towers shook his head. 'It wasn't Captain Long – Captain Saygen here called me yesterday. Did you know Terence was on my Iraq headquarters staff as a junior intelligence officer in 2004? We have stayed in touch ever since.' General Towers sighed and shook his head. 'Captain Long was in a nasty predicament, it seems. Anyway, yours is not an unfounded hypothesis – as it turns out, Long had been keeping notes and making a case, but he has other masters too, and powerful ones at that. They advised him to maintain his silence on the issue as they have some bigger fish to fry.' The general waved his hand to signal that he couldn't discuss it further.

'I see,' Matt said. 'So what about the CO then, sir?'

'Well, the SOTG CO was already under investigation by the investigative service for not taking any action the night that the camp came under direct assault. It was an easy decision to relieve him of his post pending the outcome of a full investigation.

Lieutenant Colonel Mark Hoff is in transit now. Within a day or two he will assume command. Until then, the executive officer will take over.'

'Right, I see.' It was all happening so fast, Matt could barely take it in.

'Why don't you go and get cleaned up, get some dinner and then come by the office,' the general suggested. 'We have a few things to discuss, I think.' With a nod, the general moved up the steps and entered the building.

Matt turned to look at Saygen. 'Hey, man . . . I don't really know what to say.'

'It's all good, mate; we move on.'

'We move on, sure.'

With a smile on his face, Matt headed off to the barracks to tell his platoon the good news.

40

SPECIAL FORCES MESS HALL, CAMP RUSSELL

The Special Forces eating area was teeming with operators, each sitting in their respective group. All manner of conversations were taking place, ranging from the war in Afghanistan and old Soviet tactics to fly fishing techniques to be practiced while holidaying in New Zealand, or 'anywhere green and cold for that matter,' said one guy, sick of the sand pit. It wasn't Duck a l'Orange or lobster today, but the braised beef and Singapore noodle made a nice change.

Matt noticed that the men sitting opposite him had fallen silent and were staring open-mouthed. Looking over his shoulder, he saw the source of their shock: standing behind him was Allie van Tanken. *How could anyone look so beautiful in a t-shirt and cargos?* Matt asked himself.

'Uh, sure, Allie – have a seat.' Matt moved over to make a space for her beside him.

The Dutch officer sat down with her plate of food and looked around at the other five men sitting along the table. They all watched her, the meals in front of them forgotten.

'So, guys, perhaps you could leave Matt and I to talk for a bit,' Allie suggested. 'It looks like you have finished eating.'

'So is this like a date, ma'am?' said Ben Braithwaite, clearly relishing the opportunity to have a dig at his boss.

'No, not this time, Corporal – but soon, perhaps.'

Matt laughed, simultaneously reminding himself that Allie was joking; she was a professional colleague, and he should be looking on her as nothing more.

'Clear out, lads,' Matt said. 'I'll see you back in the common room later this evening.'

With a bit of good-natured grumbling the guys did as he asked, Cinzano tripping over his own feet as he left.

'How is everything, Matt?' Allie asked, fixing him with a concerned gaze.

'Yeah, good – it turns out you were right, Allie: my guys and I were being set up as bait. But I think it's sorted now. General Towers is here at the moment and our CO has been relieved.'

'But that doesn't explain the leak, does it?'

'Does it explain the leak?' Matt frowned. 'No,' he said slowly. 'I guess it doesn't.'

Allie leaned in closer. 'Listen, Matt, I plotted the IED strikes in Uruzghan over the last couple of years onto the map this afternoon, and I found something interesting . . .' She briefly outlined what she had seen in her trends analysis.

'So what do you think this big plan might be, if it's not just ongoing combat between us and them?'

'I'm not sure, Matt. Perhaps you've already averted it by destroying his cache. Just remember, though – it seems that there is more than one bomber. Rapier's *a* guy, but he's not necessarily *the* guy. I just thought you should know.'

Matt looked at the Dutch officer intently; the mess had started to clear out now and there were only a handful of people sitting around talking over coffees. 'I have this overwhelming urge to kiss you, Allie,' he confessed. He grinned sheepishly. 'I'm sorry if that's too forward.'

'Better save that for our first date.' Allie winked, then stood up. 'See you soon, Matt.'

Matt watched Allie leave and wondered what it would be like to be in a relationship with a woman like that. She was an enigma to him; she wasn't soft at all but she was feminine. Nor was she needy. In fact, to Matt she seemed strong and, if anything, he was more attracted to her because of that. Matt thought back to Rachel, and to other girls in his life. He had loved them at the time, but there was always something missing for him. This was it; he had finally met a woman who was self-assured and demanded to be treated like an equal. That 'soon' couldn't come quickly enough for him.

• • •

Sam rose quickly from his desk and hastened to the door of the CO's office, only to remember that the CO wasn't there anymore. He took a step backwards, not really sure what to make of this new information. Perhaps it was nothing. He looked down at the handful of pink papers he was clutching then moved back to his seat. The phone report was detailed and the list of numbers on

Faisal's phone linked him to networks all over the country and abroad. Sam's junior analyst had highlighted one number in green no less than thirty times over the last five months of recorded history. It was a mobile number from Kandahar – and it belonged to Stephanie Baumer.

Sam tapped his pen on his desk and looked at his own phone. Reaching over, he picked up the handset and punched in Steph's desk extension.

It rang only once before it was picked up. 'Hello?'

Sam thought Steph sounded tired. 'Steph, it's Sam Long here. I think we need to have a chat.'

There was silence on the other end of the line then Steph gave a nervous laugh. Sam could hear the murmur of voices in the background; she obviously wasn't alone. Lowering her voice, she said, 'Really, Sam? What is there to chat about exactly?'

'Well, we could start with you telling me why it is that your phone number was found on a cell phone belonging to one of our targets, Steph.'

Steph's voice was barely a hiss as she replied, 'Is that so? Well, I've already talked to Geoff Langston about this, Sam. One of my contacts was missing at the time, perhaps in Pakistan.'

Sam glanced again at the report he was holding and leaned back in his chair. He felt himself becoming increasingly suspicious. 'Well, his phone wasn't in Pakistan. Interestingly, you called the number at almost the exact time when the assault team made entry in Tarin Kowt. That's a strange coincidence, don't you think?'

'It's a coincidence, Sam, and that's about all it is; I don't see how it's strange at all.' Steph was sounding more confident now. Her tone became aggressive. 'Sam, I'm not sure exactly what you're implying, but you had better tread carefully. I could elevate this up the chain of command, if you like?'

'There's no need to be like that, Steph. I'm merely asking for the facts. The way I see it, the SOTG cleared a building and lifted a guy who had your number in his phone, and we were not given any warning that an informant would be on the target. I just wanted to make sure that there wasn't a breakdown in procedure.'

'I have many contacts working all over Afghanistan and chances are some of them are going to get caught up in raids from time to time. I don't see the issue. Now if you've quite finished, I have reports to write.'

Sam looked over the paper again.

'Well, Sam?' she said impatiently. 'Are you done prying for today?'

Sam sat straight bolt upright, the information jumping off the page and almost knocking him from his seat. 'What the fuck?' Sam couldn't believe his eyes.

'Goodbye, Sam.'

'Not so fast, Steph.' Sam leaned over his desk, frowning as he scanned through the dates in his head. 'It looks like you've called this number the day before every operation Yankee Platoon has been on over the past three months.'

'What are you talking about, Sam?' The CIA analyst sounded anxious now.

'That's no coincidence, Steph. Jesus, have you been tipping off the Taliban?' Sam couldn't even believe he had said the words out loud.

'No, Sam, don't be stupid!' He heard her suck in a breath. 'I'm not the only intelligence officer who controls human informants,' she said meaningfully.

Sam thought about it for a moment, trying to figure out who she might mean. Then it occurred to him. 'Do you mean Allie van Tanken, the Dutch intel officer?' he asked.

'Let's not talk about this any further over an unsecure line. Perhaps we had better meet; I can explain to you what's happening, bring you into the compartment, so to speak. But you have to keep this to yourself. Can you do that, Sam?'

Sam felt uneasy. The thought of uncovering another compartmented mission was truly worrying.

'Okay, Steph,' he said finally. He looked down at the times and dates of the calls; it was a worrying coincidence indeed. Then he noticed something that his analyst had missed. In the next column of outgoing calls there was a number that Faisal would ring not long after the call from Steph. The number seemed familiar. Maybe it was a pattern in the zeros that he had seen before. He couldn't be sure, but it was familiar.

'Good. When are you in Kandahar?' asked Steph.

'Next week, I think.'

'Right, well, we can meet then and I'll explain everything.' She hung up abruptly.

Sam replaced the handset. *What the hell did it all mean?* he wondered.

Sam typed the new number that he had found into his database, not really expecting anything to come from it.

'Holy FUCK! You've got to be joking.' Sam was gobsmacked. Faisal Khan was calling Matt's terp, Nadeem Karne, not long after talking to Steph. It was clear from the report in front of him that Steph was the leak; that much was certain. But *what* was she leaking? And now it was clear that she wasn't the only leak, or the most dangerous.

Sam thought about the decisions that he now faced; expose Steph, alert Matt to the leak from inside his own platoon or deal with Faisal directly.

'Faisal Khan,' said Sam under his breath as he read the name from the top of the report. 'Hmm, perhaps if you were lifted off the street, you might be able to answer a few simple questions and shed some light on all of this, Mr Khan . . .'

41

ALEXANDRIA, EGYPT

A small beachside cafe in a quiet coastal town outside Alexandria might not seem like an obvious place to find a senior Taliban leader enjoying the morning sun. However, Mustafa Walid was not your average Taliban commander. The sixty-five-year-old had forgotten more about war than the younger Taliban would ever know. As a young man, he had studied at Cairo University, and he was there when the Soviets first entered Afghanistan. It didn't take long for the call of the Mujahedeen to reach Egypt and he answered the call to arms, as did hundreds of other young Egyptian Muslims just like him. He dreamed only of the fight when he was younger, but ideology and principle soon gave way to a sinister version of capitalism. Forty years later and Mustafa still enjoyed the fight, except these days his weapon was information. Having risen through the ranks of the Taliban, Mustafa now controlled most of the money flowing in and out of Afghanistan – as well as another, more dangerous commodity.

Mustafa looked at the watch – a Rolex Submariner – hanging loosely on his wrist.

'Cheque, thank you,' he said, squinting up at the waiter who stood silhouetted against the glare. Mustafa stretched out his legs and revelled in the cool breeze coming off the calm blue ocean. His lightweight trousers, boat shoes and collared shirt gave him the appearance of a tanned English gentleman enjoying a Mediterranean vacation.

'Certainly,' said the portly waiter as he cleared the breakfast plate and ashtray from the table. 'Your friends didn't join you again this morning, sir?'

'No, they were only here for a short holiday. They left yesterday.' Mustafa enjoyed the clumsy enquiries of the waiter, who he knew reported back to the ever-watchful Muslim Brotherhood. *They were such amateurs,* Mustafa thought. Still, he would have to see to it that the waiter met with an accident sometime in the near future; no sense taking risks. A single chime from his pocket alerted him to the SMS that had just arrived on his old Nokia phone. He reached for the phone and, holding it under the table, read the message.

Holiday booking request flashed up on the screen.

Mustafa thought about the message for a time, his attention mostly focused on a small fishing boat that was making its way out of the harbour, the crew on the deck running back and forth as they prepared for the day's fishing. After a while he turned his attention back to the phone and typed a reply.

Please send traveller details and when they would like to travel.

A message came back to Mustafa in seconds.

Traveller is a library worker from Quandha and she needs to leave soon.

Mustafa considered this. 'Library' was code for the CIA and Quandha was the ancient name for Kandahar. This would require a specialist and would not be cheap. The person on the other end of the message was not unknown to Mustafa and would know what was involved.

Approved pending payment, he replied.

Mustafa had barely typed the message and hit the send button before his iPhone, sitting on the table, vibrated.

HSBC: NOV 2010 – Credit Telegraphic
Transfer from 011–547********* USD 350,000

The accountant in Kabul was efficient, that much is true, thought Mustafa. He smiled and looked out at the fishing boats bobbing around gently in the sheltered port. He turned his attention from the iPhone back to the Nokia, looking up only briefly to check that the waiter was still behind the counter. Opening a new SMS, he typed out the name of a young Afghan soldier in Kandahar and pressed send.

Again, the response was instant.

Good, we will make the preparations to send them both on holidays next week.

Mustafa thumbed through his wallet and placed seventy Egyptian pounds on the table to cover his meal and morning coffee. Rising out of the blue wooden chair he set off and crossed over to the esplanade.

'Until tomorrow then, sir?' called the nosy waiter to Mustafa's back as he crossed the busy road.

'Sure, sure, of course, see you then,' yelled Mustafa happily, followed by 'You slimy fat prick' under his breath. The waiter wouldn't live to see the next sunrise, he decided. He would sort that out later today.

As Mustafa reached the other side of the road, he looked at the two old men who were using long rods to dab at the water; they gave Mustafa a cursory glance and then went back to their fishing. He walked on for another fifty metres and then pulled the old Nokia out of his pocket. He twisted the case, prising it apart with his thumbs. He dropped the battery on the ground and then threw the phone over the sea wall and into the water. He continued on another few metres and then dropped the SIM card into a drain grate as he passed over it.

Mustafa would take fifty thousand dollars for himself, two hundred thousand would go to the suicide bomber's family on completion of the mission – setting the family up for life – and the balance would be sent forward to the Taliban commander, Mullah Omar's, coffers. The suicide bomber would be remembered as a great martyr and the person requesting the hit would be rid of a small problem. Mustafa's vision ten years prior of establishing a network of Pakistani teenagers all infected with HIV had now given the Taliban a remorseless weapon, but this new addition to the arsenal, the Afghan police and army members who were willing to die in the name of Allah, was going to change the war.

42

CAMP RUSSELL, TARIN KOWT

Mark Hoff took a sip of the Nescafé that had been given to him moments earlier by General Towers. Sitting behind the previous CO's desk, he looked around the office and couldn't help but notice the speed at which his predecessor must have left. An open bottle of Evian still sat on the desk, half full, amid a pile of scattered official papers. The computer was on and the screen saver was requesting the Defence Restricted Network access code; in the corner of the room a drawer was open; and a couple of maps had been tossed unceremoniously onto the bottom shelf of the bookcase.

'It turns out this phone is a gold mine, sir,' Sam Long was saying. The intelligence officer was sitting on the leather couch opposite the general. The general was looking over the report that had been completed by Sam's team as he sipped his own coffee, and was showing genuine interest in the findings.

'How's that then, Sam?' asked Mark. He swept the official papers into a single pile and straightened them.

'Well, it seems that Faisal Khan was very good at deleting both his messages and the register of calls made and received, so on the face of it the phone would appear empty. However, these Nokias have a trash cache that has to be emptied as well. It's a pretty simple process, but one that Faisal seems not to have known about.'

'So there's some intelligence value to the phone then?' said Mark.

'Some! I'd say there's more than just some, sir – every message sent and received and every phone number ever to call this phone or be called by it is now on my computer. It links together most of the Taliban network across Afghanistan, including Objective Rapier and all his associates, it identifies the human network spies who are working for both sides and it identifies individuals in Quetta, Egypt and Syria who are operating with the Taliban.'

General Towers looked at Mark and then back at Sam. 'How do we move forward from here then, Sam?'

'Well, sir, we've narrowed down the areas where Faisal has been working, and we know the people he has influence with. I think if we offered the right amount of cash the human intelligence network would give him up. He's on the run; I say we pick him up – send SAS to snatch him.'

'I don't know about that, Sam; the SAS troop are bouncing all over Afghanistan with Delta Force looking for those two journalists who've gone missing. I doubt they have the capacity to do this as well.' The general looked across at Mark. 'What's your take on it, Mark?'

'I agree with Sam's assessment, sir,' said Mark. 'I think if we lift this Faisal character we might be able to target a much larger portion of the network; it might also lead us straight to Rapier. It sounds like he's had a foot in each camp for a while and it's only a matter of time before one of those camps snatches him – better that it's us. I think sending in a whole troop would be overkill though. Better to do this discreetly: a pair of operators, plainclothes, supported by a platoon acting as a Quick Reaction Force should the operators need it.'

'A platoon? Sounds like you have Rix and his men in your sights for this, Mark.'

'Rix is highly capable, sir – one of my best. Rix and his platoon sergeant can nab Khan, I'm sure of that.'

'Yes, it's a shame that the previous CO didn't share your faith in them.'

'There's just a couple more things, sir,' Sam interjected. The two superior officers turned to him. 'There's the case of Matt's interpreter and the two missing uniforms.'

'Indeed, Sam.' The general nodded. 'We can't arrest Nadeem Karne just yet as it will most probably alarm Faisal Khan.'

'Agreed, sir, we should get to him after Khan. We can loan him across to SAS for a few days, on the low down, so that we know whatever Rix is doing is going to be a secret,' suggested Hoff.

'And as to the uniforms, sir,' continued Sam, 'the results of the tests on those samples Rix and his men brought back were rather alarming. Faisal and his men certainly had a sophisticated weapon with those uniforms. Five kilograms of Semtex woven into the cotton fabric.' He whistled.

'It would have been devastating if those had ever seen the light of day as part of a wider, more orchestrated plan,' Hoff agreed.

'Rix probably changed the course of history with that find; I was as surprised as anyone else when I saw the lab results.' Sam opened his notebook to look back over his previous entry. 'The problem is, if Faisal is in possession of the last two we might lose the snatch team altogether – and it's almost certain that he does or did have them.'

'Yes, I agree, Sam . . . and that's why we're not sending in the SAS.' The general turned and looked straight at Mark. 'Isn't that right, Mark?' The general's tone was even.

Mark shifted uncomfortably in his seat. 'It's a consideration, sir, of course.'

'I'm no fool, Mark,' the general reminded him.

'No, sir, and I didn't take you as one.'

'You were an SAS troop commander, isn't that right, Mark?' The general wore a small smile now.

'Yes, sir.'

'And now you find yourself in the unenviable position of being the replacement CO of the Special Operations Task Group more than three-quarters of the way through the rotation.' General Towers stood up and rolled his shoulders as if to reinforce his point.

'I'm not sure what you mean, sir.'

'Of course you do, Mark; risk mitigation is the name of the game at this point in your career.' The general let the comment sit for a moment without elaborating.

'We need to lift Faisal, but more importantly we need those two last uniforms off the street. If Faisal delivers them to the right person then we have no way of knowing who they will hit or when they will strike. Anyway, you get settled in here, Mark, get your head around the mess that was left behind, and try to make some sense of the current operating environment. I'll brief Rix personally. Sam, you get your network searching for Faisal and keep me updated.'

'Yes, sir, we're already on it.'

As if on cue, General Towers opened the door to find Sam's intelligence corporal lurking in the corridor outside.

'Oh, g'day, sir, is Sam in there?' The corporal poked his head through the doorway and looked around.

'I'm right here, Frankie. What's up, mate?' Sam got up from the sofa. 'This is Corporal Franks,' he added for the benefit of Mark and General Towers.

'We found your boy, Faisal, sir.' Corporal Franks smiled at Sam and nodded his head towards Mark, who had risen from behind his desk and was walking over to join the others near the door.

'Really?' said Sam. 'Good timing.'

'One of the network was telling us about the raid on the motorcycle shop. He was looking for compensation and complaining that the commandos blew it sky-high. He told us that Abdul Rahman had fled to Kabul and that Faisal was with him when they left.'

'Great, he's in Kabul – it shouldn't take a couple of men too long to find him,' Mark Hoff observed sarcastically.

'Wait, sir, there's more. The informant said that Rahman's brother is a university lecturer in Kabul. Well, we have some sources in the university. The brother was overheard telling a colleague that Abdul and a friend are staying with him for a few days.'

'Bingo!' said Sam. 'Nice work, Frankie. I'll get the target packs together, General Towers. We should be able to brief Rix in about three hours, if that suits you.'

'Very good, Sam, I'll meet you in the conference room.'

The intelligence officers were heading for the door when some-thing occurred to Mark. 'Corporal Franks?' he said.

'Yes, sir?'

'Out of interest, what exactly does Abdul Rahman's brother lecture in? Do you know his speciality?'

'Finance, sir. I think he's like an accountant or something.'

'Right, I see. So he's a university lecturer and is still alive even though his brother is the friend of a high-ranking Taliban. That's fascinating. Maybe that's also worth asking Faisal about, Sam.'

43

BAGRAM AIR BASE, KABUL

It was close to 4 am when the C-27 Spartan transport landed at Kabul airport. Matt and JJ had just finished going over the plan again with Sam Long. They were together down the back of the aircraft, huddled over a cargo pallet reviewing a map of Kabul. The three of them had to shout to hear each other over the two Allison turboprops. Daniel Barnsley, the Yankee Platoon signaller, lay curled up in a ball at their feet, fast asleep.

'Seriously, how does he do that?' asked JJ.

'It's a gift he has.' Matt placed his foot on Barnsley's side to prove the point. 'He'd keep on sleeping if we fell out of the frigging sky. Speaking of which . . .'

The plane landed with a large thud and the three men braced themselves against the cargo pallet. The pilots changed the pitch of the giant propellers and the engines became deafening as they worked to assist the big plane slowing its run along the tarmac. Matt reached down and shook the signaller from his slumber.

A few minutes later, the four men were out on the runway and in the cool pre-dawn air. The fumes of aviation gas mixed with the smells emanating from a kitchen somewhere out in the darkness, where cooks hurriedly fried eggs for the ground staff already awake across the base. The commandos offloaded two black trunks into the back of a waiting white Toyota troop carrier parked at the rear of the C-27, followed by their daypacks and an array of personal weapons.

'Have we forgotten anything, JJ?'

'Nope, she's all here, boss.' JJ slapped a giant paw on the roof of the troopie to signal to the driver that they were ready. They moved along the dark runway for a few hundred metres, then turned off into the support area of the sprawling military air base.

'When we get to the hangar, JJ, we'll offload the equipment and then set up the radios for Barns so that he can talk back to the command centre in Kandahar. After that's done we'll review the mission then get our heads down for a few hours' sleep.' Matt looked at JJ and could just see him smiling in the darkness.

'I can't actually believe the general has authorised us to do this, boss,' JJ said in wonder.

'It's crazy, right? But if we're going to get these things off the street then it makes sense to go after this guy. He's either going to lead us to them or spill the beans as to where they are. Besides, this war hasn't had nearly enough real Special Forces missions.'

'Yeah, agreed. So with a bit of luck, we'll snatch him alive.'

'That's the plan, mate.'

The troopie pulled up to one of the many nondescript grey hangars lining the airfield apron. The huge roller doors slowly shuddered open, revealing a dusty and sparse area in which the guys were to set up their equipment.

They jumped out of the vehicle and moved inside to survey the area. Once the equipment was unloaded they reviewed the plan again. It was midday when the work was done and Matt and JJ crashed out on a couple of steel stretchers that Barnsley had set up for them in a side room.

. . .

A few hours later, Matt's watch alarm bleeped gently on his wrist. For a moment he forgot where he was. Looking around the small room, he could see that it had once housed big machines, though all that remained now were the giant bolts that had once secured them to the floor. Slowly Matt remembered the flight into Kabul and the plan to go catch Faisal. Rolling over, he picked up a plastic water bottle from the floor and drank. He then rose and walked out into the large hangar, where he found JJ toying with his modified M4 rifle.

'You happy with it, JJ?' Matt asked.

'I think so. This one has a shorter ten-inch barrel, ACOG sight and the latest generation laser system. I can hide it fairly easily too.' JJ adjusted the sling and let the M4 drop down by his side. His big frame meant that the rifle all but disappeared against his body. 'What are you going in with, boss?'

Matt opened one of the black trunks and pulled out an MP5K – a short-barrelled machine pistol from the Heckler & Koch range.

'I love this weapon. It's not super powerful, but with a thirty-round magazine and a couple of spares in my pockets it should do the trick. No fancy sights either; just a small IR laser to use with the NVGs and an old-school barrel sight. This gun on a bungee, hidden under my robes, will be devastating to anyone who gets in our way.'

'Awesome. A couple of grenades and a pistol each and I think we'll have enough to start a war,' JJ said.

'Or to stop one from getting any worse,' Matt replied. 'Right, let's go over the plan one more time.'

• • •

The beat-up old Hilux turned out of the base and silently made its way along the back tracks, turning left into a small settlement on the outskirts of the base. From there the vehicle slowly made its way into Kabul proper.

Matt sat in the passenger seat dressed in the traditional brown robes and pakol cap of the Afghans; with a scarf around his neck and a two-week-old beard, he could pass in the dark as a local. JJ sat quietly in the back, his huge body hidden under his black robes and a brown shemagh wrapped around his head. He was slumped low in the seat to deceive any onlookers as to his size.

The late-night traffic increased and pedestrians started to move in and around the cars as they slowed. The quiet streets had become busy arteries of commerce. People spilled from the cafes and restaurants out onto the footpath. The return of electricity to Kabul after a large scale operation to secure the power lines coming in from Uzbekistan meant that the city's streets once again had lighting. As a result, the locals now ventured out after dark.

JJ broke the silence. 'Boss, what if Sam's guy is tricking us? What if he isn't there to guide us in at all and we're about to go in the bag?'

Matt had been thinking the same thing but had reassured himself that Sam had a good handle on his informant. 'Well, it's not the first time we've had to take a gamble over here, is it?'

'No, well, when you put it that way . . .' JJ said.

Matt looked across at the smiling Afghan driver. He had once been an interpreter for the Mentoring and Reconstruction Task Force, but the intelligence community had found him to be more effective as a double agent. This suited the driver as he was quite partial to money. Matt reminded himself that the driver would understand every word that he said.

The crew cab approached a blocked roundabout and the vehicle came to a stop. Up ahead, a uniformed police officer waved cars in all directions. Overlooking the road and set back a few hundred metres was a long row of decrepit white buildings, erected in the 1950s. Seven storeys high, they contained all manner of local businesses; small takeaway shops, tailors, drycleaners, hardware shops and accountancy firms. Matt looked out at the other cars locked in all around them. Some had families in them, kids jumping around from the back seats to the front seats with the parents seeming oblivious to what was going on. Other cars had blackened windows, so you couldn't see who was inside.

Next to their car was a man in a beat-up old Nissan Sunny, sitting patiently, smoking and picking his nose. Motorbikes were streaming down the edges of the road past the stationary traffic.

'Yankee Alpha, this is Acorn One, come in – over.'

'Send it,' said Matt, adjusting the small bone mic in his right ear.

'The drone has the traffic thinning out up ahead. Location Six Three Delta is five hundred metres on the right, two hundred metres past the roundabout; I put you there in around twelve minutes. The target is confirmed to be on site.'

'Acknowledged, Acorn.'

'Good luck, Yankee Alpha – Acorn out.'

'Shit, JJ, this just got fucking real, mate,' Matt said.

The man in the Nissan Sunny looked across at Matt, his finger buried in his snout to the first knuckle, and then he looked slowly away. Matt sighed with relief. They had got this far undetected; next stop: Target Six Three Delta.

44

TARGET SIX THREE DELTA

The crew cab turned off the highway and started slowly down the narrow street. Behind them the traffic kept crawling along, oblivious to the two-man snatch team that was about to execute their task.

'That's it on the left.' The driver pulled over by the kerb. A few hundred metres down the street stood a three-storey building nestled between two larger buildings. Someone stood in front of the doorway smoking a cigarette. When he saw the vehicle he flicked the cigarette across the street and then lit another one. Once it was lit he moved slowly away, leaving an old bicycle leaning against the wall next to the closed door.

'Yep, that's the indicator there,' the driver said. 'That door leads to where Faisal has been sleeping.'

Matt felt the excitement pulse through his veins. The car moved off – past the bike, past the door and down the next side street. The driver slowed the car once more and parked.

Matt turned to him. 'Okay, listen up; there's no change to the plan that we've already gone over. Stay right here until we return. But if you hear shooting, that's when you start to count down from five minutes. Once five minutes has elapsed, you are to drive fast right up to the front door. If we're not there, then leave us. We are either dead or I have called in the Quick Response Force. You understand?'

'Of course, no problem.' The driver was nonchalant; in fact, a little too relaxed for Matt's liking. 'And if I hear an explosion,' he quipped, 'then I take it you're dead and just leave anyway.' He laughed a little and looked at the two men as if inviting them to share the joke.

Matt narrowed his eyes and looked at the driver. 'I'll let you use your own judgment – but for your own sake, if you do leave us, we had better be dead.'

The driver's smile faded at the threat.

Matt climbed out of the car and JJ followed suit. The distant highway noise covered the sound of the car's doors closing. The street was narrow and lined with rubbish and rubble from the decrepit old buildings.

'You ready, JJ?'

'Yeah, I think so. We'll soon find out, I guess.'

'We've rehearsed this sort of thing during our tactical assault training, and if it goes noisy we have the firepower to get ourselves out of any danger,' Matt assured him.

'I'm good, boss.' JJ straightened up and adjusted the sling under his robes. The M4 dropped down next to his right arm.

Matt pressed the small rubber button held by a Velcro strap on the inside of his left wrist. 'Barns, you got me, mate?'

The reply came over the bone mic inserted in Matt's left ear. 'This is Yankee Charlie, loud and clear – over.'

'Roger that, Barns. What's the news from sky view?'

The reply from the signaller took a little longer this time; Matt knew that Barnsley would need to look at the Predator feed that was being sent to a digital screen next to his radio stack.

The signaller came back over the radio. 'It's all clear, boss. No movement around or on top of Target Six Three Delta.'

Matt took a deep breath. 'Okay, JJ, I'm heading off.'

Matt moved forwards out of the moonlight and into the shadows. He had one hand inside his robes, wrapped firmly around the pistol grip of the H&K MP5K.

JJ gave him twenty seconds and then he too moved off.

The two men followed the building's wall back to the corner and then turned down into the slightly wider target street. Approaching the door, Matt could see that it was closed and that it opened out into the street. He stopped and reached into his pocket for the lock-picking tools. Moving forward again, with the thin sliver of metal in his left hand, he climbed the three steps up to the door, glancing over his shoulder to make sure there was no one watching. He slowly bent down closer to the door to manipulate the tumbler. The door jerked open abruptly and Matt looked up in surprise to be met by the equally shocked face of a man he could identify from his briefing as Abdul Rahman, the owner of the shop Yankee Platoon had rolled days before in Tarin Kowt.

Matt sprung from the crouched position, leading with his forearm and catching Rahman across the throat. Matt quickly locked his other arm around and behind Rahman's neck, closing off his windpipe.

Rahman clawed at the back of Matt's head in a futile attempt to release himself from the death grip. His mouth opened in a scream but no sound emerged.

Matt tightened his grip, putting all his strength into the hold. Rahman dropped his hands from Matt's head and scrabbled in vain for the small pistol in his belt. But he was losing oxygen quickly; his legs buckled underneath him and his eyes started to bulge. Matt kept his grip tight as the life drained from Abdul's body.

JJ came in through the door and closed it softly behind him.

Matt, still holding the dead Afghan, looked up and gave him a nod.

The sergeant pulled out his NVGs, positioned them on his head and cleared the rest of the entrance to the building.

'He's done, boss. You can let him go,' JJ whispered.

Matt released his grip on the lifeless form. JJ pulled out a small box the size and shape of an inkpad. Removing the pistol from Rahman's grip, he closed the lid over the dead man's fingers, then placed the box back in his pocket.

Matt stood up, trying to slow down his own laboured breathing. He was still shaking from the exertion; he'd forgotten the effort it took to kill a man with your bare hands. He put on his own NVGs. Both men turned on their lasers and started off down the corridor.

JJ led them slowly through the first room. The only noise was the sound of his soft footsteps. They moved noiselessly up the first flight of stairs, crossed the first landing and began to ascend the next flight. JJ had his rifle out in front covering their movement.

Matt strained hard to hear above the noise of his own heartbeat, which was taking some time to come down after the business downstairs. JJ stopped and Matt moved up and took over the lead as they approached the next landing. Then Matt stopped and JJ slowly went past as Matt covered him up to the final landing: textbook urban movement.

Matt approached JJ and squeezed his left shoulder to indicate that he was now ready to make entry into the room. JJ pushed gently on the wooden door and it creaked open to reveal a dark space. The room was small, four by four metres, and there under an open window was a steel-framed bed. Matt could just make out a figure lying on the bed. He moved to JJ's left and out of the now-open doorway, often referred to as the fatal funnel. JJ went the opposite way and the two of them methodically cleared the room. They met at the foot of the bed. JJ approached with caution and Matt saw that the person was asleep on his back, only his head visible above the blankets. Was it him? He peered through the night-vision goggles and exhaled slowly. Yes: they had found Faisal Khan.

Slowly, JJ raised his M4 to the sleeping man's head. Matt covered JJ's back, which was now facing the open door. JJ flicked a quick glance at Matt, who gave him a nod back. JJ thrust the rifle barrel straight into the man's mouth, pinning his head against the pillow. Khan woke instantly and started dry-retching against the steel barrel.

JJ whispered to him in Arabic: 'Let go of the rifle and put your hands above your head where I can see them or I will put a hole in the back of your throat.'

Faisal Khan slowly raised his arms. Matt moved behind him and secured plastic cuffs over his wrists. JJ removed the barrel from his mouth and Matt shoved a balled-up sock in and then taped Khan's mouth shut. JJ passed Matt a black hood from his trouser pocket and the platoon commander slipped it over Khan's head.

As JJ dragged their captive to his feet, Matt produced a cloth bag and went around the room. Anything that looked like a personal belonging was stuffed into the bag.

'Boss, what's that under the bed?' JJ motioned to a cardboard box.

'Bullshit, it couldn't be that easy.' Matt grabbed the box from under the bed and gently lifted the lid. 'Jackpot, JJ! Let's get out of here.' The two made their way back down the hall, JJ dragging Faisal Khan effortlessly behind him and Matt carrying the cardboard box and the bag. Matt checked out the front door. The street was quiet.

'Barns – Bondi Junction. I say again: Bondi Junction.'

'Acknowledged.'

The radio went quiet. In the car around the corner, the driver's phone vibrated three times and then went quiet. He started the car and slowly moved off from the kerb and drove around the corner towards the front door of the target. When the Hilux arrived, Matt calmly exited the building and opened the rear passenger door. JJ appeared moments later and threw Khan onto the back seat. JJ followed him in, punching Khan in the head and then sitting on his back, pinning him to the seat.

'Let's go,' said Matt as he climbed in beside the driver.

'Too easy, bro,' said the driver, sounding almost American.

Matt looked across at him; his relaxed demeanour seemed appropriate now; Matt found that he was beginning to warm to him.

45

'You can't go in there, sir.'

Matt tried the door again. It was locked.

'Sir, you're not authorised to go in there.'

'Not authorised? What the hell are you talking about?' Matt turned to face the guard, an MP sergeant who had processed Faisal Khan earlier that week. 'You saw me bring him in here only two days ago.'

'I'm just doing my job, sir. There's a process and the interrogators won't allow anyone who isn't a part of that process into the cells.'

Matt knew it was pointless to argue. For all the bad press, they were sticklers for the rules – in most cases, anyway.

• • •

Only thirty metres away, on the other side of several thick metal doors, Faisal Khan was secured to a single hook in the ceiling with rusty chains that pulled his arms above his head; the rest of his weight was on his knees on the floor.

He kneeled there in a state of constant agony. The shackles cut into his wrists and he sobbed at the pressure. His hair, once slicked back, was dirty and matted. The air of quiet confidence he had worn before the shock of his capture forty-eight hours earlier had disappeared; now he was timid and scared.

The music started again, playing very softly in the background, and Faisal let out a small sob. During the next two hours, Don McLean's 'American Pie' would be played over and over again, increasing in volume each time until it was blaring into his cell. This would herald the entry of the four huge dogs (wolves as far as Faisal was concerned) that would come in barking and snarling. The last time they'd raced right up to him, their breath hot on his skin, their teeth touching his cheeks as they threatened to tear his face off. Then the music would stop, except that Faisal would think he could still hear it. Finally, the little bald man would come in and softly ask his questions and the words would just blurt out of Faisal's mouth, he couldn't stop them; the presence of the small man, with all of his promises and suggestions, was so reassuring after the music and the dogs.

Faisal squinted up at a crack in the ceiling. In one of the corners light broke through the darkness where the cell was slightly larger than the room above it. Every time someone walked above, dust would fall down through the ceiling. It seemed to dance in the shard of light that streamed through the crack. The light brought with it the promise of a world outside the small one he now found himself in. The presence and absence of the light was only the sign of the passage of days outside this room in which time seemed random and unpredictable.

Food was forced on him when his captors felt like it and water was provided if they decided he was thirsty. The temperature never really changed down in the cell. It was always hot. It was always dusty. The air was thick with the smell of his own waste. Every now and then his captors would come down and throw another bucket of dirty water over him. The putrid water would soak his clothes. The liquid that ran off him drained to the corner of the room, leaving a muddy trail of water and waste.

Faisal wished he were dead.

• • •

Matt had left the holding area when he heard a voice behind him.

'Hey, Matt, wait up!'

He turned and watched as Sam hurried up the path towards him.

'What's news, Sam?' Matt asked.

'He's singing like a bird, mate. More information than we can use on this rotation, that's for sure.'

'What about the other uniform, the missing one with the explosives in it? Did he give any indication as to where that went?'

'No, and I'm not even sure he knows, to be honest. I think Rapier might have had a hand in that though – which is fortuitous, as he confirmed the location of Rapier's home about an hour ago.'

Matt felt his pulse quicken. 'Is this for real? Are you sure he's not just telling us what he wants us to hear?'

'Walk with me for a minute, Matt; I'm on my way to the mess hall. Something about the smell of a captive man makes me ravenous.'

'Jesus, Sam, you and JJ should swap bloody notes. You're both sick in the head.'

Sam laughed. 'Maybe you're right. Anyway, a few weeks back a drone picked up a signal from an old handset of Rapier's high up in the mountains in the province, close to the border with Pakistan. We've never been able to place Rapier there and have never had a confirmation that he is actually even from there.'

'Until now.'

'Yeah, until now; Faisal just blurted it out after we tricked him and told him that it was Ahmed Defari himself who told us where he was staying in Kabul. Seems loyalty isn't a Taliban trait.'

'What else did he have to say?'

'He mostly confirmed what we already know: the uniforms are made of a super space-age material, military-grade explosives sewn into the garment – no metal content except for an igniter disguised as a button, controlled by a special pen that is electronically matched to the uniform. It's a state-sponsored manufacture, and it seems that Iran is involved, or Pakistan; it's hard to be sure really.'

'Jesus! How many more are of those things are out there?' Matt's mind reeled at the implications.

'Well, none, other than the missing one – at least I don't think there are. It seems that some gunrunners in Libya designed them, and sold them on just before they were topped off by the Israelis – an Egyptian guy had received them. He's a Taliban facilitator and he had them delivered to Abdul Rahman's shop after

Abdul's brother, the accountant in Kabul, sorted out the funds. They had planned a massive attack across the country.'

. . .

Sam fell silent. He wasn't sure yet how he was going to use the rest of the information he had extracted from Faisal Khan, if at all. The Taliban had confessed to using Steph, who had been selling Yankee Platoon's movements in return for information that she thought could be used to show a link between Iran and Afghanistan. Khan had outsmarted her at her own game. Perhaps Sam could smooth things over with her; show her that she had been outplayed but reassure her that her secret was safe with him. After all, the intelligence community should stick together and so far everyone thought it was only Nadeem Karn who was in contact with Faisal. Nadeem had been very fast to explain how the Taliban would kill him when everyone left Afghanistan. Sam had even pitied him. The American-educated interpreter was of course right, there were no protections in place for him after this was all done, and it made sense for him to be making deals with the Taliban. It had also turned out that Nadeem had no knowledge of Steph's involvement; Faisal had kept both of them compartmented.

'So I guess we had better get planning then,' Matt was saying. He sounded excited, and Sam knew he would be relishing the opportunity to take on Rapier in Zabul, his own area.

'I'm actually going over to brief Colonel Hoff now. Why don't you come with me, Matt? I think this is grounds for a whole-of-SOTG effort. I know X-Ray Platoon is back this evening. It should make for an interesting – not to mention violent – operation.'

46

ZABUL PROVINCE

Two giant Chinook helicopters hovered a few feet above the treetops as the pilots scanned desperately through their night-vision goggles for a place to settle the birds down, their faces illuminated by a soft green glow from the instrument panels. After what felt like an eternity to the passengers, the pilots squeezed their machines down between the overhanging trees. The Chinook blades clipped and smashed the brittle branches as the pilots and passengers braced themselves for the impact that would surely follow should the metal connect with a material more robust than mere twigs.

Finally, the birds thumped down onto the dry plateau at the head of the valley. The men of Yankee Platoon pushed their two 6×6 Polaris ATVs out of the helos and the commandos sprinted off into the dark. The ATVs carried spare water, ammunition and rations, all of which would be needed in the eventuality that the platoon had to spend the next few days out here. In addition to the victualling supplies, each vehicle had a 60mm mortar and an 84mm Carl Gustaf anti-tank weapon, perfect for smashing Taliban positions or spotters taking refuge in the rocky escarpments.

The birds were gone just as fast as they had arrived and silence fell once again, except for the breathing of thirty-five soldiers peering through their fogged-up NGVs and the constant bubbling of water coming from a water source that fed the streams further down the valley.

• • •

A few hours later dawn broke, and Yankee Platoon could see the enormity of the task at hand. Matt looked down at the small piece of folded map in his hand. The sweat, mixed with camouflage cream, dripped off his forehead and onto the laminated surface. He wiped the map on his sleeve and then studied it again.

Jeez, the green belt in this valley is complex, he thought. The green belt followed a series of streams not more than four metres wide, but from recon gained already this morning Matt knew that these creeks were perilously deep in places. The streams branched off in all directions, sometimes following the natural contours of the land and at other times moving where the locals had developed canals. Matt looked up from his map to the stream in front of him. On the far side was a wall of lush green growth about ten metres deep. It looked like it contained a mixture of pomegranates, tall grasses and spiky thickets. Along the streams there were small bridges, constructed of mud and stone, crisscrossing the complex waterways, and none of these were on Matt's map.

'Yankee Alpha, this is Yankee Bravo. How far down the valley are X-Ray Platoon now, boss?' JJ asked Matt over his tactical radio. It was an all-informed net and as such every platoon member could hear the conversation, but only the team commanders could speak directly to Matt. If the soldiers wanted to talk they would have to change the settings on their radios from their team network to the platoon network.

'It's about another six k, I think. It's been about thirty minutes since Barns last spoke to them.'

'It shouldn't take us long to cover that, boss.'

'Yeah, don't be so sure about that, JJ', said Matt as he stood up and looked again at the wall of scrub in front of them. 'It's thick in there, mate.'

'Noted, boss. Bravo out.'

The plan was that X-Ray Platoon would disrupt the area to the south of Ahmed Defari's village, forcing the Taliban communicate with each other. They reasoned that the Taliban would discuss their tactics and would also ultimately ask for more support. These conversations could then be monitored through both human intelligence and communication intercepts. Once Objective Rapier popped his head above the monitoring threshold, then Yankee Platoon – fast targeting off the back of the other platoon's disruption – would vector in to his location and kill or capture him. Tactics such as this had proved highly effective at the start of the campaign, though they were becoming increasingly less so as the Taliban leadership were becoming more technology savvy.

The Special Operations Task Group was being covered by the American Green Berets and their ANA partner force. Every entry and exit into the valley was being blocked. Todd Carson and his guys could only stay on station for a day and then they were due to report back to Kandahar to support a larger US mission.

The initial movement south by Yankee Platoon was intended as a recce to get a feel for the local area. Team Two were moving to the right of the river and Matt was becoming frustrated. This area of thick trees and vegetation surrounding a compound wall to their front was limiting their progress.

'Yankee Alpha, this is Yankee Two.'

'What's up, Rob?' said Matt.

'Boss, the vegetation here starts at the side of the river and stretches across our frontage to the three-metre wall of a compound on our side of the creek,' Cinzano reported.

'Right. I can see it, mate. Just keep the guys moving forward slowly,' Matt ordered.

'Alpha, this is Yankee Four,' came the voice of Joseph Hammond over the radio. 'We're making good time on the left side and can cover Yankee Two's movement.'

'Roger that,' said Matt. He looked behind him and could see the rest of the platoon scattered behind the lead elements. The platoon was well spread out and the front guys moved off silently again, scanning for enemy and checking any tracks. The rear elements used the terrain, ensuring they could find a position to support the front teams if they needed it. The only noise that could be heard was the soft footfall of the commandos, the occasional snip of a branch by gardening secateurs carried by the forward scouts, and the dull thumping of the old water pumps around the villages as they siphoned water from the streams and irrigated the fields further away.

The tranquillity of the setting was perfect – until suddenly the air around the platoon exploded.

'CONTACT FRONT!' screamed Team Two's forward scout almost a split second after the Taliban triggered the ambush.

'What have ya got?' Cinzano yelled from behind cover, his voice almost lost in the crack and thump of supersonic rounds whizzing above and between the front sections.

The forward scout of Team Four, Jason Richards, hit the deck and crawled under the withering fire into a protected position behind a small mound of dirt. Hot lead smashed the top of his hiding place to pieces, showering him with sodden earth.

'Fuckin' arseholes,' he yelled into the ground, his lips inches from the warm earth. 'Bloody just shoot me, for Christ's sake, don't torture me with dirt and muck.'

'What have ya got, mate?' the team commander screamed.

'There's a couple of guns down the creek – I can't see where exactly,' Richards barked into his radio.

Two RPG rounds exploded, coming from enemy positions a hundred metres or so behind the guns. These were followed by another two rounds in quick succession.

As quickly as it had begun, it was over, without the commandos firing a single round. No one had seen the enemy and no one was in a position that afforded covering or return fire.

Matt, who had also hit the ground in the first moments, picked himself up out of the dirt and dusted off his face. He could see his guys slowly getting to their knees. Matt's senses were now in overdrive and he was astonished at how all the insects had taken the ambush as their cue to scream and sing in unison with each other. The silence was the loudest thing he had heard in his life and his heartbeat was banging in time to the yell of the cicadas.

'Everyone okay?' he enquired over the radio, dreading the likely response.

The teams sounded off the affirmative one after the other and his heartbeat slowed to a steady rhythm. Matt was amazed at the outcome. Given the violence of the ambush he was sure he would have lost guys.

'Want me to take after them, boss?' The request came from Joseph Hammond.

'No, let's keep this controlled, mate.' Matt moved to another covered position between two trees and a small wall while he talked in the radio. 'I have the feeling we're being drawn in here.'

Matt looked again at his map. The main stream ran down the valley for another ten kilometres and branched off into deep ravines every few hundred metres. Manoeuvring was difficult because at some point any frontal attack would have to be done either half in the open or up in the rocky escarpments. Multiple escape routes and multiple reinforcement locations ensured that a full platoon attack would result in casualties. The whole valley was locked in place by huge fissure and granite walls. Switching his GPS back on, Matt wrote the grid reference onto the side of a laminated card stuck on his rifle. He would need this later for the patrol report. Information was power and maybe later some intelligence might come from patterns that the Taliban were setting.

'Yankee Four/One, any chance you can get your team down and around this next junction? Perhaps move around over the high ground.' Matt studied his map again then keyed his mic. 'Disregard, mate, I can see that's almost impossible.'

Matt scanned the area to his front. He could see the Australians covering their areas of responsibility. It was going to be a long day.

'Boss, we need some time back here so that we can purify some water,' JJ said.

Matt thought about this. Chasing the enemy now might be suicide and was probably the effect the Taliban commander actually wanted. Holding here for a rest might make more sense tactically. Keep the enemy out there in ambush and degrading in the heat. 'Sure, let's have a break.'

Matt pulled out a packet of M&Ms and started to eat, not for enjoyment but purely for sustenance. Looking up into the high ground he grabbed his radio fist mic off the front of his chest plate. 'Kiwi, can you get your snipers and provide some overwatch up on the high ground? Don't go too high, just enough to spot any enemy that might want to cross from one green belt to the next.' Matt focused on the escarpment to his left that dominated the next few hundred metres of valley; he hated not to have the high ground.

'Moving.' The single-word response from Kiwi was expected. At times it was useful to have a guy who didn't communicate much. He just got on with it.

'Lads, when we do set off again, let's use leapfrog, one team at a time moving and one team covering. If we are going to keep getting hit like this, let's make it more difficult for them.'

Barnsley interrupted. 'Boss, that was X-Ray Platoon on the blower. They've been in contact down the valley for the past three hours. No casualties but the Taliban have taken heavy losses.'

'That's good, mate.'

'They're going firm too, boss, moving again in an hour. Also, there's an intelligence update for you. I've downloaded it onto the Toughbook.'

'Cheers, Barns. Okay, lads: all-round defence, section commanders put out early warning.'

47

THE VALLEY

An hour later JJ's admin guys had purified almost thirty litres of water from the creek and had resupplied all the teams.

Matt put down his notebook, and looked up at JJ. 'The Intelligence cell thinks that Rapier is going to try to make a run for it tomorrow morning, using the next valley as the escape route. I want to keep going down the valley until last light, JJ, so that the Taliban think we are going to continue that way tomorrow.'

'Got it, boss.'

'Thing is, JJ, we've given them a bit of time now and one thing that we know Rapier is good at . . .'

'Is IEDs,' JJ finished.

'Yep, so we have to tread carefully here.'

'Lucky we left Team Three back down the valley in that first compound, boss. There's no way we could have got the ATVs and mortars and all of our heavy equipment through here.'

'It wasn't luck, JJ – come on, mate, give me some credit.' Matt picked up his notebook and MultiCam daypack and slipped his arms through the straps.

He grabbed his fist mic again. 'Okay, let's go, guys. We have two more hours ahead of us; maybe we'll link up with X-Ray Platoon as they make their way north. Hopefully we can sandwich any remaining Taliban between us.'

• • •

Three-quarters of an hour later, Jason Richards, the Team Four scout, carefully selected where to put his foot next. He stopped and everyone travelling behind him also stopped. In unison, their noise ceased. Moving his weapon on a traverse he scanned from right to left; wherever his barrel was pointing, his eyes followed. As a scout he had no peer. The hair on the back of his neck started to rise. Richards knew this feeling well. He slowly moved his left hand away from his rifle and behind his back, making the thumbs-down field signal for enemy. He couldn't see anyone yet, but he knew that in front of him was an ambush.

Behind him, the teams started to fan out. The two lead team commanders moved their guys into frontal attack positions on either side of the river, offering the most firepower to cover Richards.

Matt saw Richards slow down and, as he did, he moved off to the corner of a compound so as to at least be protected from one side. Barnsley followed in close behind and took a knee on the ground next to an old man, who had just started a water pump. The old man sat naked but for a pair of long pants, the type a businessman would wear in the city except three times too big for him. A long brown belt was tied around his stomach, holding the pants in place. He sat cross-legged, staring at the soldiers. Barnsley mistakenly guessed he was about ninety, given the wear and tear he had endured; in fact, he was closer to seventy. Matt looked him over quickly to ensure he wasn't a threat and then turned his attention back to Richards. He watched his movements though the foliage. He could see him standing about sixty metres ahead. He had deliberately stopped in an area that was on the edge of a clearing. He stood in a shadow and in front of him was bright light that shone down through a break in the green belt. *Genius*, Matt thought.

He knew what the scout was doing. This was the spot that the Taliban must have chosen to hit them again and Richards knew it. He was buying time for the platoon to shake out and close the gap with him.

Richards held his weapon facing forwards and slowly moved his head to the right. His eyes, however, stayed looking along the barrel of his weapon.

Thirty metres away, the hidden Taliban took the bait. Thinking the Australian was looking the other way; he shifted his position to try to get a better angle with his PKM machine gun. Richards saw the movement and in an instant had unloaded his magazine into the Taliban. The M4 kicked in his hands as a murderous stream of lead ripped through the enemy.

The PKM never returned fired, but moments later the rest of the frontage erupted with the sound of AK-47s, maybe twenty or more. The air exploded in booms of rifles, snaps of rounds passing overhead and the debris of leaves and branches being stripped from plants at either end of the battle.

Matt and Barnsley threw themselves down into the dirt. Matt looked through his ACOG, trying to get a sight picture on where the firing was coming from, but his teams were already manoeuvring to give chase and crossing in front of his own command team. He looked across at Barnsley and then at the old Afghan villager, who was now squatting next to the pump. Rounds thumped into the wall overhead and the old man just sat there.

He gave Matt a toothless smile then spat on the ground between his feet. He picked up a stick, never taking his eyes off Matt, and drew lines through his saliva, mixing it into the dirt.

Matt narrowed his eyes at the old man. 'I bet they're your sons, aren't they, you old prick?'

Then, with a, 'Let's go, Barns,' Matt sprinted from his position to get in behind Cinzano's team so that he could better control the fight. This time, the commando teams gave back as good as they got. Thanks to the disciplined fire and constant pressure, the Taliban had no chance to reload. They withdrew at pace down their selected escape routes and the platoon gave chase. They fired and moved for a hundred metres or so in what developed into a rolling gunfight. The pressure on the Taliban was relentless and the commandos were vicious until the two front teams came to an overgrown creek junction. Cinzano stopped short.

'What's going on, Rob?' Matt yelled into his radio.

'It's a no-go, boss.'

'What ya talking about? We have em on the run. If we don't keep following them up they'll just ambush us again.' Matt kicked at the low stone wall that he was taking shelter behind and some of the rocks fell onto Barnsley, lying next to him.

'Jesus, boss,' Barnsley complained.

'Boss, this is a trap,' Cinzano said. 'You're going to have to trust me on this one.'

Matt was itching to finally get among these guys and make them pay for the past few months, but he knew it was true that discretion was the better part of valour.

'Acknowledged. I'm moving to your location.' And then to his team: 'Let's go, guys.' Securing the sling on his rifle, Matt started off towards Team Two's location, the rest of his team in tow.

• • •

Arriving at Cinzano's position, Matt could instantly see what the problem was. The small riverbank here dropped away into a steep cliff. The Taliban, with nothing but weapons and ammunition, had slid down it and made off across to the other side. The embankment was wet and slippery and there was no way a commando was getting up the other side with all of their kit. In fact, there was no way any team was getting across here without ropes and a good obstacle-crossing plan.

'Call X-Ray Platoon, Barns, and let them know that we won't be linking up tonight. I'll let them know tomorrow's plan when we get back to the compound.' Matt turned away from the obstacle and started to head back in the direction he had just come from.

'Oh, Rob?' he called over his shoulder. 'Get your guys sorted, and give them a rest at the back of the platoon; they've done an excellent job today.'

'Thanks, boss.'

Matt thought a moment longer and then added, 'Also, mate, take all the spark plugs out of the water pumps as you go past them on the way back up the valley. I think some of these old bastards have been marking the front line of our troops with the noise from the pumps all day.'

As Matt walked away he gave quick orders to get all of the teams turned around and heading back to the compound. They had to cover the two and a half kilometres back, and it was all uphill, but at least they'd be moving over ground they had already cleared.

48

THE VALLEY

Ahmed Defari – otherwise known as Objective Rapier – made a panicked telephone call to Quetta that evening. He begged to leave Zabul and was given the authorisation to make a run for it the next day. Up until then, he and his men had mostly remained below the occupiers' intelligence, surveillance and reconnaissance threshold. Yankee and X-Ray Platoons had put pressure on his men all day and the Taliban were reeling from the blows. With the infidel closing in on their stronghold, it was now time for them to make their escape.

What was left of Rapier's army were only simple farmhands and not the Mujahedeen of old; nor did they resemble the Taliban of a year earlier. Rapier had decided to take on the SOTG that summer. At first, thanks to the information from Steph and Nadeem, he had broken the commandos and avoided the efforts of the SAS. Now the tables had been turned. They had discovered his cache, killed Abdul Rahman, caught Faisal Khan; now

309

Rapier himself, who had once enjoyed free rein across Uruzghan, was trapped high up in the mountains of Zabul.

. . .

Matt Rix's commando platoon had been waiting for the insurgents for six hours. Word travels fast through these valleys. Most of Yankee Platoon's movements had been monitored and reported in the opposite valley, and Matt's tactics were predicated on this. The Taliban can't report what they don't see and they will report what you show them.

Matt left his engineers and a commando team behind to maintain a presence in the village, fooling the occupants into thinking that they were still there. The remainder of his men melted away and out into the black of night. They traversed the mountain range, labouring under heavy load. They avoided walking on tracks or cresting the ridges, making use of what little moonlight there was to scan for the most secure path.

The platoon had all the modern devices of warfare: night-vision goggles, global positioning systems and, importantly, overwatch provided by a silent Predator drone thousands of feet above, tracking their movements and warning them of nomadic farmers and their many goats. The drone's invisible laser, known as 'the finger of God', reached down from the heavens and illuminated potential threats. Matt's forward scouts changed their course accordingly. They arrived in their ambush location five hours later, twenty kilometres away and into the next valley, securing the route that they knew the Taliban would surely be using. It would be here that they would make a run on foot for the border. The Taliban didn't use maps, they didn't overlay weapons' effects, they didn't war-game battles and plan escape routes, and they didn't understand the huge array of technological advances stacked against them. They just followed the trails they knew. With mortars set up and snipers in position, the trap was set.

. . .

Morning broke with plumes of dark orange and deep blue appearing across a silent valley. The cool of the night was already giving way to the promised sweltering heat of the day. Ahmed's men moved forward with caution . . . too much caution. Their deliberate movements, military-type spacing and constant scanning with binoculars gave Matt the 'hostile intent' that he required under the rules of engagement. They no longer looked like farmers or Bedouin – this was Rapier and his men.

Twenty sets of ruthless eyes silently focused on the enemy, tracking their every movement. All the while, one man, Matt's number-one sniper, adjusted his sights.

'All call signs, this is Yankee Alpha.'

The platoon readied the mortars and the sniper exhaled.

'Without warning, men – ready ready . . . ready ready . . . ready ready . . . stand by . . . FIRE!'

BOOM! The Yankee Platoon sniper fired a single shot from the Blaser .338 sniper rifle. The crack echoed up and down the quiet valley. The target's head exploded some seconds before the noise reached the group. By the time they heard the shot, he was dead. His jaw was missing, blown some six metres away, and his eyes were open.

The first audible blasts of the dual mortars came in a split second later, well before the enemy group could even register the death of one of their own. The mortars rained down around them, felling a couple of the Taliban.

Ahmed and his men were terrified; the sudden rain of mortars shocked them into action as giant thumps shook the surrounding mountains and showered them with rocks and debris. The mortars chased them all the way back down the dusty valley, slamming into the ground like God himself was thumping the earth behind them, hell bent on punishing them for all of their sins. The men who were still alive after the first salvo ran screaming all the way to their hidden bikes. It was a miracle that they were not all killed. *Thanks be to God*, thought Ahmed.

X-Ray Platoon had been following Rapier's trail ever since they left Zabul; they chose the moment that the Taliban started their bikes to trigger the ambush.

The rounds, fired from only forty metres away, ripped through Ahmed and his men. Ahmed clutched his chest, now ripped open, and fell on his back in the dirt.

Ahmed watched as the clouds rolled across the morning sky. So this was his punishment for the poppy fields and the poison he had agreed to send to the people of his faith. It had never really sat well with him. A bearded face came into his view: a Westerner; his helmet was MultiCam and he still had on the goggles that gave him the green eyes in the night. His weapon was pointing at Ahmed's face. Ahmed opened his mouth to speak but no words came out. He rolled slowly to his left and tried to raise his AK-47, he heard a loud shout and then a bright light burst across his eyes, and then the world turned black.

49

KANDAHAR

'What time are we meeting the defence force investigator again, mate?' Sam stopped, admiring a stand full of Harley-Davidson brochures.

'Thirteen-thirty. We have plenty of time, in case you're thinking of making a great life choice.' Matt pointed at the Harley Softail.

'Let's go and get a brew while we wait. I can't really be bothered going around the boardwalk again.' Sam flipped through the finance brochure provided by the Armed Services Club outlining the step-by-step process to becoming the proud owner of the American legend. He placed it back in the stand.

'I guess that's why they call it the "bored" walk, right?' Matt laughed at his own joke.

'Nice one, mate.' Sam turned to roll his eyes at Matt. 'Hey, why are you still carrying your M4? Why didn't you just leave it back in the accommodation? You only need to carry a pistol around here.'

Matt tightened the Velcro quick-release strap on the weapon, holding it tighter against his shoulder, realising as he did so that he had left the rifle's suppressor back with his gear. 'There was some civilian from the defence department bunked in my room, and a couple of specialist geeks too. I didn't want to leave it in case they decided to conduct their own weapons training.'

Sam snorted. 'Paranoid much?'

Matt changed the subject. 'There's a Starbucks at the other end of the boardwalk – let's head over there. We can grab a coffee and then go over what we're going to say again.'

'You know, Matt, this is fairly cut and dried in my mind.' Sam sped up his pace to keep up with the platoon commander. 'We know for certain that the leak was Nadeem. The CO has already disappeared to a diplomatic post in the UK and probably won't reappear anytime soon, Rapier's *dead*, Saygen's now your best mate and you're considered a hero for finding these new-generation suicide vests. Easy days, I would say!' Sam slapped Matt on the shoulder.

'Yeah, right. So what time do you want to head back to TK tomorrow?'

'I'm not sure yet. The intelligence update brief is at eight and then we can get away. We can be down at the airport around ten, I guess.'

Easy days, Sam had said. Matt thought about that. It was true that everything had calmed down. Yankee Platoon had endured a lot over the last five months. Matt had been tested and for the most part he had passed – with a little help from Lady Luck. If they hadn't found those uniforms Matt would almost certainly have been sent home in disgrace and ultimately drummed out of

Special Forces. You didn't lose command and survive in this line of work. There was something though that nagged at him; a feeling that he could date back to his first meeting with Allie van Tanken in Echos. She hadn't needed to warn him, but it was her warning that had triggered the snowball of events that brought him to where he was now. She was also here for the update briefing tomorrow, he knew, and he hoped to see her after all this business with the ADFIS investigator was out of the way.

. . .

'Just park it here, Kelsey.' Steph jumped out the front of the car and turned back to talk through the window to the young female soldier on security attachment to the CIA. 'Omar should be here soon. Move the car under that tree over there and we'll come meet you when we get through security.'

Steph moved to the back of the guard box. Looking past the gate she had an unimpeded view down the road. A few minutes later, she saw the little white Corolla approach the first of the checkpoints. She watched as an old man got out of the car. He walked slowly up the dirt road and was commanded to stop by soldiers of the Afghan National Army. Some commands were shouted to him in Pashtu and his arms slowly came above his head. Even at that distance, she could tell that he was trembling. Understandable given the circumstances, she thought.

The ANA soldiers approached Omar and patted him down thoroughly and then used small metal detector wands to make sure he wasn't carrying anything that they couldn't detect by hand. His turban was also removed and unwound. Some personal things were taken from his pockets and unceremoniously dropped at his feet. The better-fed of the two soldiers held up a phone towards their commander. Something was yelled back and the phone disappeared into the ANA soldier's pocket; no doubt a receipt would be supplied for it later.

Omar slowly bent down, the way old men do, with one leg further behind the other for balance, and picked up a small notebook and pen that had been dropped in the dirt. He brushed the items off and placed them back in his pockets then proceeded cautiously the rest of the way towards the gate.

Steph stepped forward. 'Omar, good morning.'

'Oh yes, hello, Miss Steph, it is good to finally meet you.' He stretched out his hand and she took it in both of hers. The poor man was still shaking, she noticed.

'I have a vehicle here waiting that will take us to a safe place to talk,' Steph assured him. 'We can have some tea and you can tell me everything.' Steph breathed a little sigh of relief. It was always good when the target arrived and wasn't carrying a surprise, which had become all too common in recent months.

Omar and Steph climbed into the back seat of the Toyota Hilux. Kelsey slowly manoeuvred the vehicle out into the base traffic.

Omar looked out the window in silence.

'Have you been out here before, Omar?' She felt stupid asking it. Of course he hadn't; she was his first contact with Americans.

'Yes. Yes, I have,' Omar replied, gazing out the window. He looked around the base at all of the equipment and personnel.

• • •

At that moment, Allie van Tanken was walking along the dusty road towards the cafes on the boardwalk. She stopped to let a Hilux go past and had to do a double take as it went by. She recognised the old man sitting in the back instantly. She remembered him from the photos sent a few months back by Sam. Then it all clicked into place for her: there weren't two bombers at all. How could there be, if all the attacks in the east were suicide bombers? Rapier was working in Uruzghan and the man in the photo was controlling the suicide bombers. Allie broke into a sprint after the car.

· · ·

Steph watched Omar as he took it all in. His response had caught her off guard. 'But it was a lot different back then,' he said, looking across at her. 'Maybe it was forty years ago. I came here with my father. All this area was once fields and small villages stretching from Kandahar to the border regions and beyond.' He fell silent.

Steph watched as he nervously played with his pen, rolling it around his fingers and squeezing it in his fist. His hands were dry, old and rough. They were evidence of a simple man who had worked his life on the land. His English, however, indicated the hopes that his family must once have had, to invest in a Western education for him. She felt sorry for him for a brief moment, and then didn't.

The car drew to a stop out the front of six large ISO containers that had been converted into makeshift buildings. Behind these a security fence protected a demountable building that contained Steph's office and the interview room.

'Omar, this is our stop. Let's go have that tea; I'm very inter-ested to hear the information that's so sensitive you feel you need our protection.' Steph got out of the car and moved around to the other door to help the old man.

• • •

Sam placed his coffee down on the table as he looked out the window. 'See that girl, Matt?'

Matt turned his head to see where Sam was pointing. A straw-berry-blonde was getting out of the back of a Hilux. He looked back at Sam. 'What about her?'

'She's a spook for the CIA. Steph Baumer. There's just some-thing about her I find intriguing, and a little sexy. A little nuts perhaps, but . . .' Sam trailed off.

Matt looked again. He didn't see anything sexy about her at all; she walked with too much of a swagger for his liking.

'What on earth is *she* doing here?' Sam was looking down the street now, sounding puzzled. Sam's confusion was quickly replaced by a look of horror and he jumped up, knocking his coffee across the table.

'Jesus, Sam, what are you doing?'

'Fuck, Matt, she's got her gun out! She has a gun!'

'Sam, what are you talking about?' Then Matt saw it too. 'Holy shit, that's Allie.' He took off after Sam, at speed.

Sam burst through the door just in time to see Allie release two shots in Steph's direction.

'Steph!' Sam yelled. 'Steph! Watch out!'

The Hilux had pulled away now, leaving Steph and Omar standing on the dirt road. Sam, with Matt on his heels, sprinted down the boardwalk steps.

'Steph! Steph, behind you!' Sam tripped and fell down the last of the stairs, landing in a heap at the bottom. 'Fuck!'

• • •

The sudden commotion had startled Steph. She thought she had heard shooting and she swivelled around, her hand instinctively going to her hip, and she released the thumb break on her Sig Sauer. But by the time she saw Allie van Tanken, it was already too late; the Dutchwoman was aiming again, closing in fast.

From Steph's left there came a sudden cry of: 'Allahu Akbar! Allahu Akbar!' The words sent shivers down her spine, and out of the corner of her eye she saw a young soldier running straight at her and Omar from between two ISO containers.

'What the fuck?' Steph was overwhelmed by the realisation that she was caught between two threats. The soldier had only twenty metres to cover, but to Steph's surprise he didn't seem to be armed. Then a chill ran through: *he* was the weapon.

Beside her, Omar had thrust his arms up into the air and was yelling in Arabic: 'Thanks be to God! Thanks be to the one almighty God!'

'Steph!' Steph turned her head to see Allie. 'Steph!' she called again, raising her weapon. She fired.

The first round went whizzing past Steph's head, missing her by mere inches.

It was all happening so fast. Knowing she could only deal with one threat at a time, Steph decided to focus on Allie. She wouldn't be able to bring her own weapon up in time, not before Allie could adjust and find her target, but Steph's safety catch was now off and she knew where the rounds needed to go, even without bringing the weapon up to aim properly. She had been taught at 'The Farm' in Virginia by the finest firearms instructors, ex-Delta Force and Navy Seal operators, to fire instinctively; it might take more than just a double tap when you're under stress, but emptying half the magazine in a controlled manner from the holster to the line of sight would ensure something found its mark, she had been told.

She released the first round from her hip, then she squeezed four more times, each trigger pressure faster than the last, each time the weapon coming further up towards where her eyes would finally take a sight picture.

Steph never took her eyes off Allie. The first rounds missed Allie by a few inches, and Allie stopped dead in her tracks. But rather than return fire wildly, Allie steadied herself and took careful aim. Even as Steph pulled the trigger twice more, and her rounds came ever closer to Allie's body, she was surprised at how focused Allie appeared. As the Dutchwoman took careful aim and fired once more, Steph released two more rounds. This time her weapon was up in front of her face and her front sight post was the centre of Allie's chest. Bullets whizzed past Steph, again missing her by inches, just as Steph's own double tap found their target. Allie dropped straight down, clutching at her chest.

BOOM! BOOM! There was a quick double tap on Steph's right. It was the distinctive sound of a long gun. She flinched and closed her eyes, ducking to her left, remembering the Taliban as she did so. Opening her eyes, she spun to the left and raised her Sig at the same time and saw the soldier already sliding in the gravel, arriving head first at her feet – dead. His arms were outstretched as if he were reaching for something.

'Oh, shit.' Steph turned to the right and spotted a man running towards Allie. He was carrying an M4, no doubt the source of the booms she'd heard seconds earlier. It was he who had shot the Taliban now lying at Steph's feet. He pulled Allie up into his arms at the same time as Steph heard a familiar voice say, 'Steph! Are you okay?' Sam Long reached her just as she sank to her knees in shock.

'Sam! What on earth is going on? What's happening?'

'Jesus,' said Sam. 'Allie's killed that old guy who was with you.'

Omar! Steph looked around. The old man who had been standing next to her was now lying in the dirt behind her. She grabbed him by the shoulders and turned him over. He had been shot just above the mouth; his eyes were wide open and lifeless and his nose and top lip hung from his face. He was still clutching his pen in his left hand.

. . .

Allie clung to Matt, shaking in his arms as blood soaked through her t-shirt. 'Matt, that's Omar Defari – that's Rapier's brother. He's the other bomber; he has the trigger. I worked it out, Matt.' She was gasping and sobbing with pain.

Matt swore as he realised: the dead soldier was wearing the one missing vest . . . He glanced at the old man lying dead a few metres away. The pen; the pen was the trigger.

'Sam! Get away from there! That guy's got the trigger. Move!'

'Not much of a first date,' Allie joked weakly.

Sam picked Steph up and ran with her over the road. Others were arriving now, guns drawn at first and then holstered as they took orders from Matt, still sitting on the ground with Allie bleeding on his lap. Finally an American Special Forces guy arrived to secure the area as they waited for the medics.

• • •

'Sam, you saw that right?' Steph sat down on the steps next to Sam. 'She was coming straight at me with a gun. I mean, it looked like she was going to kill me.' She squeezed Sam's arm. 'She shot at me – you saw that too, right?'

Sam held Steph tight as she turned and started to cry into his shoulder. She was in shock, he realised. 'I'm not sure what I saw, Steph. It all looked pretty confusing to me.'

'I'm so sorry, Sam,' she sobbed. 'I never meant for this to happen, not like this – it just got so out of hand.'

'Don't talk about it now,' Sam said. He looked over at where Matt was sitting. He was holding Allie in his lap and a huge pool of blood was forming around his legs. Had Steph really believed Allie was trying to shoot her? And if so, did she believe Allie had cause to? Either way, the Dutchwoman had died at Steph's hands.

• • •

Allie let out a small moan and her eyes flickered and closed.

'It's going to be okay, Allie,' Matt lied. 'I've stopped the bleeding now. You're going to be fine.'

'It's over, Matt – that's the last bomb. It's over.'

Matt stroked the hair from her face then looked around. 'Where the hell are the medics?' he yelled.

He turned back to Allie, watching as the life started to drain from her, her face becoming grey. Feeling a sob rise in his chest, he lowered his face to hers and felt her last breath on his neck. She shuddered and was gone.

He looked over to where Omar and the suicide bomber lay, and then across to where Steph sat with Sam. Her head was in her hands.

Matt now put it all together. Not only had he been betrayed by those he knew and who were close to him but also by someone else, someone he knew nothing of, until now.

'No, Allie,' he whispered. 'This is not over. It's just the beginning.' He caught Steph's eye as she raised her head. She instantly looked away. No, this was a long way from being over.

• • •

'It's on a need to know basis,' Matt was told by the CIA when he pressed for details. Steph had been sent out of the country hours after the incident and the CIA had closed ranks to protect one of its own. Matt had been left to answer to the Australian army investigators once again.

Sam was of no help. 'Yes, sir; no, sir; no recollection.' He wound the investigators into knots.

Two weeks later Matt and JJ had the platoon's weapons and equipment cleaned, de-serviced and on the way to Sydney. They were going home. Yankee Platoon had been ordered to take over the responsibility for the Tactical Assault Group. Matt was given a warning by his own command, to let the issue go and stop asking questions about Steph Baumer's whereabouts. It seemed to him that she had become a ghost, much like Rapier had been in those first few months.

Matt did let it go, but he didn't forget.